THE SHIPYARD

INTRODUCTION

The following story is a fictional tale based on my own experiences working as a pipefitter.

Although some of the characters are based on real people, this story does not reflect how they are in real life.

This book is a rewrite and professionally edited version of my first book, 'Allow me to be Frank'. I have also added a few follow-up chapters and renamed it 'The Shipyard', as originally, when I first wrote it, I did not expect it to see daylight. My reason for renaming it is that 'Allow me to be Frank' sounded more like an autobiography, which wasn't my intention. I believe 'The Shipyard' represents the story a little better.

My apologies to so many characters from the yard who didn't appear in 'Allow me to be Frank'; the story could never have been written without the memories you helped me make. I found it a lot easier to write about fictional characters rather than real people, as I didn't want to say the wrong thing, or represent them in a way they wouldn't be happy with.

For some of the characters, I used their nicknames only, and this isn't a true representation of how they were, especially Blue, Dot and JJ.

If you would like to read more about the characters and who they were based on, as well as which stories are true and which are fictional, I have written a chapter at the end of this book.

Many thanks.

Andy

WARNING!

This book contains very strong language and some scenes you may find offensive.

PROLOGUE

For as long as I can remember, I've gotten into trouble and embarrassing situations, even as a kid – but as an adult, it's like someone up above is looking down and having a good old laugh at me. This is why I've been given the nickname Frank Spencer.

All my calamities and scrapes I find myself in don't surprise my friends anymore; they simply say, 'It could only happen to you' or 'You should write a book'.

I'll give you an example of a situation I found myself in just the other week while working away from home in Portsmouth.

I was living in a shared house with a workmate and a noisy, fat bloke downstairs. Anyway, this particular day was scorching hot and I'd just finished washing my work clothes. We didn't have a dryer in our digs, so I went outside into the glorious sunshine with my basket of wet clothes. Unfortunately, the fat bloke had beaten me to the washing line – his sheets and enormous boxer shorts were hanging on the line. I decided to check if they were dry, which they were, so I decided to pluck them from the line. I began to tug at the biggest purple pair of boxer shorts I'd ever seen and said out loud, 'Look at the size of them' while pulling them off the line. To my horror, when the pants were out of view, I stood looking into next door's garden, where a blonde lady in her fifties was sat sunbathing, with enormous breasts only covered with a skimpy bikini top.

She looked at me open-mouthed, covered her breasts with her hands and ran quickly for cover in the kitchen shouting, 'Geoff, Geoff, Geoff!' I ran like Usain Bolt out of the house, jumped in the car and sped off. Knowing my luck, Geoff will be Hampshire's hardest man and be built like a brick shithouse!

CHAPTER 1

Hammer horror

Friday
September 1997

I was starting my apprenticeship on Monday in a shipyard called Wear Dock in Sunderland, so I quit my job at McDonald's before they had the chance to sack me for my calamities.

It was Friday, and I was sat at home with my mam watching 'This Morning' in our house on our rough council estate in Sunderland.

The estate back then was well known for its villains and drug dealers. Our little square was the exception. It was a quiet little cul-de-sac; it was a friendly, well-kept, nice-looking square. Well, that was until the family from hell moved in next door!

They were well-known drug dealers. They were a young couple in their early twenties – friendly enough and always said 'Hello' when we passed them in the square, but it was obvious to everyone they were dealing drugs, as cars came and went all day and night.

Anyway, this particular day, my mam and me were sitting having a coffee and watching telly when a rough-looking lad in his early twenties appeared on a BMX bike. He was very dodgy looking, wearing a tatty old tracksuit and a hooded top pulled over his head. As he cycled closer, my mam said, 'Here comes the drugs!'

'You what?' I replied, quite shocked at my mother's outburst.

'Every day at about this time, someone turns up with a package for the druggies next door, gives them the package, then leaves,' my Mam said, pointing to the scruffy lad outside.

Today, unexpectedly, he stopped outside our house and pulled his hood down
while climbing off his BMX as me and my mam looked on in horror. He unzipped his hooded top and pulled a claw hammer out, walked towards our door and rang the bell. My mam screamed, 'Go! Get out the back door!' Before I knew it, my mam had bolted the front door and practically dragged me into the kitchen to the back door.

My 14-year-old sister came rushing down from upstairs to see what all the commotion was about. My Mam wasted no time, grabbed my sister by the arm, dragged her into the back garden and shoved her into the old shed. She then pushed me to the back wall and shouted, 'Jump up! Go find a phone and ring the police! Quick!' she screamed, while shoving me towards the back wall.

Somehow, I managed to scramble up the six-foot wall, but to add to my worries once I was at the top, I realized the other side was a good twelve-foot drop into thorny rose bushes. Without a lot of time to think and adrenaline pumping, I jumped into the rose bushes, which sent pains all over my body as the thorns tore into my flesh, and worse still, I was now dangling like a puppet by my ripped Sunderland home shirt.

I eventually managed to wriggle myself free and drop-landed into a pile of mud beneath my feet. I ran like Linford Christie to the new estate behind our house, where my best mate Pikey lived.

Within a few minutes, I was at his house. I jumped over the gate and burst into his front door, where Pikey was sitting in his boxer shorts watching Richard and Judy. He looked at me and suddenly burst out laughing.

'Fuck sake, Andy – what you done now!'

I tried to explain as quickly as I could, but he just sat there laughing at me, with my Sunderland shirt ripped to shreds and covered in blood and muck. As I didn't get the help I was looking for, I ran into his kitchen and saw his golf club set, and I picked up the biggest-looking club I could find and bolted out the door. Aware that Pikey didn't have a phone, I ran next door to his neighbour's house where Rose lived. I banged on her front door and shouted, 'Help!', as Pikey looked on out of the window laughing his head off. Rose came to the door eventually and looked at me with shock.

'Are you okay, son? What's happened?' she said, pulling a twig out of my hair.

I explained as quickly as I could and told her to ring the police, which she did immediately.

In my state of panic, I suddenly realised my sister and mother were at the mercy of this maniac, so I shot off out the door with the golf club to my family's aid. I somehow gathered my thoughts as I got to the edge of our square and became aware of the danger I was in and decided to peek around the corner towards our house.

He was still there at our door, hammer in hand with his back to me. I sprinted as fast as I could towards him, made a quick grab for his hood and swung him around onto the grass, where he fell into a heap and dropped the hammer. I raised the club above my head ready to take a swing at him. He looked up at me with a look of fear etched across his spotty face.

'What the hell are you doing?' I screamed into his increasingly familiar face.

In that moment, three police cars came screeching into the square, followed by a van with its sirens blaring. My mam opened the front door and shouted, 'That's him! That's the druggie!' pointing to the panic-stricken lad on the grass.

Then he looked at me and said, 'I've only come to bring your dad his hammer back.'

My mam suddenly looked over all confused at the lad on the grass and said, 'John? Is that you?'

I looked at my mam lost for words. My mam read my confused look and shouted, 'John! It's Lisa's John!'

My heart sank as I looked at all the police cars in the square, the realisation filtering through that my cousin's new boyfriend, John, had come to return my dad's hammer that he must have borrowed.

CHAPTER 2

Day one at the shipyard

The induction

The sun was shining as I was standing in the number eleven bus shelter over the road from my house. I would almost be able to enjoy the weather if it wasn't for the smell of stale piss in the old stone bus shelter.

I was suddenly awoken from my thoughts as the double-decker bus hissed to a stop and nearly made me shit my pants in fright. It was my first day at the dockyard as an apprentice plumber. I felt I'd finally succeeded in life – no more working in McDonald's or burger vans. As much as I loved the food and the female attention, it was now time for a 'proper job', as my dad would say.

Yes, today this 20-year-old, lanky, skinny boy was going to be a marine pipefitter – after my apprenticeship, that is.

As I boarded the bus, I noticed Ricky, a lad of 16 who lived around the corner from me. He was at the job interview the day I had mine a few months back.

'Areet, mate,' he said.

'You got the job then?'

'Aye, pipefitter. What about you?'

'Welder,' he replied.

Ricky had just left school this year and this was to be his first job. I knew this, as he was at the same school as my sister, Natalie, who fancied him.

It was the starring role as Danny in Pennywell School's production of Grease that 'clinched her undying love', as she put it.

How could he play Danny, I thought, with a blonde curtains haircut?

'I thought your dad worked at the dock. What ya doing getting the bus?' Ricky asked.

'He's useless – he was on the drink last night. Can't get him up and I don't want to be late on my first day,' I replied.

We chatted for a while, mainly about football and how useless Sunderland were at the weekend. We finally got off the bus at the city Centre as far as the bus went. A quick stop-off for fags and papers and we headed down Hendon bank. Hendon at the time was a run-down area of Sunderland that lead us to the docks.

Suddenly, a clapped-out maroon Ford Fiesta pulled up next to us and beeped its horn.

'Jump in, lads!' a voice shouted out the window.

'Aright Blue? How's it going?' Ricky said to the old, grey-haired, scruffy-looking driver. As I climbed over the back seat, I recognised the driver as one of my mates from school Wayne's dad.

'Cheers,' I said as I struggled to climb in over the bent-over front seat into the back.

'Fawlty's son, ain't ya?' Blue asked as Ricky pushed the front seat back too quick, nearly breaking my legs in the process.

'Aaaaaaaaiii!' I struggled to reply as the pain shot down my leg.

'Fawlty?' Ricky muttered as Blue interrupted.

'Thought it was you – I heard you were starting. You used to hang around with our Wayne years ago, didn't ya?' Blue asked.

'That's right,' I said, remembering what a nutter his son was at school.

'He's a bailiff now. Still daft as a brush though. He was up at the flats up Gilly law repossessing someone's telly the other week and was banging like fuck on someone's door on the top floor. They wouldn't answer, so he just gave up. When he got to the bottom, the bloke threw his telly over the balcony and shouted, 'There's the fucking telly!' It only just missed him – it smashed to pieces on the ground. Our Wayne shouted up, 'You got the remote, mate?"

We all started laughing as the car stopped at the security gate house.

'Areet, Adolf,' Blue said to one of the security blokes.

'Who are those two?' The security asked, pointing to me and Ricky.

'Couple of new saveloys starting today,' Blue replied. Ricky and I looked at each other, puzzled, as he opened up the gate crossing the road. 'Thick as the Yellow Pages, him,' Blue said as he drove through the gate.

'Never guess what happened the other week! One of the lads, Billy - mad he is, always nicking stuff. Anyway, he was walking up the bank every night with a wheelbarrow with an old rag covering the top. Every night, the security lifted the rag and shone the torch inside – he sees it was empty and let him through. This happened every night for a fortnight – he was too thick to realise he was only nicking wheelbarrows!'

'Here we are boys! Welcome to Wear Dock!' Blue said.

'Cheers,' Ricky and I both said as Blue headed off towards a manky-looking canteen.

'Hey, why do they call him Blue?' I asked Ricky.

'Blue Peter! He's a right dirty old bastard. Sound, though – couldn't meet a nicer bloke. He's a good mate of my dad's'.

An hour later, we found ourselves in the health and safety induction room – a small, stuffy room with no windows or ventilation, only a door at either end, an overhead projector lighting the room and six sweaty, bored-looking new apprentices sat around a big white table.

A tall, skinny Clark Kent, a geeky-looking bloke, came in wearing white overalls and a shirt and tie underneath.

'Good morning, lads! My name's Gavin. I am your shafety officer. I'm here today to teach you all about shafety in the workplace,' he said with a lisp, which made a few of the lads chuckle. 'Let's leave all the jokes outside. I'm here today on serious business to teach you about shafety!' Gavin said, looking annoyed, which added to the giggles, especially every time he used the word 'shafety'.

We all sat nodding off, listening to Gavin's boring voice babbling on about the various hazards of working in a shipyard. He made it sound like we were stepping into the world of bomb disposal. His gory slideshow of various injuries that can happen was the only thing that kept us from nodding off, with the exception of Ricky, whom I kept nudging with my elbow in his ribs each time he fell asleep.

After an hour of gory slideshows and health questionnaires, Gavin shouted, 'Okay lads, we're going to take a short break. Help yourself to tea and coffee next door, and those of you who want to kill yourselves, feel free to smoke in the workshop,' he said, pointing to the other door.

Three of us headed for a fag out of one door, and Ricky and the other two headed out the opposite door for drinks.

'Wanna tube?' one of the lads said in a thick Geordie accent, passing a cigarette to me and a small, strange-looking kid with dark hair and beady eyes.

'Cheers! Andy by the way, mate," I said as I pulled a lighter out of my pocket and passed it around.

'I'm Iain,' he replied, lighting his fag up.

'You both Mackems?' Iain asked.

'Why, aye!' I replied.

The other lad muttered something about needing a dump and wandered off.

'What planet he's from, I've no idea,' I said, pointing to the strange kid as he wandered out the workshop.

'You a Geordie?' I asked Iain.

'I'm a sand dancer, me man. I'm from South Shields,' he said, proudly.

Suddenly, my dad wandered through the big gates leading to the workshop. I quickly dropped my fag and covered it with me foot.

'Shit, my dad!' I whispered.

'Does he not know ya smoke, like? Iain asked, laughing.

'Na, and he'd fucking kill me if he found out,' I said, with a worried look on my face.

'Aright, son,' my dad said.

'Aright,' I replied.

'Iain, dad – dad, Iain,' I said.

'Bit of a tosser, that Gavin bloke, isn't he?' Iain said, while taking another drag on his fag.

'Gavin? Na! He's alright him, man Bit of a job's worth, like, but he's okay. Wait til ya meet Photo Finish – now he's a tosser,' my dad said.

'Photo Finish?' Iain said at the same time, looking puzzled.

'You'll understand when you see him. John West is his name, or 'Tuna' as some of the lads call him. Right prick, though – watch him. He's been known to sack lads for fuck all,' my dad muttered.

I looked a bit shocked, not used to hearing my dad swear. Iain laughed, looking at me.

'Those things will kill you, son,' my dad said, watching Iain put his fag out.

'Disgusting habit,' I said, smirking.

Just as Iain looked as if he was about to spill the beans, Gavin's voice shouted, 'Right, ladies, back to business. Get your arses back in.'

My dad winked and walked out of workshop with a pipe over his shoulder, and Iain and I wandered back into induction room.

'Where's Colin?' Gavin asked me and Iain, and we both shrugged our shoulders.

'Dunno. Who's Colin?' Iain muttered.

'Right, anyway lads, we've got the head of shafety in this yard coming in to give you all a talk, so I want you to show him a bit more respect than you've shown me,' Gavin snapped as the door opened and a bloke in his late fifties walked through the door with an unbelievable hunch in his back, his head almost looking down to the ground.

Suddenly, Iain started laughing his head off. I looked over as he pointed at the bloke who just walked in and muttered, 'Photo Finish', which set me off, and I suddenly burst out laughing. The laughter became infectious, and before long, the whole room was in stitches.

Just then, a nervous-looking woman in her late forties walked in, smartly dressed, with a tray of sandwiches. She carefully placed the tray of sandwiches in the middle of the table, looking puzzled as to why everyone was in hysterics.

'What on earth is so funny?' Photo Finish asked, looking straight into my eyes.

'Erm, erm – Father Ted!' I replied with the first thing that entered my head. 'We were just talking about Father Ted that was on last night.'

'I seen it,' Ricky laughed. 'Chris the sheep,' to which one of the other lads made sheep noises. 'Baaaa.'

'Baaaaaa.' One of the other lads joined in with an amazingly accurate impersonation of a sheep, which sent the room into hysterics again.

'I shagged a sheep once. Was gonna stop, but it kept asking for maaaaaa!' Iain shouted, now with tears of laughter rolling down his cheeks.

The rest of the lads were starting to see how pissed off Photo Finish and Gavin were, and they were trying to stop themselves laughing, but to no avail, when suddenly, Photo Finish slammed his fist on the table, sending the plate of sandwiches everywhere.

The room was suddenly silent, except for Iain, who burst out laughing, pointing to the sandwiches scattered all over the table. He shouted, 'They're fucking tuna!'

The room was in uproar now. Everyone was in kinks of laughter. Suddenly, the door to the workshop opened and in walked the strange, beady-eyed kid looking puzzled as to why everyone was laughing. Gavin shouted over to him, 'Where the hell have you been, Colin?'

'For a shite – I got locked in', he replied.

Gavin looked at Photo Finish and said, 'Where in God's name did they drag this lot from?'

'Cherry Knowle mental hospital?' Photo Finish muttered under his breath and stormed out.

When things eventually settled down, Gavin told us how lucky we were to be given the opportunity to earn a trade, and how Photo Finish (John West) was so close to sacking the lot of us over the outbursts. The mood in the stuffy room was now as cold as the coffee.

'Right, now I want you all to go and collect your P.P.E from the store,' shouted Gavin.

'P.P.E?' Colin replied, with a confused look on his face.

'Personal protective equipment,' replied Gavin, angrily. 'Which you would have known if you had the intelligence to open a toilet door,' he snapped.

'Head through the workshop door, turn left into the big shed and you will see a big sign – if you can read! It says, 'General Stores'.'

As we all stepped into the workshop, I noticed a group of scruffy-looking blokes, including my dad, gathered around the work bench giving us the once-over.

A small, fat, dark-haired bloke in his forties shouted, 'Which one is your boy, Fawlty? Wait, see if I can guess,' he said, pointing to Colin. 'Him.'

'No, he looks more like your kid, him,' my dad said, laughing.

He did too; both had dark hair, beady eyes and were quite chubby. In fact, Colin was his spitting double.

'Him,' he said pointing to me.

'That's my boy!' my dad smiled.

'Looks nothing like you – must be the milkman's,' he laughed.

Then he came over.

'Na, just kidding son. I'm John Cotton, or Dot as the lads call me,' he said with an outstretched hand.

'Andy,' I replied, shaking his, while thinking, has everyone got a nickname here?

'How's it going?' he asked.

'Aright,' I replied. 'Just off to get our P.P.E from the stores.'

'You couldn't do me a favour, could ya?' he asked. 'Will you pick something up for me while you're there?'

Before I could answer, he blurted out, 'Cheers. Just ask for a long stand. Ask Larry – he will know what I'm on about. Cheers, young'un – just leave it on the bench for me!' he said, pointing to a work bench in the corner.

By now all the apprentices had wandered out the workshop. I quickly ran after them and spotted them gathered inside one of the main, manky-looking old buildings. I wandered through the big double doors and joined the back of the queue to the store.

A friendly old face popped through the hatch asking for each apprentice's name and each time shortly after handing them a big cardboard box. The boxes contained two pairs of overalls, a helmet, safety glasses and a bag of other bits and bobs, I wondered how the hell I was going to manage to carry all that as well as the long stand thing for Dot.

My turn eventually came and the friendly-looking old bloke who had 'Ron' written in black marker pen on his hat said, 'Hello, bonny lad. What's your name?' smiling as he asked.

'Andy Carter,' I replied.

'Ah, you must be Fawlty's son! He said you were starting. Good lad, your old man,' he said smiling.

Then I remembered about Dot. 'Is Larry about?' I asked.

'I'm your man,' he said. 'What can I do you for?' he laughed.

Puzzled as to why he had 'Ron' on his hat, I asked, 'How come you have Ron on your hat if you're called Larry?'

'That's my helmet's name,' he laughed. 'Only joking. The cheeky buggers here call me Larry because I'm always happy – you know the term 'happy as Larry'? he laughed. 'Well, that's me, Larry,' he said, trailing off, chuckling away to himself.

'Anyway,' I said. 'Dot asked me to ask you if I can have a long stand for him.'

'No problem,' he said. 'Just give me a few ticks while I quickly serve these other lads here and I'll sort you out, bonny lad,' he said, then proceeded to serve one of the scruffy-looking blokes in the queue.

After about ten minutes, all the lads had wandered back to the induction room. I was starting to get a bit worried.

'What's happening, Larry?' I asked.

'Don't worry, bonny lad – I haven't forgot about you. I'll be with you shortly.' Larry laughed.

About another ten or fifteen minutes later, a scruffy black-and-white cat wandered up to me, brushing its head up my leg and moving between my legs making a loud-pitched 'meow'.

Larry popped his head out the hatch.

'Ah, here he comes for his dinner,' and disappeared again for a few minutes. He eventually came back out with two bowls; one had cat food in and the other had milk, with the word 'Bastard' written on each bowl in marker pen.

'Here, son – put these on the floor for Bastard, will ya?' Larry said, handing me the two bowls.

I placed them on the floor and the cat shot from my leg and started happily munching on his dinner. I went back to the hatch and noticed Larry had gone.

'Larry! Larry!' I shouted through the hatch.

'Coming!' he shouted.

Five minutes later, Larry appeared with my boxes of P.P.E. He dropped them into my open arms.

'Give me two minutes,' he said, 'And I'll get your long stand.'

Shit, I thought. It's been ages already.

Suddenly, there was a very loud bang as the double doors at the front of the building slammed open. Bastard, the cat, quickly ran off in fright. I looked up and noticed Gavin walking towards me with a well-pissed-off-looking face on him.

'What the hell's taking you so long? You've been gone over half an hour.' Gavin snarled.

'I've been getting something for Dot,' I replied sheepishly, trying to calm him down.

'Let me guess – tartan paint, solar power torch?' he shouted.

'No,' I replied. 'Long stand.' The penny dropped as soon as I opened my mouth.

'Long stand!' Gavin hissed. 'Oldest one in the book! Hey, you're as thick as your fatha, you boy! Has your stand been long enough?' Gavin asked, charging off ahead, not waiting for my answer.

Back in the induction room, it was form filling in time.

'Right, lads. I want you all to fill one of these forms in,' Gavin said, passing the forms around to each of the apprentices. 'Hand them back in and then you can go for your dinner.
One of you can pop out of the yard to get sandwiches for the rest of the lads.'

We all finished filling forms in, except Colin, who seemed to be struggling. Gavin wandered over to see what was taking so long.

'What's happening, Colin?' Gavin asked.

'Erm, er – I haven't got my glasses,' he replied. 'I can't make out what it says.'

'Here,' Gavin said and handed him a magnifying glass from his top drawer.

Colin pulled a panicked face, so Iain and I went over, putting two and two together that he couldn't read or write. Luckily, Gavin left the room, and we helped him fill out the form. I had to alter it a couple of times, as Iain kept writing things he shouldn't; for instance, where it said, 'Address', he wrote, 'No thanks, I wear trousers.'

The other lads were too busy to notice. They were deciding what they were having for dinner and writing it on a sheet of A4 paper Gavin had given them.

After a few minutes or so, Dan, one of the apprentices, came over asking us what we wanted for dinner and gave us the pen and the paper to write down our orders. Iain shouted, 'Just get me a crocodile sandwich, and make it snappy!'

I grabbed the piece of paper and wrote, 'Andy – cheese chip buttie'. Iain grabbed the paper and scribbled something on it. He then asked Colin what he wanted.

'I'll just have a sausage roll, please,' Colin replied.

Iain folded the sheet of paper over and wrote something on the front.

'Right, Colin, you get yourself up the shop out the way,' Iain said and gave him the note. 'Just give the note to the woman in the shop, mate,' Iain said as Colin picked up the pile of money off the table, reluctantly agreed and wandered out the room.

Gavin returned to the room and shouted, 'Where's he gone?'

'He's gone to the shop – ya said he could! There are his forms – he's filled them in,' I said, giving Gavin Colin's forms.

'Look at the state of that! There's more scribble on there than writing,' Gavin moaned. 'Why the hell did you send that numpty to the shop? He'll probably get lost,' Gavin snapped, shaking his head while walking out the room.

Thirty minutes later, we were all sitting in our bait hut, hungry, wondering where the hell Colin was.

'Where the fuck's he gone to get the bait? Newcastle?' Ricky shouted.

'I'm starving. Wish he'd fucking hurry up!' one of the other lads snapped.

Just then the bait room door opened.

'Right, lads, back to induction,' Gavin shouted. 'Haway, man.'

'Fuck off!'

'We've never had nee bait yet!' came the shouts from the apprentices.

'What you on about? Where's Colin?' Gavin shouted.

'He hasn't come back yet!' shouted one of the quieter apprentices.

'Told you he'd get lost.' Gavin laughed for the first time that day. 'Anyway, come on lads. Soon as we get this paperwork done, the sooner you can go!'

Suddenly, the canteen emptied, everyone getting the impression we could go home when we were finished with the induction.

'She seems in a happier mood,' said Iain.

Gavin's good mood didn't last long. As soon as we stepped outside, a police car turned up with Colin sat in the back.

'Good god, what's he done now?' Gavin shouted, looking on shocked.

Back in the induction room, ten minutes later: 'Of all the stupid pranks! I can't believe one of you could do this,' Photo Finish ranted.

'Immature and downright disgraceful,' added Gavin. 'And you, Colin – you should have told us you can't read or write,' he yelled.

Colin sat there like he had the world on his shoulders.

'Give me all your money. I have a gun in my pocket! You're lucky they're not pressing charges!' Photo Finish yelled, with a face of bewilderment.

'Tomorrow I want whoever is responsible to go up to the shop and apologise to the poor girl. Otherwise, this will not be the end of this. I may even think of getting the lot of you replaced.' Photo Finish yelled, and then walked out and slammed the door behind him.

'Right, lads,' Gavin snapped. 'Get out of my sight! Tomorrow is a new day. Any more stupidity and you're out,' Gavin shouted pointing to the door.

As we were walking out the door, my dad stopped me. 'What's this about an armed robbery at the greasy spoon cafe?' he said, laughing.

'One of the lads sent Colin, who can't read, with a note saying, 'I have a gun in my pocket – give me all your money',' I replied.

'Wasn't anything to do with you, was it?' he said, trying to stop himself laughing.

'No.'

'Good. Your mam will go mental if you get sacked!' he said. 'Tell her I'm going to be late home – I'm working 'til six,' he said, walking away and laughing.

I noticed Iain and Ricky walking up ahead, laughing and carrying on, so I jogged to catch them up.

'Go on, bet ya can't do it again,' Ricky was shouting at Iain.

'Fiver says I can,' Iain replied.

'Go on then,' taunted Ricky.

'Right,' Iain said, opening out his arms out preparing himself. Then he suddenly spat out his chewing gum, caught it sweetly on his right foot, kicked it up in the air and caught it in his mouth. Ricky and I started laughing as we headed up the bank towards the security gate. Just then Ricky started giggling.

'What's up?' Iain asked.

'Look!' Ricky said, pointing to the bloke with the wheelbarrow with the old rag over it, which set me off laughing.

Iain looked puzzled as Ricky and I walked through the security gate in kinks of laughter.

CHAPTER 3

Day two at the shipyard

Tools of the trade

Johnny Cash was blasting out of my dad's clapped-out Volvo, my dad singing at the top of his voice, with me in the passenger seat as we headed through the security gates to the dockyard.

'Morning Adolf,' my dad shouted out the window to the security guard as he waved us through.

As we pulled into the car park, a bright yellow, souped-up Citroen Saxo skidded to a stop next to us with hard-core dance music blasting out the windows.

'Morning Fawlty,' said the tall, stocky lad in his early twenties, leaping out of the car.

'Morning Decka,' my dad shouted back, sticking his head out the window.

'Watch out for him, Andrew – he's a nutcase,' my dad told me as the lad walked on ahead.

'How's that, like?' I asked as we climbed out of the car.

'He smacked his boss at Amec,' he said. 'Knocked him clean out.'

'Why?' I asked.

'His mam rang him in sick because his dog died, and his boss said, 'Tell the soft git to get himself in.' He got himself in alright and chinned his boss! The lads drew around him in chalk as he lay on the shop floor!' my dad laughed.

'It was there for months after, Decka got the sack, like, halfway through his apprenticeship, but these felt sorry for him and gave him a chance to finish his apprenticeship here. Canny kid – just a bit radio rental,' he said.

'Radio rental?' I asked.

'Bloody mental!' my dad replied, heading off towards his canteen.

I walked into the apprentices' bait room, but I didn't notice Iain sneaking up behind me shouting, 'Morning lads' in a camp, squeaky voice then jumping out of sight, so it looked to everyone inside that I'd said it. Everyone stopped talking and looked at me like a weirdo, then carried on talking.

Iain walked in a couple minutes later with a serious face. 'Morning lads.'

'Twat,' I said, laughing.

'Hey, you'll not believe what I've just seen,' Iain shouted.

'What?' Colin asked.

'Seen Bastard the cat having a shit, and you never guess what it did afterwards? It only started burying its shit!' Iain said, looking astonished.

'All cats do that, man!' Colin shouted back.

'What, with a shovel?' Iain said, laughing.

Everyone started laughing, except Colin, who just looked out of the window puzzled.

'You going for the bait today, Colin?' Dan asked Colin with a cheeky grin.

'I don't think so,' Colin snapped.

'Hey, where's Ricky?' Iain asked me.

'He's not coming in – he's got chicken pox,' I replied.

'Chicken pox? How old is he? Ten?' Iain laughed.

'Pringles!' Colin shouted.

'Eh? What's he on about?' Dan shouted.

'Adults don't get chicken pox. They get Pringles,' Colin stated.

'Pringles?' Iain laughed.

'Shingles, you daft twat!' Dan shouted, with everyone laughing.

'Hope he doesn't pop his spots if he's got Pringles, hey Colin?' Iain laughed. 'Because once you pop, you can't stop!' Iain shouted, which sent the rest of the lads in fits of laughter as the bait room door opened and Gavin stood in the doorway looking bemused.

'Alright lads! Just a quick word,' Gavin said. 'Right! Quiet down. Today's the day you start work. Pipefitters, stay here and wait for John; welders, come with me. I'll take you to the welders' bays to meet Ronnie. All other trades, follow me,' Gavin shouted, turning to walk out, leaving only me and Iain left in the cabin.

I lit a cigarette and passed it to Iain, then lit one for myself. I took one drag and then the door opened, and my dad walked in. I quickly dropped the fag onto the floor and covered it with my foot.

'You'll get shot smoking in here, young'un, if they catch ya,' my dad said to Iain. 'Anyway, Andrew, ya mam said she put my bait in your rucksack,' he said, grabbing my rucksack off the table and starting to rummage through it.

'Yours is the Morrisons carrier bag,' I said.

'How come you get a yoghurt, like?' he muttered, while raking through my bag. 'Salt and vinegar!' my dad yelled. 'How come I get bloody ready salted?' he said, looking annoyed, while still raking round. 'And a bloody Twix,' he shouted, shaking his head. 'Going to have words with her! Shocking,' he muttered, while storming out the bait room with his Morrisons carrier and slamming the door.

Iain started laughing. 'Must be mad working with your dad,' Iain said.

'I know. It's going to be mental,' I replied.

Suddenly, the door slammed open and a tall, stocky bloke with penny glasses and 'J.J' written on his helmet stormed in. 'You the pipefitters?' he shouted.

'Yes. You John?' I asked.

'Names', he shouted, with a touch of venom in his voice. I immediately took a disliking to this bloke.

'Andy Carter,' I replied, coldly.

'Andy? What, you were christened with Andy, were you?' he muttered, while writing in a notepad. 'Fawlty's son, aren't you?' he asked.

'Yep,' I replied.

'Most of the lads got in here because they stuck in at school, but you got in through the backdoor, eh Andrew?' he replied with a sinister look in his eyes.

'Bloody hell, who is this knob-head?' I whispered to Iain as John wrote something in his notepad.

'Your name?' he said, looking over the top of his glasses in Iain's direction.

'Iain,' he replied.

'Fuck's sake! Iain who?' John snapped back.

'Hunt,' Iain replied, looking at me with a look of, 'What the hell is this guy's problem?'

'You can wipe those dumb looks off your faces, Laurel and Hardy – you're not at school now,' he shouted and walked out, slamming the door.

Iain and I looked at each other. 'Does the prick want us to follow him?' I asked.

Iain shrugged his shoulders. 'He never said – fuck him,' he said, passing me a fag.

Just as we sat back down enjoying our smokes, the door burst open and John, looking furious, ran over and grabbed me and Iain by our ears, dragging us outside screaming. He dragged us to a manky-looking, dark and dingy workshop with all shapes and sizes of pipe on various benches and a stench of oil and dust.

'This is your home for three years, kids. While you're here, you do as I say. Understood?' John shouted.

We shrugged our shoulders.

'Understood?' John snapped, grabbing our elbows and squeezing our funny bones, which sent shooting pains up our arms.

'Aghhhhh! What ya deeing, man?" Iain shouted.

Decka walked into the workshop and saw him latched onto mine and Iain's arms. 'Hey, John, are you bullying kids again?'

'Decka, they're worse than you, these useless twats. Look at them – it's Dumb and Dumber!' John snapped back, shaking his head and looking at us. 'Right! Andrew, you get me a shifter, and Iain, you get me a hacksaw, and see me on the office roof in five minutes.'

John stormed out of the plumber's workshop.

'What a bell-end!' Decka laughed, looking at me and Iain stood there looking gob smacked.

'Don't let the prick get to you. He was like that with the second-year apprentices, the lads told me. Try that with me, I'll knock his teeth out!' Decka said.

'He can't get away with that, can he?' I asked.

'Bloody hell, man, you better deal with it,' Decka snapped.

'He threw a lettuce at me yesterday, and that was just the tip of the iceberg.'

Decka laughed and walked out. I laughed at the size of this guy rather than his joke. He was only in his early twenties, but he was built like a brick shithouse; his shoulders were huge.

'What the fuck's a shifter?' Iain looked at me, puzzled.

'Where we gonna get this stuff?' I asked Iain back.

We walked out of the plumber's shop not knowing what to do next.

'What a prick. How can he get away with talking to us like that?' I said.

'Fuck him. Just take the money,' Iain said, looking unaffected by the whole scenario, and wandered off muttering, 'I'm going for a shite.'

I headed into the big fitters' shed – I knew the store was in there somewhere. As I walked through the door, I forgot there was a bottom part to it and tripped over, sending my helmet rolling and me crashing to the ground nose first. Roars of laughter erupted from inside as I lifted my head off the oily floor.

'Young Fawlty!' Dot shouted. 'Just like ya fatha,' he said, as the rest laughed.

I slipped and slid trying to get up off the oily floor, each time falling back down; now my overalls were covered in oil.

'Where will I get a hacksaw from?' I asked, struggling to my feet.

'B&Q,' one of the lads gathered round Dot shouted as the other blokes all laughed.

'Haway,' I shouted. 'I went to the store to get your long stand – the least you can do is lend me a hacksaw!' I snapped back, amazed at my attitude, thinking the fall must have unlocked some long-awaited confidence as I finally managed to get to my feet, dripping with oil.

Dot laughed, reaching over into a big blue box, and as he opened it, a yoghurt shot out and covered him.

'What the fuck!' Dot shouted, looking at his toolbox, with all the lads gathered around him laughing their heads off.

Seeing a now empty yoghurt pot taped to a hacksaw blade, which was bent back under the weight of the lid and duct-taped to the front end of the box, I got the impression Dot liked being the prankster, not the victim. He was looking on with a mixture of embarrassment and anger when he handed me the hacksaw. 'Look after it, and remember where it lives,'
he said, handing it to me with yogurt dripping from his chin.

'Cheers,' I replied, trying to contain my laughter after seeing of one of the best practical jokes I'd ever seen, and feeling a little triumphant after the long stand incident, I hurried out of the fitters' shed, knowing John didn't seem like the patient type.

I wandered down towards the office and to the right of me I noticed a scarily big, old wooden ladder leading up to the roof. Then I noticed John stick his horrible head over the side of the roof, shouting 'Where you been? Bloody hell, man – just like your fatha!'

Shit, I thought. I wish I had a quid for every time I heard that since I started here.

'Get up here then! What are you waiting for?' shouted John.

At this point, I felt like saying, 'Enough is enough – I'm going home', but I remembered my days at McDonald's being shouted at by some jumped-up prick. At least this dickhead has been there and learned how to be a dick, I thought. No matter how hard it's going to be, these three years had to be done! I'm sick of being treated like shit. I'm going to be someone, even if it is just a pipefitter, I thought.

My thoughts where rudely interrupted by John shouting down the ladder, 'You on something?'

Here goes, I thought, as I climbed the ladder, shitting myself, thinking, 'I can't give this prick the satisfaction of knowing I'm scared of heights.' I climbed the ladder, grabbing on as if my life depended on it, while shaking like a shitting dog all the way up, leaving a trail of oil behind me.

'Scared of heights as well as thick as shit? God help us,' he shouted, shaking his head, looking down the ladder at me clinging on for dear life.

I climbed to the top of the ladder and headed over to the opposite side of the roof, where John was bent over the opposite edge doing something with the drainpipe.

'Give me the hacksaw, young'un,' John shouted. 'What's with all the oil?' he asked.

'I tripped over in the shed. The bloody floor's covered in oil!' I said, hoping for a twinge of sympathy.

'Bloody hopeless,' John muttered to himself as I walked over to him, handing out the hacksaw.

'Where did you get this? Look at the state of it! Covered in bloody oil!' he moaned as he bent over the edge of the roof and began cutting out the old drainpipe.

'Where's your mate?' He shouted.

'Dunno,' I replied, on the verge of turning around and going back down the ladder and never seeing this shithole again.

After twenty minutes or so of him handing me bits of plastic pipe bunged up with muddy green slurry and insults that made me feel like jumping off the roof, John suddenly shouted, 'Where the fuck's your mate?'

'I don't know!' I shouted back, defensively trying to escape further wrath from this prick.

'Thirty minutes he's been gone to get a shifter,' John shouted, spraying my face with spit.

What seemed like an hour later, I peered over the edge and saw Iain walking in our direction as John paced behind me shouting abuse, and, to my horror, I looked at Iain's right hand and saw what he was carrying – a hacksaw.

'Oh shit,' I thought as I reached over the side, trying to do my best mime act, signalling to ditch the hacksaw and go get a shifter, whatever the bloody hell that was! But it was too late – Iain just strolled towards the ladder without a care in the world.

John noticed me looking over the side, curious as to what I was looking at. He peeped over my shoulder and spotted it.

'Hacksaw! That's it! Go! Get out my sight, useless!' he shouted, pushing me towards the ladder.

Iain grabbed the ladder and began to climb up. I looked John straight in the eye, only for him to shout, 'Go on, fuck off! Hopeless. Hopeless!'

John took off his helmet and threw it in my direction, missing me by inches.

I quickly descended the ladder, wanting to get as far away from this prick as soon as possible. Iain screamed up to me, 'Ahhhhh! What ya deeing, man?' as I stood on his hand.

'Sorry, mate!' I shouted down. Iain let out another shout and fell about three metres to the ground,

'You alright, mate?' I yelled, genuinely concerned, looking at Iain lying on the muddy ground

'Aye. Hard as nails, me, man!' Iain shouted back, dusting himself off, shaking the hand I just stood on. I started laughing so bad it made Iain start laughing; the two of us were buckled over laughing. After finally calming down after a proper giggling fit, I said, 'Bloody hell, we drew the short straw with him, haven't we?' and jumped off the ladder.

'Unreal him, like!' Iain said.

'Fancy a belly buster?' Iain asked, changing the subject.

'Aye, why not,' I replied.

As we walked, Iain kicked a stone, which whizzed off ahead. 'Hey, did ya see that, man? These steel-toe-capped boots are quality for kicking stones.'

'Bet I can send one further,' I said.

Iain took a run and kicked a stone, sending it shooting towards the crane.

'Beat that!' he said, proudly.

I braced myself, and seeing a steel nut on the ground, I thought that would do better than a stone. I swung back my right foot with all the power I could muster, and I kicked it. Unexpectedly, it was somehow fixed to the ground, and when I kicked it, the thing didn't move! I did, however, and screamed like a baby and fell, grabbing my possibly broken toe. 'Ahhhhhhhh!' I screamed.

Iain was bent over with laughter. I finally got myself to my feet, my right foot in agony. I looked behind me. John was staring from the rooftop, open-mouthed, shaking his head with his hands on his hips.

'Frank Spencer, you man,' Iain laughed as John looked on, gobsmacked.

We eventually arrived at the very scruffy-looking burger van. A woman in her fifties, who was incredibly small, stuck her head out the hatch.

'What can I get you boys?' she said in a broad Scottish accent.

Decka burst through the queue and shouted, 'Two chicken legs, open!'

Iain and I laughed, but the Scottish woman looked at Decka unamused.

'New boys?' she said, looking towards us with a pervy grin.

'Aye, new apprentices. Full of horny young hormones, just for you, Alyson!' Decka laughed.

Iain and I grinned shyly.

A couple of minutes later, the burger woman handed Decka the biggest sandwich I'd ever seen, in a half stottie bun with bacon, sausage, egg, tomato, beans, black pudding and anything else that could possibly be fried.

'One belly buster,' Alyson shouted and handed it to Decka.

He opened his mouth and took a bite, sending egg yolk dripping down his chin

'Lovely, that, sweetheart' Decka shouted with his mouth full and handed her two pound coins and walked off.

I stepped up. 'One belly buster without tomato or black pudding, with brown sauce,' I said, reluctantly, seeing the size of the thing and thinking it would take me a week to finish it.

She nodded and turned to make my sandwich.

Iain shoved his way forward. 'I'll just have a chip buttie. And is your vinegar free?' he asked, winking at me.

'Of course, it is,' Alyson replied.

'Well, I'll take four bottles then,' Iain replied, laughing.

Again, I erupted into fits of laughter.

Iain laughed as Alison turned away to make his chip buttie. Iain, seizing his chance, undid the vinegar bottle top, leaving it loosely sitting on top of the bottle.

Behind us, Colin shouted over, 'Can I have cheesy chip buttie, please?'

'You can wait your bloody turn first,' Alyson snapped at Colin, handing me my belly buster.

I had to use both hands it was so big. I squashed it down with my hands, so I could get my mouth around it, sending egg and beans dribbling all over the counter.

'Look at the bloody mess you made on my counter!' Alyson screamed as she handed Iain his chip buttie.

I grabbed some serviettes and began wiping up my mess, just as Alyson handed Colin his cheesy chip buttie, Colin grabbed the vinegar, pouring it all over the chips. The top fell on his chips and the vinegar went everywhere, all over the counter I'd just cleaned, and Colin was covered in it.

'Bloody hell, man' he shouted. 'I'm going to stink.'

'That's it. Clear off, the lot of you!' Alyson shouted.

Iain and I set off in kinks of laughter again.

'What about me? My chip buttie! My bun's all soggy!' we heard Colin shouting at Alyson as we walked away, still giggling to ourselves.

'Who's serving at the burger van today?' Blue shouted to us from a distance.

'Alyson, I think her name is,' I shouted back.

'Get in!' Blue shouted, pulling a comb out of his pocket and running it through his scruffy grey hair and sprinted off towards the burger van.

Iain and I both laughed as we headed over to the bait room.

As we burst into the bait room, I made loud cat squeal noise, which made everyone jump. Just as we sat down, Colin walked in shortly after with a face like thunder.

'What's up with Colin?' Dan asked.

'He got covered in vinegar at the burger van. Iain loosened the top and Col used it,' I laughed, as Colin stripped off his overalls and wandered to the sink, washing the vinegar off his hands and face.

Dan laughed with a mouthful of coke dribbling down his chin.

John suddenly came bursting through the door, reaching over and grabbing Iain's ear, and then mine.

'Agghhh, what now?' Iain shouted.

'Break's over – out!' he shouted, dragging me and Iain to the door by our ears. Finally, letting go outside the plumber's shop, he said, 'Right, there's a ship come in. Get yourselves down to the dock, and I'll see you by the man rider in five minutes,' he shouted, storming off towards the fitters' shed.

'Bloody hell, I can't take much more of him,' I said, looking at Iain lighting a fag.

'Want one mate?' he asked.

'Cheers,' I replied, taking one out of his outstretched packet.

We walked along the dockside smoking and chatting. We passed the crane and saw the big, grey naval ship sitting in the dock with a big sign painted on the side: 'Orange leaf'. We walked out of the sunlight into the shade of the crane, when we suddenly felt little spots of water on our faces.

'Is that rain?' I said, looking at Iain, confused, as there didn't seem to be a cloud in the sky.

'Ughhhh! That tastes like piss!' Iain shouted, spitting out what just went in his mouth.

As we got to the edge of the crane, we made the mistake of looking up and saw Billy Animal, the crane driver, pissing over the rail at the top of the crane, singing, 'We're singing in the rain! We're singing in the rain!' at the top of his voice.

'Haway, man,' Iain shouted up, brushing the spray off his overalls with the back of his hand.

'Dirty bastard!' I said, shaking the piss off my helmet as we walked further forward alongside the ship.

'How we going to get on board?' I said, looking around, noticing there was no gangway to the boat.

'Didn't John say something about a man rider?' Iain replied as I spotted John storming towards us.

'Right, get in,' John ordered, pointing to a big cage with a door either side with a wooden floor.

We walked through the door as John attached a hook to the top and waved up to Billy to lower the crane down to pick up the hook.

'Bloody hell, are we going in this?' I screeched.

'Stop being such a fanny,' John snapped back, while hooking the crane to the top of our man rider.

Suddenly, it lifted sharply off the ground and swung left and right as it got higher and higher. I gripped as tight as possible onto the handrail as Iain looked on, laughing at me looking petrified.

John pulled a little black walkie talkie out of his overall pocket. 'Billy Animal. Call back,' he shouted into it, while holding onto the button.

'Billy Animal, eh!' came the muffled reply on the radio.

'Stop mucking about Billy and drop us on the aft end!' John shouted, as we seemed to be heading towards the end of the dock, swinging and swaying as the crane moved down the tracks, with Billy shouting something out of the window and laughing.

We looked down over the edge; we were now being lowered down over the water at the end of the dock gate.

'What's he doing, the bloody idiot', John shouted as he raised his radio to his mouth. 'Billy Jonson – call back'.

'Can't quite hear you, John!' came the reply as we got closer to the water.

'Lift us on the aft end,' John shouted down the radio. He was getting redder and redder in the face by the minute. The crane eased down really slowly towards the water. I looked over the dockside and looked at a crowd of blokes, including my Dad and Dot, laughing their heads off as the cage dipped into the water. Our boots underwater, now it kept on going til the water got to our knees, and then John's radio crackled, and Billy's voice came over.

'Is that aft enough for you John?'

'Stop clowning about and get us on deck, you bloody idiot,' John shouted down the radio.

After a couple of minutes, the crane finally lifted us onto the back end of the boat, with John shouting and swearing up to Billy in the crane.

'Bloody idiot! Speaking of which, Andrew, Iain, there are a couple of shifters. I want you to take that pipe out. We have got to take it back to pipe shop to remake it. I'll be back in five minutes,' he shouted, pointing to a small, copper looking pipe that ran along the side of the ship, and he walked away leaving us looking puzzled.

'And make sure you isolate it first,' John shouted, sticking his neck around the corner.

'What's he on about, 'isolate' it?' asked Iain.

'No idea,' I replied.

After about five minutes of wondering what to do, I opened the shifting spanner to the same size as the nut on the pipe and began to turn it. I couldn't get it to move, so Iain had a go, and it eventually started to turn. He kept turning the nut slowly until the pipe started to feel loose and a few drops of water started to come out.

'I'll see if I can find a bucket,' Iain said, giving me the spanners.

I carried on where he left off, turning the nut slowly, when all of a sudden, the spanner flew out of my hand and water started gushing out everywhere, soaking me and everything in the area, and it wasn't stopping.

'Iain!' I screamed, but there was no sign of him,

The water kept gushing out. I was now up to my ankles in water, with the water showing no signs of stopping.

'What the bloody hell you done now?' John shouted, running around the corner.

He ran towards me and shoved me aside, sending me flying into the water flat on my back.

'I told you to isolate it, you bloody idiot!' he shouted.

He quickly moved his hand about a metre from where the water was gushing out and turned a valve, and the water stopped. John turned to me with water dripping down his face. 'Get away from me now!'

I jumped to my soggy feet, and just as I was about to get out of there, Iain came around the corner with the smallest bucket I've ever seen. It was the size of a teacup. 'Found one,' he said.

John took one look at him and shot towards him. Iain dropped the bucket and ran away from him

'Get here!' he shouted, while chasing him down the corridor, swinging his foot to try and kick him up the arse.

I decided to run off in the other direction. Luckily, I noticed there was now a gangway in place, which I quickly ran across to the dockside. As I looked across, I saw John chasing Iain along the side of the boat. Finally, John gave up the chase, and Iain saw the gangway and quickly ran towards it. As he saw me on the dockside, he started laughing, and that set me off. We headed towards the pipe shop again, laughing hysterically.

'I'm going for a shit,' Iain said, thinking it was probably best if we kept out of John's way for the rest of the day. I thought I'd better go too.

'So am I,' I said and followed Iain into a manky-looking toilet block. It had a vile stench, five or six cubicles and a urinal overflowing, obviously blocked, but nobody had bothered to fix.

Iain went for the end cubicle; all the others were full, apart from the one next door, so I went to that one.

As I walked in, I saw Iain's head, as the cubicle walls were so low. He looked at me and laughed. I sat on the manky bog, not needing to go, just hiding from John, so I just sat reading the graffiti on the wall. The bit that caught my eye was, 'Toilet tennis. Look right.' I looked right, and on the other wall, in the same handwriting, 'Look left.'

'Hughhhhhh!!' I heard coming from Iain's bog, an extra-loud strain noise he made, then a plop, and then he shouted, 'Areeet!'

'Areeet?' I shouted back.

'Ya hughhhhhhhh! Going out tonight,' he shouted while straining again, with a plop sound at the end. 'After the nightmare today, I need a drink. Hughhhhhhh!'

'Me too,' I shouted back.

'Are you coming around mine then?' Iain shouted.

'You what? You live miles away,' I shouted back.

Suddenly, Iain popped his head over the side and said, 'I'm on the phone to my lass here you know. Can you keep it down a bit!'

About an hour later, I was on my way to my dad's car to head home after a nightmare day. I was walking with my dad and Decka

'Don't know if I can handle working here much longer,' I said.

'Don't let that prick spoil it for you,' Decka replied.

'I've heard he's going in for Photo Finish's job anyway as a shafety manager, so he'll not be bothering you for much longer,' my dad said, imitating Gavin's lisp.

Thank god for that, I thought, as we jumped in the car and Johnny Cash's 'Ring of Fire' came blasting on.

CHAPTER 4

Day 3

Wet dream

I was woken from my deep sleep by heavy thumping on my bedroom door and my dad yelling, 'Get up, ya tit! We've slept in.'

Good start to my day, I thought, as I climbed out of bed and headed towards the bathroom.

'No time for a wash – we're late man!' my dad shouted, while struggling to pull his jumper on.'

'You work in a shipyard, not The Ritz, ya handbag!' he screamed as he ran downstairs.

I ran into my room, sprayed on some Lynx and quickly jumped into a pair of old jeans and an old naff jumper and pulled on my old trainers. I ran down the stairs past my younger sister smirking on the settee and ran into the kitchen. My mam handed me my rucksack and put a piece of toast in my mouth.

'Hurry up – your dad will be going mad,' she said, quickly pushing me towards the door and kissing me on the cheek.

I charged out the door, ignoring my sister shaking her head at me. After slamming the door shut, I ran towards my dad's clapped-out Volvo. He was beeping the horn, shouting out the window, 'Haway, man – hurry up!'

I was just about to get in when my foot slipped on something soft and squishy and I fell to the ground. I quickly got myself up off the ground, dusted myself down and jumped into the passenger seat of the car, and before I'd even had a chance to get my seat belt on, my dad skidded out of our cul de sac with Johnny Cash's 'Boy named Sue' playing full blast.

'Have you shit?' my dad shouted at me.

'No,' I snapped back.

'Well, something stinks in here. You'd better have not trod dog shit in!' My dad looked at me with a suspicious look on his face.

A couple of minutes later, my dad pulled in at a bus stop.

'What are we stopping here for, like?' I asked.

'We're picking Dicky Don King up,' my dad snapped back.

'Hey, what you snapping at me for? It's not my fault we're late,' I shouted.

'You're the one with the decent alarm clock. You know ours is cream crackered!' my dad snapped.

'If the druggies next door's dog shut up, I might have gotten some sleep. The noise was worse than when you come in pissed!' I snapped back.

'You can less ya lip and all, or you can walk to work,' he snarled.

The back door of the car opened and a grey-haired bloke in his late fifties jumped in.

'Aright, Basil. You must be young Fawlty?' he shouted, reaching across to shake my hand.

'What's that smell?' Dicky asked.

'You bloody have shit, haven't you?' my dad screamed at me. 'Open that window – it stinks,' he shouted at me, pointing to my window.

'How was your weekend away, like, Dicky? Amsterdam ya went, wasn't it? On the ferry?' my dad asked, peering in his rear-view mirror.

'You don't wanna know, Billy. Bloody nightmare from the start,' Dicky replied.

'How's that, like?' my dad asked, then slammed the breaks on and shouted out the window, 'Watch where you're going, you silly cow! Bloody women drivers – should be banned, the lot of 'em,' my dad muttered under his breath as he looked up to Dicky in the mirror.

'Aye, the wife insisted on taking the bloody dog! We only just set sail and the bloody thing jumped off the aft end into the water!'

'Bloody hell, you're joking?' my dad replied, half laughing.

'Honest! They wouldn't turn around, the bastards, so I had to put up with her crying all weekend about the dog. Ruined our weekend,' Dicky moaned. 'But hey, you'll never guess what was waiting for us on the doorstep when we got back home?'

'The dog,' I shouted, excitedly.

'No,' replied Dicky. 'Six pints of milk! The silly cow only forgot to cancel the milk as well.'

I climbed out of the car and headed for the bait room, leaving my dad and Dicky at the car, as knowing what John was like, I was bound to be in trouble.

I got to the bait hut and opened the door. There wasn't a soul in sight. They all must be already out at work, I thought.

I got to my locker, which now had a cock drawn on it in marker, I noticed. I opened the locker, took off my jacket, threw it in the locker and kicked off my trainers into the locker. Forgetting about my earlier incident, I now noticed the brown, sticky dog shit all over my trainers, and now all over my jacket and locker. 'Bollocks!' I shouted.

Then I heard Iain's voice coming through the door. He walked in to see what was happening and started laughing his head off when I showed him the mess.

'Never mind that. John's going mental that you're late! You better get your finger out,'
Iain warned.

I quickly put on my boots, overalls and helmet and threw my rucksack in the locker, without thinking, straight on top of the shitty trainers.

'Ahhhh, bollocks!' I shouted again and slammed the locker door.

Iain lit two fags, passing me one while laughing. Just as I took a drag, the door burst open. I panicked, thinking it was my Dad, and dropped it to the floor, covering it with my boot. Iain, however, wasn't so quick.

'Smoking in here, you animal. People eat in here, ya dick!' John shouted.

He then grabbed the two of us and shoved us to the door and kicked me up the arse. When we got outside, John said to Iain, 'Right, you piss off to see Tommy the Brush. Tell him you're gonna clean the bogs,' pointing him in the direction of the big shed doors. 'And you, young Basil, I have a job even you couldn't fuck up,' he said, while dragging me towards the ship.

When he eventually let go, we walked side by side in an awkward silence. John broke the silence with an insult, surprisingly. 'So, how come you can't get to work on time like everyone else?'

'I was kept up all night with next door's dog barking,' I replied.

He reached into his pocket, pulled out a small packet of ear plugs and handed them to me. 'Put them in tonight, because if you're late again, you're getting a warning.'

I really can't stand this bloke, I thought, as we headed for the gangway. Once on the ship, he took me down a few sets of stairs into a small room with a metal hatch open on the deck.

'Right, listen to me,' John shouted, while shining the torch into the tank. 'This is a freshwater tank. We have to fill it manually.'

He pointed to a big blue hosepipe that was already hanging over the edge into the tank, tied loosely to a metal handle to stop it moving.

'Night shift have filled three quarters of it. Now you're going to fill it to that mark there.'

He pointed to a line clearly marked inside the tank. He gave me a little walkie talkie-type radio. 'Here, take this. Now, I'm going to turn the water on, and all you have to do is sit here, don't move, and soon as the water reaches that level, you shout me on the radio, and I'll turn the water off. It's probably going to take a couple of hours, so get comfortable,' he said, and began to walk away.

'Any problems, radio for me. You think you can manage that?' John shouted sarcastically.

'Yes,' I answered, and he stormed out.

'Dick,' I said.

He immediately came back in and slapped me across the back of my neck.

‘Take your finger off the button. The whole yard just heard you calling me a dick!’ he said, pointing to the radio I had in my hand.

'Shit. Sorry,' I said.

'You will be,' he said with a deadly serious looking face and stormed out.

'Dick,' I said again, this time making sure I didn't have my finger on the radio button.

After a few seconds, water came gushing out of the hose and into the tank. I was no mathematician, but I figured this was going to take hours. I pulled up a bag of rags and plonked it onto a wooden shelf about a metre above the deck and sat on it, staring at the water coming out of the hose.

It is going to be a long day, I thought, and began chucking bolts into a bucket to amuse myself. Once I got bored of that, I sat back, got myself comfortable on the bag of rags and began pondering life.

I awoke suddenly with a jump, realising I must have dozed off. I looked down and, to my horror, the tank wasn't only full, it was overflowing, and the room I was in was flooded.

'Shit, shit, shit! Think, think!' I shouted out.

I tried to think what I could do, but I quickly gave up. I picked up the radio and braced myself. I was in trouble big trouble, I thought. All I could do was admit what I'd done and apologise.

'John, call back,' I shouted into the radio, pressing the button. 'I don't fucking believe this. That baldy prick is going to kill me!' Then, to add to my woes, I realised I never released the button!

'John, the tank’s full,' I shouted, panicking, trying to redeem myself.

Then the call came back. 'I heard everything you said, Andrew. I'm on my way over.'

Shit, my life is over, I thought. I sat there terrified, awaiting his wrath.

After a few minutes of waiting, Decka walked in the door above the stairs and immediately started laughing. 'What the fuck's happened here?'

'I fell asleep. John's going to kill me, and I called him a baldy prick over the radio.'

Suddenly, John came barging past Decka, charged down the stairs, plunged into the water and splodged his way towards me, his face red and a look of intense rage on his face. He tried to climb onto the shelf, but slipped into the water and fell, totally submerged, into the water. He threw his helmet across the room and charged again at me, this time getting onto the shelf and grabbing my legs as I tried to wriggle away. He yanked me off the shelf and into the water and raised his fist to punch me.

Decka quickly hurtled down the stairs, dove on John and dragged him off me, jabbing him in the ribs. John was raging, but he saw sense; he knew he was out of his depth and couldn't fight Decka, who stood over him, fist raised.

'You're gonna get sacked for this!' he screamed at Decka as he winced in pain. Then he looked at me. 'And you!'

I was in panic mode. I apologised and pleaded with John not to sack Decka. 'It was me at fault, not him,' I explained, but Decka looked at me and winked, smiling, and suddenly backhanded me across the face.

I looked at him, shocked, already feeling a bruise swelling under my right eye.

'That's going to leave a mark that on young Fawlty's face where you smacked him, John,' Decka said.

'Who's going to believe I did that?' John shouted back.

'Well, I saw you with my own eyes, and so did he, didn't you, Andy?' Decka looked at me, urging the answer out of me.

'Yes,' I said quickly, fearing Decka's look in his eyes.

'I'm a fair man, John. You say nothing about this. We will get this water pumped out, and I'll not break every bone in your body if you keep schtum,' Decka snarled, staring intensely into John's eyes.

John weighed up his options, gave me the filthiest look, and said, 'This place better be spotless before today's out or you're a gonna!' He quickly stormed out, leaving me and Decka knee-deep in water.

As soon as John was out of sight, Decka burst out laughing, pulling a box of soaking wet fags out of his pocket. He handed one to me all soggy and bent and said, 'You got a light?', which set me off laughing.

After ten minutes or so, Decka left and came back shortly after with a big, heavy hose on his broad shoulders and threw it to the deck into the water, making an almighty splash.

'That should do it,' Decka said, wiping a spot of mud off his shoulder.

'Jesus, that looked like it weighed a ton!' I said, looking on amazed. Already the water was disappearing into the hose.

'Decka, I'm sorry for getting you in this mess with me. I appreciate the help, though. Cheers mate,' I said.

'It's no bother, man! Besides, I got to take that dickhead down a peg or two. If there's one thing I can't stand, it's bullies, and that prick's been getting away with it for years.'

My opinion of Decka changed as we sat watching the water suck up the hose. He seemed like a nice lad, a sort of gentle giant, but I'd seen today that he's not to be messed with.

'Sorry about the backhander, by the way. Looks like you're gonna get a black eye. I hit you harder than I meant too,' he said, looking at the swelling around my right eye.

'No bother. Hey, you don't reckon John will say owt, do ya?' I asked.

'Na, not if he knows what's good for him, but hey, let's keep this to ourselves. I know what he's like. He won't want to lose face. If word gets out, he might see his arse and grass us.'

'I'll not say a word, mate, cheers. I owe you one,' I replied.

The water now was nearing the point where it should have been originally, and I was going around sucking excess water out of corners of the room with a wet vac just as John walked in. He looked on as I was busy mopping up my mess and Decka was manhandling the hose out of the tank.

'Is that level okay, John, or do you want more water out?' Decka asked John, as if nothing had happened.

'Aye, that's fine. Cheers Decka,' John replied nervously.

'Look, John – sorry about earlier. It went a bit too far, but hey, look, it's spotless in here. No harm done, eh? And we won't say nowt if you don't.'

John thought for a second and said, 'Aye, I suppose so,' and walked out.

Decka looked at me and winked. 'See, told you. Sweet as a nut.'

Half an hour later, I headed into the bait hut. As soon as I walked in, the other apprentices looked at me and laughed at me dripping wet.

'You been swimming?' Dan asked.

'You could say that,' I replied as the door burst open and Iain came bursting in with a fish in his hands on a bit of fishing wire.

'Hey, look what I've just caught,' he announced, proudly.

'Where did you catch that? The river?' Colin asked.

'No, it was running along the jetty,' Iain replied, sarcastically. 'Obviously the river, you thick twat!'

Everyone burst out laughing.

Iain headed to the fridge and popped the fish on the shelf just as John, Photo Finish and the welding foreman walked in the door. My heart sank. I had the feeling John had blabbed about the flood incident.

'Right, quiet lads and sit down,' Photo Finish shouted in a very serious tone.

I sat there, fearing the worst, when to my surprise, Photo Finish announced there was going to be an owner's walkaround, so they wanted the place spotless. All the apprentices were to be given different areas to sweep up. John slammed a list on the table.

'Right, Dumb and Dumber, you two sweep the outer decks,' and he handed me and Iain a dustpan and brush each. 'Colin, you sweep the bridge,' and he gave him a dustpan and brush, and then stood staring at us. 'What are you waiting for? Go on, piss off!' and shoved us out the door.

Iain, Colin and I did as we were told and headed down towards the boat, kicking stones as we went. We approached the gangway and walked on board, but Colin wandered off straight past the gangway. Iain looked at me and gave me a puzzled look. 'Where's he going?'

I shrugged my shoulders and we started sweeping the deck. Iain started doing pull-ups on a pipe that ran across the deck head. After about five or six, he said, 'How many can you do?'

I gave it a try, struggling to get even one. Iain started laughing. 'You can't even do one?'

He jumped up and did another six or seven with ease.

'Watch out, here's John,' I shouted as I saw him walking down towards the gangway.

Iain quickly dropped down and dropped to his knees with the dustpan, gathering the muck while I swept it onto his pan. Suddenly, out of character, John started laughing his head off. Iain and I looked at each other, shocked, until John pointed over to Colin in the distance sweeping the bridge over the river.

John took off his penny glasses and wiped a tear from his eye. Seeing him without his glasses on for the first time gave me a surprise, and seeing his beady, nasty little eyes made me chuckle. He shot a look at me and said, 'What?'

'Colin sweeping the bridge rather than the one on the ship,' I replied, looking across at Iain. He was pulling a funny face. I suddenly burst out laughing again. John glared at me again.

'You laughing at me?'

'No, no! Colin,' I replied and suddenly got a fit of giggles, which I couldn't stop. I looked over at Iain, who had turned away, but I could see his shoulders moving up and down. Shit, he's got them too, I thought, while John stared at me.

'You are fucking laughing at me.'

'I'm not…' I tried to get the words out, but I couldn't contain my laughter. Then I heard Iain give a big howl.

John grabbed his shoulder and spun him around to see him in hysterics, red faced and tears rolling down his eyes

'What are you laughing at?' he screamed at Iain. 'Have you opened your mouth?' John asked, staring at me.

'No, honest!' I said, trying to stop myself laughing, but then seeing Iain in the corner of my eye, I couldn't stop myself. I was in kinks. and the harder I tried. the worse it got.

'You fucking have, haven't you,' John snapped and swung a kick at me. I swerved out of the way and ran to try and get away from him as he chased me around the deck. I ran as quickly as I could, turning as many corners as I could, until he was out of sight. John eventually gave up and walked off the boat, red faced. Iain looked on confused and creased with laughter.

About an hour later, I headed up to the workshop. I'd been hiding on the ship out of John's way for what felt like ages, but I had to head up there to get ready to go. As I crept into the bait hut, I spotted Iain in my locker.

'What you doing?'

He started laughing and removed the fish he'd caught earlier. 'I was going to hide this in your locker.' Then he pulled a face as if he'd just remembered something. 'Hey, Ricky's off, isn't he?'

He grabbed a knife from the sink and began working it on Ricky's locker, and after a little wiggle here and there, he popped the lock. 'Champion!' he said as the door swung open. He then popped the fish in Ricky's right rigger boot and placed his overalls neatly over the top. We laughed then got ready to leave.

As we were walking out the door, I noticed my dad's car just outside the plumber's shop to my right. 'Hurry up, ya tit!' my dad shouted.

'See you in the morning, bud,' I laughed as I jumped in the car.

Another day over, thank god, I thought. Only another two years, eleven months and twenty days to go 'til my apprenticeship was over. If only I knew then what I know now: that time would go by so quickly, and when it's over, you'll wish it was back again.

CHAPTER 5

Family matters

'It's 3 o'clock in the bastard morning man!'

I awoke hearing my dad screaming out his bedroom window. I jumped out of bed and pulled back my curtains to see what was going on. Just outside the square were about four or five kids in their late teens drinking bottles of cheap cider with rave music blaring out of a ghetto blaster in the old bus shelter. One of my neighbour's lights came on, and Harry from two doors down appeared at his front door with only his boxer shorts and slippers on and a cricket bat over his shoulder. He charged out towards the bus stop with a look of pure rage on his face.

'Bit late to be playing cricket, isn't it, Harry?' my dad yelled out the window as Harry stormed out of the square and crossed the road to the bus stop. He walked up to the kids' stereo and smashed it to bits with the cricket bat, and then began swinging it towards one of the kid's heads, missing only by an inch at the most.

The kids dispersed and ran off in different directions as Harry kept on swinging away at them. He smashed one across the back of the head as he ran off. Then he charged back towards the square. My dad applauded out the window and whistled, as did somebody else a couple of doors up the other way. Harry didn't even acknowledge them; he just walked in the house and slammed the front door behind him, nearly smashing the little windows on the top with the force.

I jumped back into bed, pulled the quilt over my head and tried to get back to sleep. Just as I was dozing off, the bastard dog next door started barking.

After tossing and turning for hours, I finally decided to give up and get out of bed. The carry-on at the bus stop, then the dog barking, then the bloody house phone ringing all meant I had absolutely no sleep, and I was knackered.

I jumped out of bed, chucked a T shirt on and headed downstairs. To my surprise, my dad was sat on the settee drinking a cup of coffee, fully dressed.

'What are you doing up? It's only 5 o'clock?' I asked my dad, while rubbing the sleep out of my eyes.

'You're going to have to get the bus in today – I've got to go in early. Night shift rang.

One of my pipes leaked. There'll be hell on if it's not fixed before the day shift come in. They're meant to be going on sea trials at the weekend!' He yawned.

'I'll just come in early. I can't sleep anyway with that bloody dog next door. I'll just drink coffee and read my book in the bait room,' I replied.

'You'd better hurry up then, because I'm leaving in a minute.'

I quickly darted upstairs, got ready, ran out the door within minutes and jumped in the car.

The journey to work was quiet, with my dad yawning and Radio 2 playing and a posh woman's voice talking about how there was going to be heavy rain up and down the country. It seemed strange pulling into the security gate in the dark, but the security guard just waved us through.

We pulled up in the car park to the dockyard and my Dad jumped out and wandered towards his locker room. I wandered in the opposite direction towards our bait hut.

I nearly jumped out of my skin when I opened the door and noticed somebody was lying on one of the long wooden seats with jackets laying on top of him.

'Shit, sorry,' I shouted with a jump, assuming one of the night shift lads was having a kip.

To my surprise, Colin popped his head out from beneath the jackets and said, 'Shit, have I slept in?'

'What are you doing here, Col?' I asked as Colin sat up and the jackets fell to the floor.

Colin sat up, put his elbows on the table, put his head in his hands and started sobbing.

'What's up, mate?' I asked, while sitting down next to him and putting my hand on his shoulder.

'Nothing,' Colin snapped and hid his face.

'I'm going to make a coffee. Do you want one?' I asked.

'Aye, please,' Colin replied, rubbing his face and looking embarrassed.

I boiled the kettle and poured a spoon full of cheap coffee into two manky cups that I found next to the sink.

'How many sugars, Colin?'

'Six,' came his reply.

Six! I laughed to myself.

I took the two cups over to the table and Colin shot a look at the cup with disgust. 'I'm not drinking out of that!'

'Sorry, I should have cleaned it mate.'

'It's not that,' he said. 'Look, it's got a Newcastle badge on.' He pushed the cup away.

'So, what's up mate? Haway, you can tell me – I won't say a word, I promise,' I said, looking at Colin, genuinely meaning every word.

Colin sat for a little while staring at the table, flicking a crumb.

'Things aren't so good at home. My stepdad is a pisshead and keeps hitting my mam and picking on me. I've had enough of it – that's why I've been sleeping here.'

'Shit, sorry mate,' I replied, shocked.

'Have you not told your real dad?' I asked. 'Maybe he'll sort him out.'

Colin stared at the table and said, 'I don't know my real dad. He pissed off years before I was born.'

I was a bit confused, but then carried on. 'Is your mam okay? Does he beat her bad, like?'

Colin looked at me and put his head down. We sat in silence for a little while I drank my coffee, and he looked up and said, 'Please don't say anything.'

'I won't,' I replied, offering him a fag. Just then, the door burst open and Dot appeared. I quickly dropped my fag in my coffee. 'Where's my hacksaw, young Fawlty?'

Shit, I'd forgotten all about that, I thought. 'John's got it, I think,' I told him.

'I want it back. I needed it this morning, you prick! We had to cut your dad's cowboy job out!'

'I'll have a look on the roof. John was cutting the guttering up there – he had it last.'

'Don't go blaming JJ – you fucking borrowed it,' Dot snapped back, storming out and slamming the door behind him.

'Fancy coming down the office with me, like, Col? I'm going to have to see if I can find his hacksaw.'

'Aye, might as well,' he said, standing up and grabbing his jacket off the floor.

We headed out the door and slowly walked down towards the office.

'So, how did you manage to get the job in here, Colin?' thinking it couldn't be down to his academic skills.

'My mam knows a bloke that works here. Not sure who, but he got me an interview and my charm did the rest,' he smiled and winked at me.

'It'll be worth it, all this, you know. My dad reckons once you get a trade, you can work anywhere Europe, America, Saudi,' I told him, watching his eyes light up.

'My brother, Alan, emigrated to Australia. I'd love to go there,' Colin said.

As we got to the office, I looked up at the roof and thought, shit, I really don't like heights. I hunted around the area looking for a ladder, and then I spotted the old wooden set that John used lying next to a big, green skip next to the dock. I picked up one end and Colin came over and grabbed the other end, just as I spotted my dad coming off the gangway.

We lay the ladder against the roof and noticed my dad looking over from the dock with a pipe on his shoulder. 'What are you up to?' He shouted over.

Colin and I walked over, and I explained about Dot's hacksaw.

'Be careful up there,' he said.

'Hey, you know what this is by the way, son?' he asked, nudging his head to the heavy-looking steel pipe on his shoulder. 'It's what's known as a spladunge pipe!'

'A what?' I asked.

Then he chucked the pipe over the fence into the water in the dock.

'Listen,' he said, with his hand on his ear. There was a big splash.

'Did ya hear that? Spladunge!' he said, laughing, and then walked off towards the plumber's shop.

I climbed up onto the ladder, while Colin held the bottom steady for me while I nervously made it to the top. I climbed over the ledge and up over onto the rooftop. The sun was rising over the sea in the distance I stopped and admired the view for a minute and shouted down to Colin, 'Lovely view up here, Col!'

Then I spotted the hacksaw over where John repaired the guttering on the opposite side of the roof. There was a big puddle in the middle, so I walked around the long way and picked up the hacksaw, all rusty and wet.

'I bet that baldy prick left it up here on purpose,' I thought to myself as I picked it up.

'Wow, it is a good view up here,' Colin said.

'What are you doing up here, man? Who's footing the ladder now?' I looked at him, shaking my head.

I started to head back over to the ladder, but rather than walk around the puddle I decided to jump over it. Suddenly, CRASH! The roof gave in as I landed. I crashed through the roof, falling completely through, bouncing off an office desk and onto the floor of the office.

Colin looked down the hole, shocked, and saw me lying on the office floor in a heap covered in papers and bits off the roof.

'You all right?' he asked as I looked up in horror, seeing what I'd done to the ceiling. All the plaster was hanging down and there was a big gaping hole where I fell. Paula, the office secretary, came running in. She had only just arrived to work and hadn't even taken off her jacket yet, and to her shock, she saw me come crashing through the roof.

'Are you okay?' she asked as she knelt down beside me, giving me the once over.

'Yeah, I think so,' I said, sitting up as bits of plaster fell from my lap.

'What on earth were you doing up there?' she asked, looking up to the gaping hole in the ceiling.

I explained the full story about the hacksaw, and she looked on, full of concern. 'You're gonna have to go to the first aid room – make sure you're okay,' as she helped me up onto my feet.

Colin popped his head through the hole. 'It looks like it's gonna piss down out here!'

I burst out laughing, but I immediately stopped when I saw the look on Paula's face. She told Colin to stay put and not to move while she took me to the first aid room. As we walked away from the office, I noticed Dot was walking towards us with a scruffy-looking bloke with a big, red, angry-looking face and a massive beer belly sticking out of his overalls.

'Aright, Paula,' the big bloke grunted in a husky voice.

'Could you lads do me a favour and foot the ladder down there. One of the apprentices is up on the roof that Andy's just fell through.'

'Aye, no bother, pet!' the other bloke said and headed down towards the office.

'Cheers Duncan,' Paula shouted.

Dot just stood there, open mouthed, looking at me.

I handed him his hacksaw and said, 'Sorry about that. John left it on the roof.'

He burst out laughing. 'Just like your fatha,' he said and followed Duncan down towards the office.

Paula took me into a small room, which looked a bit like my doctor's surgery, apart from it being a bit scruffy and white paint

peeling off the walls.
Paula gave me the once-over, stating that the nurse didn't start 'til nine o'clock, but she was a trained first aider herself.

After checking my blood pressure, shining a torch in my eyes and a few other checks, she was happy to let me go, so I thanked her and apologised for the mess I'd made of her office.

'Don't worry. I'll get Andy, the joiner, to fix the roof, but this will have to go in the accident book. Make sure you come back and see Gavin when he comes in.'

'Okay,' I replied, walking out the door and heading for the bait hut.

As I walked into the cabin, Iain was stood there with his Newcastle cup in one hand and a fag in the other. He saw me covered in plaster and looking in a bit of a state and burst out laughing. 'What the hell has happened now?'

Suddenly, the door burst open and John came storming over. 'What's this? You fell through the office roof?'

The place erupted as the other apprentices all burst out laughing. He looked at Iain, took his fag out of his mouth and dropped it in his coffee. 'What have I told you about smoking in here?' he ranted. 'And what's that smell of bloody fish?' he shouted with his nose in the air.

'You two, follow me,' he said, grabbing mine and Iain's arms. 'The rest of you, clean this shithole up – it bloody stinks!'

As we got outside, John noticed I didn't have my overalls on. 'Oh, for fuck's sake! Get in there and get ready,' he screamed, shoving me back towards the door. I got my gear on as quick as I could and joined John and Iain in the plumbing shop.

'What the hell were you doing on the roof, ya lunatic?' John said, angrily. 'Is there something wrong with you?'

I tried to explain about Dot's hacksaw, but he quickly dismissed what I said and started a new rant.

'Right, the boat is going on sea trials tomorrow, so we have loads of work on today – no more piss farting about! Iain, you're coming with me, and Andrew, you're going to give Duncan a hand.'

Iain looked devastated at the thought of being stuck with that miserable git all day. I winked and give him a sly grin when John's back was turned.

Shortly after, Duncan came storming in, ranting and raving about how the pipes are rotten. 'They should be all ripped out and started again,' he shouted and threw a pipe in temper across the floor. 'I've been here since 5 o'clock this bastard morning!'

'Aright, Dunc, calm down. The boy here is gonna give you a hand', John shouted back.

'Well, I hope he's got a magic wand!' Duncan said, giving me a filthy look.

Iain looked over and smirked. Looks like I got the short straw – again – I thought.

Iain and John walked out of the shop and left me alone with this angry, scary bloke. He started going through the pipe rack, throwing bits of pipe around in a rage.

'Grab hold of that,' he shouted at me, pointing to a length of pipe hanging in the rack. I tried pulling at it, but it wouldn't budge.

Duncan came over and shouted in my face. 'Grab hold of it, man!'

His breath stank of booze and his red face looked even redder close up, and his eyes were bulging. This man looked like a serious drinker and a very scary bloke. He shoved me out of the way, grabbed the pipe, pulled it out of the rack and threw it effortlessly on the steel bench, cursing and swearing as he did so.

Dot came walking in and was smirking as I stood there, gobsmacked, while Duncan grabbed the pipe, slamming it into what looked like a pipe-bending machine, throwing bits of pipe about in a tantrum.

Dot whispered in my ear, 'Don't wind him up – he's a bloody lunatic. Duncan Disorderly, they call him,' he said, smirking.

I'd already gathered as much as I tried helping him, but he just lost his temper and swore at me. He eventually got the bending machine working and was pumping on a handle, making the pipe bend.

'Pump that 'til I tell you to stop,' Duncan shouted.

I did as I was told and kept pushing on this handle while Duncan looked on. 'Right, stop!'

I stopped, and Duncan grabbed the pipe out of the machine and threw it on the bench with a big crash and bang. He started measuring the pipe and made two black marks on each end of the pipe with his marker pen and shouted at me, 'Cut there and there,' pointing to the marks he'd just made and stormed out, leaving me looking at Dot puzzled.

Dot laughed and gave me a hand lifting the pipe into the saw and showed me how to work it. He gripped the pipe in the machine vice. He pressed the green button and the machine began cutting the pipe.

'Cheers Dot,' I said, grateful for his help.

'If I didn't, he'd only go off on one! He's like a spoilt little kid, Drunken Duncan – right bad-tempered bastard,' Dot said.

My day just gets worse, I thought, as I undid the vice and turned the pipe around to cut the other end. Dot gripped the vice and told me to press the green button, which I did, and the saw started cutting the pipe.

Duncan came back in and seeing the pipe in the saw seemed to calm him down a bit. He went over to a big wooden box in the corner, looking for something, and shouted to Dot, 'Where are all the fucking flanges?'

Dot said, 'I'll go and get you a couple. Do you want me to weld them on for ya?'

'Aye, please mate,' Duncan said, sounding like a normal person again.

After a few minutes, Dot came back with two metal disks with holes in them and placed them on the bench. He grabbed a grinder and cleaned the paint off each end of the pipe and explained to me what he was doing as he pulled out his spirit level and put the flanges on the pipe two holes square. He then put on a welding screen on and shouted, 'Eyes!'

I didn't know what he was on about 'til he sparked up the welding machine, almost blinding me. Duncan looked on, laughing, and shouted, 'He said eyes! Cover your eyes, you idiot.'

He shook his head, got the level, placed it on the flange and said to Dot, 'Okay, mate.' Again, Dot shouted, 'Eyes!' This time I covered my eyes as he welded the flange to the pipe, and then Dot flipped the pipe around and did the same again.

A few minutes later, Dot had finished and cooled the pipe down in a big tin container full of water. Duncan told me to grab the pipe as he headed out of the pipe shop towards the ship with his tool bag.

'You're welcome, Dunc!' Dot shouted, sarcastically, as I followed Duncan out of the shop with the pipe on my shoulder.

As I walked out the door, the pipe seemed to get heavier on my shoulder. I tried to keep up with Duncan, but I couldn't. I had to stop and rest. After a minute or so, I lifted the pipe onto my other shoulder and continued walking towards the ship. I stopped at the gangway and swapped shoulders again, and eventually walked on board. I looked around and Duncan was nowhere to be seen. Iain came out of a door to my left. I asked him if he'd seen Drunken Duncan. He said, 'Aye, is that the pisshead who looks like his heads gonna explode?'

'That's him,' I explained and told him what a nutcase he is.

'He's over there, look,' Iain said, laughing as Duncan was mid-tantrum, throwing rubbish bags and old pipes.

'Look at the state of this place, man!' he screamed from the hanger.

I wandered over and Duncan pointed to the space where the pipe was going that we just made.

'If this doesn't fit, I'm away!' he shouted as he grabbed the pipe off my shoulder. 'Give me the bolts and gaskets.'

'What bolts and gaskets?' I asked.

Duncan went into a rage, screaming that I was supposed to have picked the bag up off the bench.

'You never told me too,' I answered back, immediately regretting it.

He looked at me and said, 'Go and get them now!' with an evil look on his face.

I ran as quick as I could up to the plumber's shop, but Gavin stopped me.

'Mr Carter! Come with me' he shouted.

'I can't. Drunken Duncan...'

I tried to blurt out the words, but he grabbed me and pulled me towards the office. He told me to sit down while he pulled out a letter and passed it to me. Before I had a chance to read it, he said, 'I'm issuing you with a written warning.'

I couldn't believe it. I was gutted. It was only my first week and I was getting a warning.

'Gavin, I'm sorry. It was an accident. I was just trying to get Dot's hacksaw back.'

'You disregarded safety, Andrew – that's the main issue here.' Gavin explained how I could have been killed and that this hasn't been the only incident.

I just kept quiet, thinking John must have opened his mouth.

After about ten minutes of filling in forms, I was free to head back to work. I headed to the plumber's shop and saw Duncan grab a bag off the bench.

'Where the hell have you been?' he screamed at me.

'I got dragged into the office,' I tried to explain, but he was in one of his tantrums, throwing things about and not listening to me.

He grabbed the bag of bolts and gaskets and stormed out, so I followed him, almost running to catch him up.

'I'm sorry. Gavin dragged me into the office and gave me a written warning,' I said, trying to calm things down.

'You deserve a warning. You're useless, like your dad'.

I was close to losing it myself now. I stopped for a second and tried to calm myself down. I took a deep breath and then followed the dickhead on board.

Back on board, Duncan told me to grab one end of the pipe as he grabbed the other. We tried it in the space the old pipe came out of, but even I could see the pipe wasn't at the right angle and looked way too short. Duncan insisted it would fit. We continued to struggle to get the pipe to fit for about five minutes, when suddenly, Duncan grabbed the pipe and threw it across the hanger, smashing it against an electrical box that cracked, and a big chunk fell off.
'That's it, fuck it. I've had enough!' he screamed and walked out.

I walked to the hanger door and saw him wandering off the gangway to the dockside, kicking a bin at the bottom of the gangway over in a rage. I stood there wondering what to do next when Decka crept up on me and gave me the shock of my life when he made a scream sound in my ear.

'You're jumpy, aren't ya?' Decka chuckled.

I explained the day I'd had – the roof, Duncan's tantrums, the warning. He just laughed. 'I'm on my third written warning, man! They give them out for no reason here.'

He explained how he drove a forklift truck into the river while he and the lads were messing about. 'Hey man, you'd have to kill someone to get sacked from here,' he laughed.

'Some of the dickheads here, I just might,' I replied.

Dinner time finally arrived. I headed into the bait cabin with Decka. As soon as we walked in, we noticed the smell of rotten fish was getting stronger.

'That honks!' Decka shouted as he sat down next to Iain, who was arm wrestling Dan.

'Get in!' Iain shouted as he slammed Dan's hand down on the table. 'Next!'

I jumped in the seat opposite him, thinking I would try my luck. Before we started, Decka explained my arm was in the wrong position. He straightened up my arm, and then we started. Within seconds, my arm has been slammed down. I was beaten easily.

I sat down next to Dan as Decka took the position in front of Iain to take him on.

'Where's Colin?' I asked Dan.

'He's gone home for dinner. He only lives up the road,' Dan explained.

Iain jumped up celebrating as he beat a gobsmacked Decka.

Five minutes later, Colin came limping through the door black and blue, blood pouring from his nose.

'Bloody hell, Col, you okay?' Dan asked.

Everyone rushed over to see if he was okay.

'You should see the other bloke,' he laughed as he winced in pain, holding his ribs.

Colin sat down. Decka handed him a bottle of water and told Dan to get some bog roll.

'Who did this to you?' Decka asked.

'Nobody,' Colin said and looked at me.

Decka noticed him looking at me and said, 'Haway, I'll take you to see the nurse,' and walked him outside.

'Bloody hell, who'd do that? He wouldn't hurt a fly, Colin!' Dan shouted.

Everyone sat in silence, wondering what had happened, but I knew, and I was raging. I kept quiet, keeping Colin's promise, but I was a bit unsure what to do for the best.

John came bursting through the door and grabbed me by the ear and shouted of Iain to get his finger out. He dragged me to the plumber's shop and started ranting. 'What the hell happened with Duncan Disorderly? He's packed his tools and gone.'

'Nothing to do with me – the bloke's a lunatic.'

I explained what had happened. Dot came in, caught half the story and joined in the conversation. 'He's off his head, man! He couldn't fit a pipe in a snowman's mouth. All he's bothered about is drink!'

John nodded along with Dot and had to agree.

'Look, Dot, take the lad here and fit that pipe, will ya? Remake it – whatever you have to do, bud.' John walked out, leaving me with Dot.

I wasn't listening as Dot rambled on about the pipe and what we were going to do; my thoughts were with Colin. There must be something I could do, I thought.

My thoughts were broken by Decka, who said to me, 'Word, outside. Now!'

I wandered outside, while Dot nodded that it was okay. As soon as I got outside, Decka had his nose right in my face with a scary look on his face. 'Has this got something to do with you? I saw the way Colin looked at you.'

'No honest, but…'

'But what?' Decka interrupted. 'You'd better start talking!'

I explained to Decka that I'd made a promise to Colin that I wouldn't say anything, but I could see from the look in his eyes he wasn't going anywhere 'til I told him, so I explained everything.

'Any idea where he lives?' Decka asked.

'No idea. Dan reckons he lives locally, like,' I replied.

Dot headed out of the plumber's shop. I explained to Decka that I'd better go, and I quickly ran to catch up with Dot, who was heading towards the ship. I caught up with him near the crane just as Gavin was walking towards us with Colin all battered and bruised, holding his ribs. They walked off towards the bait hut.

'They must be sending him home,' I said to Dot.

Dot's face looked full of concern. 'What's happened?' Dot screamed, looking at me.

'I don't know,' I said, but he sensed I wasn't telling the truth.

'You'd better start talking,' Dot said, grabbing my overalls and pinning me up against the wall with a look of rage on his face.

I was shocked, but I told him what I knew, and that I'd told Decka after promising Colin I wouldn't. Dot ran towards the plumber's shop and shouted at Decka. Within a couple of minutes, Decka and Dot came running out of the shop and quickly jumped in Decka's Saxo.

Decka sped away, but quickly spun the car around when he saw me and pulled up next to me.

'Get in!' Decka shouted.

I quickly jumped in the back seat and we sped off towards the gate.

'Where are we going?' I asked.

Decka looked in his mirror and said, 'To pay somebody a little visit.'

A few minutes later, we skidded to a stop outside a scruffy-looking block of flats.

'Which way, Dot?' Decka shouted.

'Up there. Number 44,' Dot said, pointing up to the fourth level.

Decka charged up the concrete steps with me and Dot following, trying to keep up.

'Smells worse than the bait cabin in here,' I commented, as the stairwell stank of stale piss.

We got to the fourth floor and Dot said, 'Hang on, Decka, let me. He might not even be in.'

Decka stepped aside and let Dot knock on the big blue door with a crack in the frosted glass window. A couple of seconds later, the door opened and a small, chubby, dark-haired woman in her mid-forties opened the door with the biggest black eye I'd ever seen.

'What the hell are you doing here?' the woman screamed at Dot.

'Have you looked in the mirror? And Colin's in a worse state than Russia!'

The woman replied, 'Look, you gave up your right to care when you pissed off all those years ago. We don't need you!'.

Dot stood staring at her in disbelief. 'Pam, look at the state of you, man! Where's that drunken prick?'

Suddenly and without warning, Decka went storming past Pam and headed into the flat. We heard a big crash and bang and then shouting and screaming; then, before we knew it, Decka came through the door with a battered-looking Duncan Disorderly.

I looked at Dot, stunned, as Decka had the heavy-built bloke by the throat and dragged him to the railing that looked down over where we parked the car four storeys down. Decka had Duncan by the throat, leaning him over the balcony, with Duncan now pleading for his life and Pam screaming.

'You listen carefully, Duncan.' Decka had his nose in Duncan's face, staring into his eyes. 'You leave here now, and if you ever show your face around here again, you're going headfirst over there. You hear me?'

Duncan screamed, in tears, 'Yes, yes, please – just let me go!'

Decka pulled him away from the balcony and slammed him against the wall next to the door, then head-butted him in the nose. Duncan fell to the floor, clutching his bloodied nose. Pam screamed, 'Enough!' and grabbed Decka, who was about to kick Duncan while he was on the floor.

Pam shouted at Duncan, 'Just get your things and go, please!' Tears streamed down her face.

Decka picked him up off the floor and shoved him towards the front door. He quickly scrambled to his feet and staggered in the house, doing as he was told. Colin appeared from the stairwell, went running to his Mam and hugged her. 'You ok, mam? What's happening?'

'It's okay, son. It's all going to be okay now.' She hugged him and kissed him on the forehead.

A few minutes later, Duncan came staggering out the house with a tatty old brown suitcase and a big bag of tools. Decka grabbed the tool bag and threw it over the balcony, then suddenly heard a big crash and a car alarm going off.

'Bollocks!' Decka screamed as he looked over the balcony and realised the tool bag had just smashed through the windscreen of his pride and joy.

Duncan saw the angry look on Decka's face and ran as fast as he could, clutching his nose and headed down the stairwell out of sight.

I shouted after him, 'You've forgot ya case!' and threw it over the balcony with another big crash. Decka looked at me, and this time, I started running for the stairwell, but Decka just looked at Dot and the two of them burst out laughing.

Colin and his mam headed inside, and Pam turned and looked at Decka and Dot and gave a smile. 'Thanks lads.'

CHAPTER 6

Last laughs and photographs

For once, I woke up early. I even shouted my Dad to get up out of bed. The only reply I got was, 'Piss off!'

I sat waiting in the car, bored, so I ejected my cassette out of my Walkman and stuck it in the car cassette player. My dad jumped in the driver's seat eventually and said, 'You shit the bed? Not like you to be up at this time!'

As he turned out of the square, my cassette came on and Cornershop's 'Brimful of Asha' started playing. I sat waiting for him to say something; it seems as though I was always criticising his choice in music.

A minute or so later, the rant came, just as my dad pulled over at the bus stop and Dicky jumped in the back. 'What's this shit? Everybody needs a bosom for a pillow?'

Dicky also joined in. 'It's all boy band shite now, Fawlty. No taste in music, the kids of today!'

The Verve's 'Bittersweet Symphony' came on next and not a word between them. My dad even hummed along at one point. I sat there looking all smug, knowing that song won them over. Then the next track came on: Aqua, 'Barbie Girl.' My dad ejected the tape, threw it out the window and looked at me in disgust. He then raked about in his side door while keeping one eye on the road and eventually found what he was looking for. He popped in the cassette and Johnny Cash, 'Ring of Fire', came on.

'That's more like it, Fawlty,' Dicky shouted as I sat there, sulking.

As we pulled into the car park at the dockyard, JJ was walking past. He stopped and looked at us in shock, rubbing his eyes and started clapping his hands.

'On time for once?' he shouted as we got out the car, then started laughing to himself as he walked down towards the plumber's shop.

My dad and Dicky headed down to their locker room as I walked over towards the bait hut. I noticed Ricky heading in the door before me.

'Alright mate – welcome back,' I said, patting him on the back.

'Bloody hell, it stinks in here!' he said as he headed in towards his locker.

I sat down opposite Colin, next to Iain.

'Good thing he got over that bad case of Pringles, eh Colin!' Iain laughed.

Ricky kicked off his trainers and popped on his overalls, then slipped his foot into his left rigger boot as we all looked on in anticipation, knowing Iain had stuffed a fish in his right rigger boot the other day. Ricky stopped what he was doing and looked round at Iain. 'Pringles?' he said, looking puzzled.

He then carried on and popped his right foot in his boot, and there was a crunchy, squishy sound accompanied by a horrendous smell of rotten fish. Ricky started retching to be sick as he pulled his foot out of the boot and saw what remained of the fish. He ran to the door with his hand over his mouth, quickly opened the door and vomited. He looked up in horror to see John stood there, now with puke all over his white overalls. We all howled with laughter as Ricky was dragged out the cabin by his ear.

Ten minutes later, John came back in wearing a new pair of overalls and looking well pissed off.

'Right, Dumb and Dumber!' he shouted. 'You're going to do your NVQs today. You have to meet Davey Chocolate at the induction office in ten minutes.'

He stormed out, slamming the door behind him.

'Davey Chocolate?' I said, looking at Iain and wondering if the name was a wind-up.

Ricky came bursting back in five minutes later rubbing his hands together and grinning from ear to ear.

'Get in! They've just said they're sending me home on full pay!' he laughed.

'After seeing me vomiting, they think I'm still bad,' Dan shouted from the other table. 'You're going to miss the crane game final.'

'The what?' Iain asked.

Dan explained how there's an overhead crane in the big shed. You have to grab the hook, and someone lifts you up using the controller 'til your bottle goes, and you shout stop. Then they then bring you back down.

'It's the final today between Colin and Whopper Napper!'

'Who's Whopper Napper?' I asked, laughing.

'You know, man. Gaz, that Sparky with the massive head.'

'Who, Sniper's Dream?' Iain shouted.

'Aye, that's him. Anyway, he beat me yesterday, and I got about six metres up. Fearless, he is. Mind you, Colin beat Fat Kev, so it'll be those two in the final. It'll be some match, like!' Dan explained.

'We have to go do our NVQs with Davey Chocolate! Hopefully, we don't miss it,' I replied, wondering if I should have a go myself.

Ten minutes later, Iain and I were sat in the induction room playing coin football and waiting for Davey Whoever-he-was. Just as I was celebrating my two-nil lead, the door opened and a huge guy, well over six-feet tall, came in dressed in a smart pinstriped suit. He was a strange-looking bloke in his forties, with jet black hair, a big pointy nose and a massive beer belly.

'Hello boys. My name's David Rowntree. I'm the yard's NVQ manager. I'm here with you every Friday to help you do your books,' he said in a very camp voice.

He explained how every week, we had to keep a diary of the pipework we had done, and we were to take pictures using the company camera.

'This week, one of you will have the camera, and next week, the other, right? Which one of you is Andrew?' he asked.

Seeing me with my hand up, he handed me the camera. It was an old silver, rectangular Kodak camera, similar to the one my dad had at home.

'It's already got the film in. All you have to do is take the pictures and give it back to me next Friday, and I'll get them developed and get a new film put in for Iain,' Davey said, showing me how to work the camera.

David seemed like a nice guy and offered us tea and coffee and sat chatting to us, asking how work was so far, and even came outside for a smoke with us, smoking his old wooden pipe. He seemed very laid back; he even gave Iain a smoke of his pipe, as he kept pestering him for a go and asking what it was like.

Back in the induction room, he gave us both a big blue folder with about 300 empty pages. 'These folders will be full three years from now. I want you to put in each job you do, with a little description and a photo or sketch with each job,' Dave said, handing us the information packs and a few forms to fill in.

After about thirty minutes or so, he told us we could get back to work, so we started heading out the door. Dave handed me the camera, which I'd totally forgotten about, leaving it on the table.

'Please be careful with the camera, lads. It's the only one they've given me and use it wisely!' Dave said, before heading off to his maroon Rover parked outside the office.

We were just about to head to the plumber's shop when Iain suddenly remembered the crane game final.

We quickly ran past the plumber's shop door hoping John wasn't in there and headed into the big shed. As we ran through the door, I tripped again over the same bottom part of the bastard door frame that got me the other day and I fell to the ground to roars of laughter from the lads standing round the toolboxes. Iain picked up the camera that fell out of my hand, ran in front of me and took a picture as I struggled to get to my feet. Dot, my dad and a few others stood laughing as I got to my feet. Luckily, today there wasn't a big puddle of oil, so I just dusted myself down, shook my head and headed over to the crane, where Dan and a few others were preparing for the big finale.

We had missed Colin's attempt, but it was a very respectable ten metres up, Dan informed us. Now was Gary's turn, or 'Whopper Napper', as the lads call him.

My god, I thought – he did have a big head. He was tall and of average build, but he had a massive head that wasn't really in proportion with the rest of his body. Gaz cracked his knuckles, then reached up and grabbed the crane hook as Dan pressed the up button on the controls and he began to move up slowly – one metre, then two. He continued going up with nothing to cushion his fall if he fell. I stood rooted to the spot, watching open-mouthed as Whopper Napper showed no fear and smashed Colin's record.

Dan announced, 'I reckon twelve meters. Well done, Gaz,' he shouted up and started bringing him down. When his feet finally touched the ground safely, I breathed a sigh of relief.

Everyone shouted, 'Well done!' and whistled and patted him on the back as he walked by, arms raised in triumph.

'Well done, Whopper Napper,' I shouted as he walked past.

'You what? Dickhead!' he shouted over to me and had a look in his eye like he was going to whack me, but he just walked over to Dot and my dad and the rest and shook his head.

Dan looked at me, stunned, and informed me that people don't normally call him that to his face.

As all the other apprentices left, it was only me and Iain. I was feeling brave, and my competitive side was beating my fear of heights.

'Haway, let's give it a shot,' I said, walking over to the hook.

Iain grabbed the controller that hung down on a thick, black cable, 'Ready?' he shouted.

'Aye.'

I grabbed the hook and off I went, heading upwards. As soon as I got about a metre up, I started panicking, but Iain kept pushing the up button, eventually stopped about five metres up and then took my picture with the camera.

Whopper Napper came running over and snatched the controller.

'Whopper Napper, eh?' he shouted and started moving the crane towards the back of the shed, with me clinging on, screaming 'Stop!'

He kept going. I was finding it hard to keep grip as the crane bumped along, and I started swinging and swaying. He finally started slowing down as my dad shouted over, 'Hey man, be careful!'

Whopper Napper noticed my dad was pissed off, so he lowered me down a little bit to a safer height and manoeuvred me over the cooling tank. The cooling tank was basically a big steel tank that the sheet metal workers used. It was full of water to cool hot metals down. I looked down below me. There was only a metre's drop and then another metre or so of dirty, rusty-coloured water.

Whopper Napper left me to hang above the water and walked away laughing, handing the controller to Iain. My dad came over as Iain began taking more pictures with his free hand.

'Haway!' my dad said. 'Give me the controller.'

He grabbed it off Iain and was just about to manoeuvre me away from the water, but my arms were aching, and my fingers were starting to slip down the hook. As soon as my dad got the crane moving, I couldn't hold on any longer; my fingers started slipping, and I fell. There was a massive splash as I fell feet first into the water up to my waist, and then fell backwards, fully submerging myself in the rusty, smelly water.

I was drenched. The water felt freezing cold and my overalls and wet clothes felt so heavy as they clung to my skin. I quickly scrambled to my feet and climbed up onto the edge of the tank and jumped out. The sounds of hysterical laughter came from my dad, Iain and the others as I climbed up off the floor and stood there, soaked through to my skin. Iain began again taking pictures of me stood there freezing and drenched.

Back at the bait room for dinner time, I'd taken all my wet clothes off and jumped into Ricky's spare pair of overalls, which were about three sizes too small and looked ridiculously tight. I hung my wet clothes over various chairs and turned the electric heaters on full blast to try and dry them out.

'It's like a sauna in here!' Dan shouted as he burst through the door.

I ignored him, as I was too busy trying to hang my soaking wet boxer shorts next to my wet socks along the top of my locker door.

Iain burst in and started laughing, seeing all my wet clothes hanging around the place.

'Good thing I had the camera!' he shouted.

'Look man, Davey is going to go mad. That's supposed to be for my work,' I snapped at Iain.

'Look, it's no bother. We will get your mate Whopper Napper to delete the pictures. He's a sparky, isn't he? He'll know how to do it. Then we can take some pictures of pipes in the plumber's shop – there are loads of pipes in there. We can just pretend you made them,' Iain said.

'Good thinking, Batman!' Dan shouted.

'Thank you, Robin!' Iain replied with a wink and a nod.

It's worth a try, I suppose, and it will give me a chance to apologise, I thought.

After about ten minutes of rooting around old lockers to find some old boots, I used Ricky's left rigger boot and a random right boot that didn't match and had laces unlike my left. We headed over to the electrician's place, which was situated just opposite the plumber's shop, so we ran, hoping John wouldn't see us. We opened the big wooden door with a sign on that said, 'Keep out. Skilled tradesman only.'

We walked into the stuffy little shed. There were coils of cables hung up everywhere and four scruffy-looking blokes sitting on a wooden bench drinking tea. One of them was Whopper Napper, who looked at me with an angry glare. Iain passed me the camera and nudged me forward.

'Sorry to bother you, lads. Just wondering if any of you know anything about cameras?' I asked, nervously.

I explained the situation and told him there were pictures on there that needed deleting. Whopper Napper took the camera from me. 'And I'm very sorry about earlier,' I said as I watched him giving it the once-over.

'There's nothing you can do once you've taken the pictures, but you still have twenty left,' he explained. 'Don't know why you're so bothered. Davey is sound anyway – he'll probably just laugh about it. Just take some random pictures of pipes on the boat and pretend you made them,' Whopper said.

'Good thinking, Batman,' I said for some reason. God knows why.

'Did you just call me fat man?' he screamed and stood up.

'No, no! I said Batman,' I replied, nervously.

'Batman? Why the fuck did you just call me Batman?' he asked as I stood there, cringing.

I looked over at Iain. He was hiding his face in an embarrassing, cringe-stricken way.

'You were supposed to say, 'Thank you, Robin…'' I stuttered, struggling to get my words out.

'Should I have? Sorry,' he said, obviously being sarcastic.

Cheeks now glowing red with embarrassment, the four blokes looked at me like I was some sort of weirdo as I stood there with odd boots and naked under my skin-tight overalls. I quickly snatched the camera and ran out the door.

Iain followed me out, looked at me and just burst out laughing. 'That was the most horrible, cringeworthy moment I've ever witnessed,' he said, tears streaming down his face with laughter.

We headed back to the plumber's shop, where John stood with his hands on his hips.

'Where the hell have you two been?' he screamed.

'Taking pictures of our work,' I said, showing him the camera.

'What work? You've done no work!' he shouted. 'It's a shame you didn't have the camera earlier in the week – you could have taken a picture of the floods you caused, or even the big hole in the office roof you fell through.'

John stared at me with a confused look, probably wondering why I was wearing odd boots and had no clothes on under my overalls.

'Anyway, there's a toolbox talk in the big shed at two o'clock this afternoon, so be there. It's pointless giving you a job now. Just wait here and try not to break anything or flood the place!' he shouted as he stormed out the door, passing Decka on his way in.

'Aright, ladies. You got the camera this week, young Fawlty?' Decka said, noticing the camera in my hand.

I explained all the pictures Iain took. He laughed and said, 'Hey, just do what I did. Watch this.'

He picked up a pipe with a flange on one end, got his spirit level out and popped it on the top. He gave Iain the camera and directed me where to stand, holding the spirit level over the bolt holes of the flange. He stepped behind me out of my view. 'Left arm up a bit,' he said from behind me and told Iain to take the picture. I didn't realise he was behind me undoing his pants, bending over and showing his arse as Iain took the picture.

Then he guided me to a pipe that had been completed by someone else. He turned away from me briefly, then handed me the pipe and told me to stand holding it to the camera. I should have realised something was going on when Iain started smirking, but I happily posed for the picture. Written in black marker on the side of the pipe facing the camera was, 'I have a tiny penis', which I didn't see.

Then he guided me to the welding machine, switched it on and gave me a welding mask to put on my head. He grabbed the pipe with the flange on and put it on the workbench.

'Right, get ready to weld. Just bend over and tap it on the pipe and it will spark up and look like your welding. Iain, you take the picture,' he shouted to Iain as I leaned over the table, sparking the torch to life, not realising Decka was posing as if he had me bent over the table.

'There you go. That's three jobs you've done now. Davey will be okay about the other pictures, man! He's a good bloke, Chocolate,' Decka said, putting my mind at rest.

'Aye, he's sound. He even let me smoke his pipe,' Iain replied Decka and I grinned.

'Aye, I bet he did,' laughed Decka.

'Cheers for this,' I said, thinking again that this lad had saved the day.

'Haway, lads, it's two o'clock toolbox talk,' he said, looking at his watch and quickly darting out the door.

'What's a toolbox talk?' I asked Iain.

He opened the lid of a toolbox on the bench and muttered, 'Hello, I'm a toolbox' in a squeaky voice, lifting the lid up and down as he spoke.

Iain and I eventually walked into the big shed and the meeting was already under way. About a hundred blokes were gathered around Gavin, Paula, Photo Finish and some other bloke I'd never seen before.

Everybody turned to look at me as I followed Iain in, as the wind suddenly picked up and slammed the big metal door behind me with a massive bang. There I was, stood with odd boots and clearly naked under my overalls. There were a few odd looks and a few scattered laughs as I stood there, red-faced, wanting the ground to swallow me up.

'Thanks for that entrance, lads,' Gavin shouted with an angry look on his face.

Then the other bloke looked at me in a strange way and began shouting, 'As I was saying – until I was rudely interrupted – we have no more work on the order books here, unfortunately. As soon as the orange leaf goes, we will have to let a lot of you go, but the Hebburn yard has a requirement for a few trades, so if that interests any of you, please sign the sheet that is being passed around, and make a note next to your name that you're interested and we will contact you in due course. Now again, lads, I'd like to take this opportunity to thank you for all your hard work, and I assure you all, as soon as work picks up here, we will be in touch.'

'So, when are we getting our notice?' one of the platers at the back shouted.

'Paula here has some letters for a lot of you. Again, I'm sorry,' the bloke shouted, holding his hand up apologetically.

Iain and I headed back to the bait room a little shocked at what we had just heard. The other apprentices were sat around wondering where that left us.

After about ten minutes or so, Gavin came in and informed us all we were all being transferred to the Hepburn yard on Monday to continue our apprenticeships there, as it was going to be a while before another ship came in.

'Take the rest of the afternoon off, lads, to make arrangements to get there on Monday. Here is the full address and all the information needed,' he said and handed us all a little handbook.

'Take this opportunity as a fresh start, lads, and no more mucking about.'

He walked out, slamming the door. We all stripped off our overalls ready to leave. I hid behind the locker door, as I had nothing underneath.

I reached over to get my overalls from the top of the heater when suddenly Iain slammed my locker door shut and started taking pictures of me naked.

'Ow, man!' I shouted, quickly pulling my boxer shorts on. I grabbed the camera, and suddenly, the door opened and Photo Finish popped his head in.

'I'll need that camera back, Andrew – it's property of Wear Dock,' Gavin said, snatching the camera from me. 'Don't worry, I'll get the film to David,' he said, seeing the worried expression on my face.

'Cheers,' I replied, and Iain burst out laughing.

My dad popped his head into the bait room just as Gavin left and said, 'We are all off to the boozer if you fancy it, lads. Nice farewell drinks. Seems as though the bastards have laid us off. Are you coming?'

Most of the lads agreed, and we arranged to meet in Cheers, a pub about half a mile up the bank. Iain, Dan, Colin and I stuffed our overalls and boots into the back of my dad's car, and we all squeezed in the back seat, with my dad and Dicky singing along to Johnny Cash, 'Ring of Fire' again.

My dad mounted the curb right outside the pub door and we all climbed out.

'I wouldn't leave your car there, Fawlty. It'll get nicked around here,' Dicky warned my dad.

'You're having a laugh, aren't you? Who'd want to nick that?' I shouted as we all walked into the pub, and my dad slapped me on the back of the head.

My dad pulled out his wallet and said, 'I'll get this round in, lads,' just as Blue Peter and Decka walked through the door.

'Good man, Fawlty,' Decka shouted.

'Eight pints of lager, please, pet,' my dad shouted over to the rough-looking, blonde, busty barmaid wiping down the bar with a cloth.

Peter sat on the stool next to my dad ogling at the barmaid as she began pouring the drinks. She noticed him staring and shouted over, 'Having a good look there, Blue?'

Not fazed at all, Blue replied, 'I bet you a fiver I can make your tits move without touching them, Lil.'

She stopped pouring the drinks and walked over to Blue with her hands on her hips. 'You what?'

'I'm serious, I bet you five pounds I can make your tits move without even touching them,'
Peter replied, slamming a five-pound note on the bar.

She looked at him curiously, picked up the fiver to see if it was real and threw it back on the bar. 'You reckon you can make my tits move without touching them? And you'll give me a fiver if you can't?' she said, looking at Blue nodding.

'Okay then, you're on,' she said, standing there looking confused.

Peter stood up and started rubbing his forehead with his thumbs, making a quiet humming noise as we all looked on. He suddenly reached across the bar, grabbed her breasts, squeezed them and moved them up and down as everyone looked on, shocked.

'Best fiver I've ever spent,' he shouted, handing her the five-pound note.

'You cheeky bastard!' she screamed, throwing half a pint of lager at him while laughing her head off as Peter scarpered towards the pool table.

My dad paid for the drinks, handing her a twenty-pound note and telling her to keep the change. Lil could see him struggling to carry four of the beers to a table opposite the bar.

'Do you want a tray?' she asked.

'Do you not think I've got enough to carry?' my dad replied as he carried the other four and plonked them on the table.

The eight of us were getting ready to play killer pool as Blue explained the rules, which were: Each player was given one life. We take turns, and if you pot a ball, you stay in, and if you miss, you lose your life and you're out. We each pay a pound, and the winner (the last one with a life left) wins the money. The first person to lose a life must do a forfeit, which the winner decides. If the loser doesn't do the forfeit he has been given, he has to buy every player a drink of their choice.

We all agreed to the rules and put a pound in an empty pint glass that sat on the edge of the pool table. A few other lads came through the doors and Blue asked if they wanted to join in.

'Na, you're alright, mate. I'm not running around naked again like last time!' Fat Kev shouted over.

My heart sank. It sounded like these forfeits get pretty extreme, and I was hopeless at pool I thought.

'No silly dares or you're all out!' Lil the barmaid shouted over at Blue. 'This is a respectable pub. No-one wants to see fat, naked men in their fifties running about again!' she yelled, pointing at Fat Kev.

'Hey, it's not a brick in there, ya know, Lil! I've got feelings,' Kev snapped back, pointing to his chest and giving Lil a wink.

A couple of the other lads who came in joined the game and Blue wrote their names on the blackboard by the dartboard. I was up first, as Zack, the welder, came up with the idea that alphabetical order was the fairest way to go.

I was feeling quite confident as I broke off and potted two balls, but what I didn't see was the white ball roll into the top-right pocket.

'Bollocks!' I shouted.

'Right, that's young Fawlty first one out; the winner decides his forfeit,' Blue shouted, rubbing my name out that was written in chalk on the blackboard. I could only watch and hope somebody sensible won, like my dad or Dan. God help me if Billy Animal or Blue won, I thought.

It was a tense game. Colin missed a really easy black that lay over the pocket – his name was also scrubbed off the chalkboard. Dan missed a tricky blue spot, undercutting it so it only just missed the middle pocket. My dad miscued and didn't even hit a ball; he was also out.

As the game went on, more lads missed and dropped out, and soon, there were only two left. Iain was facing Billy Animal in the final as I looked on in horror.

Billy had a tricky shot, as the white was tight up against the top cushion, and the only two balls left to pot were two spotted balls, both sitting in the middle of the table touching each other. Billy stared at the table thinking of his next move while scratching his chin, weighing up his options.

'I'm just gonna have to blast them,' he said, looking very serious.

He squatted down and carefully prepared to take his shot. Suddenly, he stopped and said to Iain, 'Right, fancy a wager? I bet you all the money in the jar I can hit every cushion, kiss that ball on the left and drop the other ball in the middle bag.'

Iain looked on confused, thinking Steve Davis couldn't pull that shot off. 'So, I get eighteen quid?' he replied.

'Only if I don't do it, but if I do, I win the game and win the eighteen quid in the pot.'

Iain looked at the balls on the table, looked at Billy and agreed. They shook hands on it, and Billy squatted down again, ready to take his shot as we all looked on in anticipation thinking that surely this can't be done. Billy moved the cue backwards and forwards as everyone watched in silence. Suddenly, he stood up, threw the cue to the floor, ran around the table, punched every cushion, then reached over and picked up one of the balls off the table, held it to his lips, kissed it, then picked the other ball up and dropped it in the middle pocket.

'There ya go, son,' Billy shouted, then poured all the pound coins out of the pint glass into his hand as everyone looked on and howled with laughter, while Iain just stood there, open mouthed.

Iain eventually saw the funny side and he and I sat giggling as my fate was being decided by Billy and the rest of the lads still crowded around the pool table.

Billy eventually came over and said, 'Right, son! With it being the first dare, we're going to go easy on you. All you have to do is go over to that bus stop over the road there,' he said, pointing to a bus stop out the window where about six people stood waiting for the bus. 'You have to go over, lie down on the ground and not say a word for five minutes. If you talk to anyone, you lose, and you have to buy everyone a drink.'

It didn't seem too bad, I thought – at least it didn't involve getting naked, and it's not like I had a choice. I only had about a fiver left in my pocket, so I reluctantly agreed, and headed out the door as everyone crowded around the window to witness my dare.

I had hoped the bus would have come by the time I'd crossed the road, but there was no sign of it, only more people at the bus stop. There were now about a dozen or so people standing there. I glanced at my watch and, to everyone's amazement; I walked into the bus shelter, lay down on the ground, crossed my legs and put my hands behind my head. A couple of teenage girls laughed and whispered to each other. I tried to ignore them and just stared at the bus shelter roof.

A little old lady wandered over asked me if I was okay, to which I nodded. She sat back down, looking puzzled. A dark-haired woman moved her pram, so she could see my face and said, 'Are you okay, son?'

Again, I replied by nodding.

Then, out of nowhere, Whopper Napper appeared and knelt down next to me. 'You alright?'

I gave him a nod and a smile. He looked at me with a very strange look and said, 'Are you on drugs?'

I shook my head and looked at my watch. Still four more minutes to go.

Whopper Napper explained to everyone that I worked at the dockyard, that I'd been acting weird all day and said I must be on something. Suddenly, a bus pulled up and everyone got on except Whopper Napper, who kept asking me questions like: how many fingers am I holding up?

Then the bus driver got out of his booth and got off the bus to see what was happening. He knelt down next to me, saying, 'Are you okay, son?'

I nodded again.

'Maybe we should take him to the hospital,' the driver said. 'I go past the General.'

I shook my head to the driver, but he looked at Whopper Napper and said, 'Come on, let's get the lad up.'

The driver and Whopper Napper tried to get me to my feet, but I wriggled around, determined to stop them picking me up.

Eventually, I gave up and screamed, 'It's a dare!', pointing over to the pub window, where there were about twenty faces pressed up against it, laughing their heads off.

'And now you owe everyone a drink!' Whopper Napper shouted, arms raised, and ran over the road into the pub.

'Prick!' I shouted after him, realising he must have been in the bar and knew what was going to happen if I spoke. I looked at my watch, thinking surely, I'd gone over five minutes, but there were still only three minutes gone.

The bus driver stepped away from me and got back onto the bus. 'Bloody idiot!' he yelled as he shut the doors and drove away.

I got back to my feet and headed over to the pub. There was a big cheer as I walked into the bar and a crowd of people shouting what drinks they wanted. I felt cheated. I would have done it without speaking easily had Whopper Napper not turned up.

I borrowed twenty quid off my dad and went to the bar to get the drinks in. I slumped over the bar and waved the twenty-pound note to Lil, who came over. I looked over to my left and noticed Billy Animal was sat on the bar stool next to me. He grabbed my hand and winked. 'Put your money, away, son. I'm getting these in.'

The look on his face said it all as he smiled and told me he wouldn't let an apprentice pay for the drinks, and he patted me on the back. 'You're a good kid, just like ya fatha! Just enjoy yourself and don't stress about money.'

Figuring he must have seen me borrowing money off my dad, I thanked him and shook his hand.

'I'll get the next ones,' I said.

He jumped up off his barstool and said, 'No, ya won't! Stop being such a tart and go and join ya mates,' he shouted, pointing over to Iain doing something strange with a coke can.

I walked over to Iain and patted him on the back. 'What's happening here, like?'

Iain explained how he can make an empty can of coke move with the power of his mind.

'Bollocks!' I shouted, but Colin looked at me as serious as I've ever seen him.

'It's true,' he said. 'I've seen it with my own eyes. It's like some sort of gift.'

'Haway, you have to show me this, Iain' I said, sitting in the chair opposite him.

'Very well, but my powers may struggle with such scepticism,' Iain said.

He then picked up the empty coke can and poured the remaining few drops from the can onto the table and sat it upright on the puddle of cola. He began rubbing his forehead and started chanting quietly.

'Are these the same powers Blue summoned when he made the barmaid's tits move?' I asked.

'Look, non-believer,' Iain shouted, nodding towards the can.

I looked at the coke can and noticed, surprisingly, that it was actually turning.

I looked under the table to see if anything was going on, but – nothing.

'How's he doing this?' I said to Colin.

He just looked at me and nodded. 'It's a gift.'

The night went on with more dares and laughs; in fact, I don't think I've ever laughed so much.

'I'm away son – the taxi is here. Are you coming?' my dad slurred, being held upright by Dicky.

'I'll just stay a bit longer, dad,' I said.

I was still too busy trying to get the truth out of Iain, wondering how he got the coke can to turn. I wasn't convinced, like Colin was, that he had some sort of super-human powers.

He finally gave in and said, 'Go and get us a double Aftershock, and I'll teach you my powers.'

I stumbled my way to the bar, bumping into Whopper Napper on the way, making him spill his drink a little down his jumper. He turned and squared up to me, but I just backed away from him, held my hands up and apologised and quickly headed to the bar. A few minutes later, I returned to the table with the doubles.

'Cheers,' Iain said.

We sank the two red Aftershocks and slammed them on the table.

'Right, sit there.' Iain guided me to the seat where he'd sat. He poured a little drop of his pint onto the table and plonked the coke can down in the puddle.

'Right, focus. Imagine the coke can turning,' he said.

'Okay.' I focused on the can for a few seconds and suddenly, to my amazement, the can began turning, really slowly.

'Bloody hell, I'm doing it,' I shouted. 'How is this possible?'

Iain eventually looked up to the ceiling and pointed to the fan above. It turned out the combination of the ceiling fan and the liquid on the table makes the can turn. I swore my secrecy to the Iain and the magic circle and carried on drinking, raising a glass to Iain's trick. The rest of the night became a bit of a blur, and at some point, I left in a taxi a bit worse for wear.

I woke up in the back of a taxi with a jump and very little recollection of how I got there.

'That'll be four pound fifty,' the driver told me.

I rooted about in my pocket and eventually found five pound coins and handed them to the driver. 'Keep the change,' I said as I tried to crawl out of the taxi.

I climbed out of the cab, but I couldn't get my legs to work properly, and I fell to the ground. The driver got out and helped me to my feet. I thanked him and stumbled towards our house in the square. I noticed I was uncontrollably veering over to the left, so I decided to make a run for it. I gained a little more speed than I'd planned, and I smashed into Harry's wooden fence and privet bushes and fell headfirst into his neatly kept rose bush, sending rose petals and leaves everywhere. I let out a scream as the thorns scratched at my face and my head got wedged solid in the base of the rose bush.

The following morning, I woke up with the sun shining through my bedroom window, stinging my eyes. I also had a raging thirst and a pounding headache.

I sat up and realised the pillow was stuck to my face. I peeled off the pillow and noticed it was covered in splashes of blood. I put my hands on my face, trying to find where the blood had come from, and found three or four little thorns sticking out of my face. I tried to remember what happened to me last night, but I couldn't piece it together; I could only remember little bits.

I checked my alarm clock. It said 8:10.

I jumped out of bed screaming, 'Dad, we've slept in!'

Noticing I still had my work clothes on, luckily, I quickly sprayed some Lynx under my armpits and ran to the bathroom.

I splashed some cold water on my face and glanced in the mirror; there was dried blood everywhere and about ten different scratches on my face and neck. I washed the blood off, pulled a thorn out of my forehead, headed to the landing and banged on mam and dad's bedroom door.

My dad came to the bedroom door and shouted, 'It's Saturday, man, ya tit! And you'd better go over to Harry's and apologise and fix his fence, ya bloody idiot!'

I wasn't sure what he was on about, so I headed back into my room and pulled back the curtains to see the carnage below. Harry's beloved normally immaculately kept garden was completely ruined. His little wooden picket fence was smashed into pieces and the middle of his privet hedge bush now had a big gaping hole in the middle, and his rose bush was completely ruined.

It all came flooding back: the dares in the pub, putting a request in on the karaoke for Whopper Napper to sing a Talking Heads song, the fall, the rose bush. I remembered vaguely my mam dragging me to the toilet after finding me pissing in the kitchen.

I climbed back into bed, covered my sore head with my quilt cover and tried to put my final day at Wear Dockyard behind me.

CHAPTER 7

A fresh start

I got out of bed, full of the joys of spring, knowing I was starting at the Hepburn yard and thinking, 'No more John making my life a misery.' At least, I hoped that was the case. I was sure he would be staying at Wear dock.

'Your bloody calamities are getting worse! Please be careful – no more falling through roofs!' my mam screamed as I headed out the door.

My dad was sat behind the wheel, glaring at me impatiently as I ran out the door. I quickly jumped in the passenger seat.

Harry, our neighbour, came running over to the car. I'd purposely avoided him since crashing through his fence that drunken night.

'Where are you off to like, Billy? I thought you got paid off,' Harry asked.

'I got a start at Hepburn with the boy,' my dad replied, trying to rush his answer, as we were running late.

Harry looked at me. 'Look, son, I'm going to need a hand tonight to fit Mrs Patterson's bathroom,' he said, pointing over to our elderly neighbour's house, 'Seeing as though you wrecked my garden last week, it's the least you can do!'

'Aye, no bother. I'm really sorry by the way,' I grovelled, as my dad started driving away.

'Bloody hell, man! I was supposed to be playing five-a-side tonight with Pikey and them!' I moaned as we drove off.

'You should learn to handle your bloody drink,' my dad said, while raking about in the side door for his Johnny Cash cassette. He was getting pissed off, as he couldn't find it.

'You're one to talk! That taxi driver thought you were disabled Friday night – mam told me. He was asking how long you've been like that and what happened to you.'

My dad just shook his head.

'I've got my charts tape here,' I offered, as dad pulled into the bus stop to pick up Dicky.

'I'm not listening to your shite!' he screamed as Dicky climbed in the back seat.

'Morning lads,' he shouted.

'Morning Dicky,' I replied, as my dad was still too busy raking about for his tape to acknowledge Dicky.

'Where's that bloody tape?' he shouted, leaning over me and hunting in the glove box.

'Had four numbers on the lottery on Saturday!' Dicky said. 'Guess how much?'

'Hundred quid?' my dad replied.

'I wish! Twenty-eight bloody quid! Only two more numbers and I would have won ten million!'

'Disgrace, that,' my dad shouted. 'Nice villa in Benidorm,' he muttered.

'Eh? What ya on about?' I asked.

'The lottery, man! If I won the lottery, that's what I'd buy,' my dad screamed. 'Where's that bastard tape?'

He finally gave up and put Radio 2 on.

Dicky piped up, 'You know what I'd do if I scooped ten million?'

'What's that, Dicky,' I asked.

'I'd give the wife a million pounds, and I'd tell her if I ever see her again, I'll take it off her!'

As we whizzed down the A19, my dad's fan belt was screeching.

'It doesn't sound right, that, dad. Have you heard the noise it's making?'

My dad turned the radio up full blast. 'There ya go. Problem solved!'

Dicky reached over and pointed to the temperature gauge that was showing the engine was red hot.

'It'll be areet man,' my dad shouted, as we headed past the Tyne tunnel with Chumbawamba's 'Tubthumping' blaring out of the speakers.

We drove towards Jarrow city centre, and I noticed smoke coming out of the bonnet. 'Dad, were gonna have to pull over – it's gonna catch fire man!'

'You're a right fanny, you are! It's only a bit of smoke!' my dad moaned, but eventually gave in and pulled into a Shell garage when Dicky also joined in nagging him to stop.

There was a sign up next to the air and water saying, 'Out of order', so he pulled up next to a petrol pump.

'You in the AA, Fawlty?' Dicky asked.

'It's him who can't handle his drink, not me!' my dad replied, nodding towards me.

'Shall I go buy some water?' I asked my dad.

Dicky handed over a two-litre bottle of strawberry-flavoured fizzy water. 'There ya go, Fawlty. Use that.'

I jumped out and headed into the garage shop to see if I could buy a bottle of water.

'Get that car away from the pump!!' the garage bloke screamed over the tannoy.

My dad ignored him, got out of the car and popped the bonnet. The smoke was now hurling out of the engine as my dad began pouring Dicky's strawberry fizzy water into the cooling tank.

I stood in line waiting to be served with my two-litre bottle of Volvic and a red marker pen that was in the bargain bucket for 50p. I'd been meaning to buy one for marking pipes at work. The bloke behind the counter screamed over a mic, 'Please move your car away from the petrol pump immediately!'

My face was burning red with embarrassment as a few people started slagging my dad off while waiting in line to be served behind me. I noticed my dad drop the bonnet and give the bloke behind the counter the finger.

'Haway, man, ya tit!' he screamed out the window and sounding his horn to me as I was about to be served.

I threw £1.50 on the counter, apologising, and ran out without my change.

I quickly jumped in the car. I'd barely got in the passenger seat as my dad sped off shouting, 'Tosser!' to the pissed-off bloke behind the counter.

'Hey, that smells nice, that, Dicky,' my dad laughed, as the smell from the water mixed with the smoke coming through the vents.

We pulled up at the security gate with smoke hurling out of the bonnet. The guard pointed us towards the car park with a look of, 'What the fuck?' on his face.

We jumped out the car with relief at somehow making it, although we were half an hour late.

'It'll be alright man – it just needs to cool down a bit, that's all,' my dad said, looking at Dicky and me staring at the smoke billowing from the car.

We finally got into the yard after the journey from hell, and the security guard drew us a little map of where to find the induction centre. We followed the map down the big, long bank towards the River Tyne. I noticed there was a massive green ship sitting in the quay to our right, and to our left, we could see a massive dry dock, which was about three times the size of Wear Dock, and sitting in it was an old-style white cruise ship.

'That's the Edinburgh Castle, that there,' Dicky pointed out. 'I worked on it years ago, but they're making it into a hospital boat now'.

'Some size, like,' my dad looked on.

We followed the map, which lead us to a set of stone steps that took us down to loads of cabins and old workshops. Then my life took a turn for the worse as I looked over to the building painted green and John Jenkins was stood talking to Whopper Napper.

'Late again.' John looked at us, shaking his head.

'Aye, we had a bit of bother on the road, like,' my dad replied.

'Where's the induction centre, like, John?' Dicky asked.

John pointed over to a little portable office. 'Just as well for you lot the safety induction isn't until nine o clock! he said, and he walked off with Whopper Napper towards the office, both of them looking at me like a piece of shit.

We opened the door to the pokey little office and there was a load of familiar faces squeezed into the room, which cheered me up immediately. Colin, Dan, Blue, Decka, Billy Animal, Fat Kev, Dot and Iain were all there, along with a few others, and they all cheered as we walked in.

'You brought the Evening Echo, in Fawlty?' Blue shouted as we sat down in the only available seats at the front next to Larry, who was sat on his own right next to the overhead projector.

The projector looked onto a big white screen, which had a big photograph of the yard, and in big letters, it said, 'Welcome to Tyne Tees Dockyard.'

I looked back at Iain. 'You seen JJ yet?'

He frowned and looked at me. 'Aye, the tosser!'

Shortly after, the room fell silent as a ginger-haired bloke walked through the door.

'Alright, lads, I'm Lenny Douglas. I'm going to do your safety induction. It was supposed to be at nine o'clock, but it looks like it's going to be this afternoon now, as I have to attend an important meeting this morning. Sorry lads.'

'What we supposed to do 'til then, like?' Billy Animal shouted.

He explained how we could all go and sit in the canteen where there are tea and coffee facilities, and he explained how he needed two apprentices to take the van to Wear Dock to pick up some tools and stuff. Iain put his hand up and tapped me on the shoulder, so I raised my hand too.

'Can one of you drive?' Lenny asked.

'Aye, I can,' Iain said, which was news to me.

Lenny threw Iain the keys and said, 'Haway, lads, I'll show you the van.'

He led us out the side door and pointed to a big, white Transit van parked up the road.

'Cheers lads,' he said. 'There are a few toolboxes to pick up – they should be sitting outside the plumber's ready to go,' he said and walked away, leaving me and Iain with the keys.

'I didn't know you could drive.' I looked at Iain suspiciously.

'Why, aye. I drive my dad's car all the time!'

'Have you passed your test?' I asked.

'Not yet, but they don't know that,' he winked.

We opened the big double doors at the back of the van and chucked our rucksacks in, then shut the doors, climbed in the front seat and headed up the bank. Iain pressed a button and there was a locking sound and he sat smiling.

'What?' I asked, wondering why he was smiling. Then suddenly it hit me. The most horrendous fart I'd ever smelled.

I began reaching to wind down the window to get rid of the smell, but it was locked shut. Iain started laughing his head off, leaned over and let out another loud fart. He pulled out an AA road map that was on the dashboard and began wafting the smell towards me. Luckily, he had to open his window to ask the security to lift the gate. The young security guard popped his head in the window.

'Dear me, who died in there?' he shouted, covering his nose.

'Him!' I said, pointing to Iain while nipping my nostrils with my other hand.

We headed down towards the A19 with the smell still lingering in the air. 'What you been eating?' I asked.

'I was out on the lash all day yesterday. We stopped off for a curry. My guts are rotten!' Iain said, holding his stomach.

'You got any pop? I'm choking for a drink!' Iain asked as we sped down the dual carriageway.

'I've got a bottle of water in the back. If you pull over, I'll get it,' I replied, thinking I might get the opportunity to get some fresh air.

Iain eventually pulled over onto the hard shoulder of the A19 overlooking the Nissan factory. I jumped out, taking my chance to take in the fresh air. I tried to open the back doors to the van, but they were locked. Iain tried pressing different buttons, but it didn't work, so he eventually got out with the keys, tried one in the lock and one of the doors popped open. My rucksack had slid to the back of the van with Iain's dodgy driving, so I climbed up onto the van to get it.

Suddenly, I tripped on a metal hook sticking out of the wooden floor, and I went flying forward, crashing to the floor. I got a really sharp pain in my index finger and shrieked as Iain stood, laughing, holding the door open.

'Shit. Shit!' I shouted in horror, looking at my finger.

'What's happened?' Iain shouted, jumping in the van and running to my aid.

I showed him my finger and he winced in shock as a splinter about two inches long had somehow managed to go right under my nail and blood was trickling out.

'It's bloody killing!' I screamed, as I looked in horror at how deep the splinter went.

'Shit, it's gone right past the nail,' Iain squirmed, turning away.

'Shall I pull it out?' I shrieked.

Iain suddenly grabbed my hand turned away from me and quickly pulled the splinter out. I screamed at the top of my voice in pain.

'There ya gan – sorted! Now, where's that water?' he said, rummaging through my rucksack.

He loosened the top, took a massive swig and said, 'Ahhhh, liquid gold!'

Suddenly, a gust of wind slammed the van door shut and we were in darkness. I got myself back to my feet, my hand still throbbing but easing a bit since Iain's doctoring.

Iain was fumbling with the door, then looked at me and shook his head.

'What's up?' I asked, barely able to see him in the darkness.

'I think we're locked in,' Iain said, feeling around the door for some sort of leaver.

'There must be a way to open it from inside, surely?' I said.

'I can't find it, and don't call me Shirley!' he laughed. 'There probably is, but it's been boarded out – it's all screwed down!'

I joined Iain in trying to feel around for a way out. 'Where are the keys?' I asked.

'In the door,' he replied.

'Shit, we're screwed! Have you got your phone?' I asked.

'Aye, it's in the front!' he said, and then burst out laughing.

After about ten minutes, I was starting to feel very claustrophobic, especially with the smell of Iain's constant farting. I started banging on the side of the van, shouting 'Help!' at the top of my voice.

'We're on a dual carriageway, man – who's gonna hear ya?' Iain shouted. 'Calm down, here's a fag!' He handed me a cigarette.

'You got a light?' I asked.

'Aye, in the front,' he said and burst out laughing again.

After another twenty minutes or so, I noticed Iain had gone very quiet.

'You okay, mate?' I asked.

'No, I need a shit!' he said, sending me into a blind panic. I felt around every square inch of the van again, but all I could find was a paint brush and an empty plastic bucket.

Suddenly, Iain broke the silence with a fart and a laugh.

'Haway, man, if it isn't bad enough!' I shouted, covering my nose.

Twenty minutes later, we were still stuck in the van, with no way out and Iain complaining that he was growing a tail and touching cloth.

'Please mate, hang on!' I pleaded.

'I can't for much longer. I'm gonna have to use that bucket.'

I could tell by his voice he was deadly serious. Again, I felt around to try and find a leaver, but nothing. I started kicking the door, but all I heard was the keys fall to the ground outside, teasing me.

Another ten minutes later, I heard the unthinkable – Iain fumbling around with his belt and then a zip. 'Sorry, mate,' he said.

I sat in the opposite corner of the van, reaching to be sick as I heard the farts and thuds as his shit hit the bucket. I had my T shirt shoved up my nostrils to try and stop the horrendous smell, and I had my fingers in my ears trying to blank out the noise. Suddenly, I was hit in the head with a paintbrush.

'Ow! What was that for?' I asked, rubbing my sore head.

'I was trying to get your attention, man! Have you got a paper in your bag?'

'No, why? It's too dark to read anyway,' I said, not thinking.

'I want to wipe my arse, man! I don't wanna read Dear Deidre!' he snapped back.

'I'm gonna have to use my socks!' he said, giving in.

Eventually, when Iain finished, I think my nose forgot about the putrid smell and we began chatting.

'I can't believe that prick, John, has been transferred. Gutted! And Whopper Napper,' I moaned, and Iain started laughing.

'He was gonna kill you when you put that song request in at the karaoke. If it wasn't for Decka, he would have,' he laughed. 'Talking Heads – classic that, Reg.'

'Who's Reg?' I asked, but Iain shushed me. 'Listen! A car has just pulled up.'

'Help!' I screamed, banging on the door, and then I heard a muffled voice and a crackle over a walkie talkie.

'It's the coppers!' I said to Iain.

'Shit!' Iain muttered.

'Is there somebody in there?' shouted a voice with authority.

'Aye, we're locked in,' I shouted back.

I heard a rustling of keys and then the key going into the lock, and then the door opened, blinding me with the light.

A young female police officer with blonde hair tied back popped her head in the van and immediately covered her mouth and nose. 'Jesus wept!' she shouted and disappeared out of view.

Then a second policeman – a bloke in his fifties – popped open the other door, looked in and said, 'What's going on here?'

He covered his mouth and stepped back. I spotted the female officer over his shoulder throwing up on the grass.

The police were surprisingly lenient when we explained what had happened. I'm not sure if it was the embarrassment, the smell, or the fact that we were parked on the hard shoulder, but they just quickly hurried us on our way, to Iain's relief, seeing as though he only had a provisional licence.

We finally arrived at Wear Dockyard and quickly loaded the van with the heavy toolboxes.
Although the bucket had gone in the bushes on the A19, the smell was still lingering.

'It's the last time I have a jalfrezi from that place!' Iain laughed as we loaded the last of the boxes into the van. 'Fancy a McDonald's?'

'I'm never eating again after smelling your arse!' I shouted back.

About an hour or so later, we ended up back at the Hepburn yard just in time for the induction. We handed Lenny the keys.

'Bloody hell, it would have been quicker to get the bus!' Lenny laughed, as we walked in and took a seat in the induction room.

John looked over, shaking his head at Lenny. 'Can't be trusted with nothing, those two – thick as shit!'

'Right lads, we're gonna get started in a minute, so if anyone needs the bog, go now. They are just in the building opposite,' Lenny pointed out.

I jumped out and headed over to the bogs while John looked on, shaking his head. 'Bet he gets lost!'

I entered the big, blue toilet block and was surprised that it was a lot cleaner than Wear Dock and actually had soap and paper towels, unlike Wear Dock, where such luxuries were rare.

I entered the first cubicle, which was covered in graffiti – mainly taunts between Mackems and Geordies about football, but I kept seeing writing slagging John off, like 'Mickey Mouse wears a JJ watch!' and 'JJ is a baldy prick!', and there was a big picture drawn of him with a cock on his head.

At least I'm not the only one who hates him, I thought, and took a bit of comfort in knowing that he's hated here as much as at Wear Dock. There was also loads of writing about a so-called 'Krusty' – 'Krusty was here!' – and also loads of pictures of Krusty, the clown from The Simpsons.

I could have sat there all day reading all the graffiti. I decided to add my own bit with my newly purchased red pen and wrote, 'Whopper Napper's head has three orbiting moons!' and drew a picture of the prick on the toilet door.

I eventually headed back to the induction room, where nobody said a word, as they were too busy laughing at Billy Animal, who was taking the piss out of Fat Kev because of how tight he is with money.

'He's so tight, he turns the gas off when he flips his bacon man!' he shouted, as the room erupted into laughter.

Lenny was banging on about safety, but he could hardly be heard over the laughing and carrying on. He didn't seem too bothered, but John's face was becoming increasingly redder, and then he suddenly stood up and yelled, 'Haway, man, for fuck sake, shut up! Give Lenny some respect, you bunch of children!'

'What's it to you, ya baldy prick. You're not the gaffer here!' Decka shouted over, and John sat down quietly two seats along from us.

Iain and I we were both smirking on hearing the news for the first time that John was working on the tools. The room fell silent after the outburst and Lenny carried on talking about working at heights and harnesses. Shortly after, he moved onto smoking.

'Right, lads, from April, they're stopping smoking on all ships, as the company is having a bit of a no smoking campaign, so any ideas you have about helping people stop would be a good help. We're going to be giving away free nicotine patches, that sort of stuff, so if anyone is interested, see me.'

Blue raised his hand. 'Women are like cigarettes.'

'How?' Lenny asked, looking confused, wondering what the hell he was talking about.

'Well, they cost a fortune, one's never enough, and they'll bloody kill you in the end! he laughed.

'And they make your fingers stink!' Billy Animal chipped in.

'And you wanna set fire to them!' John shouted.

'No, that's just you, John, because you're a horrible, bullying twat!' Decka shouted, which set the whole room off laughing.

After an hour or so of boring videos and form filling-in, we were allowed to start work and meet our new bosses. We were pointed in the direction of the plumber's shop, which was over the other side of the dock. The eight of us pipefitters headed over there, while the others went to their places of work.

When we got to the plumber's shop, we walked in the big main door, and it was huge compared to the little workshop at Wear Dock. There were about ten work benches with blokes stood around chatting, there were also loads of machine saws, drills and benders. I also noticed the place was spotlessly clean compared to our old shop. All the pipes were stacked up neatly on racks in order of size, and there was even an overhead crane, which one of the lads was using to lift a pipe out of the rack.

'This is more like it,' said Decka, as we headed into the office in the middle of the workshop. 'Alright, lads, here come the Mackems! Proper pipefitters.'

A little grey-haired bloke stood up to greet us, shaking our hands and asking our names. He got to my dad and said, 'I don't need your name, Fawlty!' and started laughing, shaking his hand. 'I worked with you in Thompson's years ago! Jimmy Whistler, remember me?'

'Why, aye! Alright, mate – how's it going!' my dad laughed. 'This is my son, Andrew,' he said, patting me on the shoulder.

I shook his hand, and he told me how he once met me when I was about three years old.

After we had made our introductions to Jimmy, our new boss, he told us to just hang around the workshop for the day, make ourselves at home and meet the other lads.

My dad, Dot and Dicky knew quite a few of the lads from the shipyards in Sunderland from back in the seventies and eighties, and they seemed to have a little story attached to each person, like Big Brian who, in his day, was more accident prone than me.

My dad said, 'Hey, remember that time you were up dancing in Steel's club!' Both of them were in stitches of laughter.

Big Brian told us he was once dancing, swinging his legs about that much that he got his foot caught in a bloke's pocket! Unlucky for the bloke at the time, he was carrying a full tray of drinks. Brian was a tall, thin bloke in his early fifties and was a dead ringer for Russ Abbott, an eighties comedian.

'Take notice of this bloke, here, lads! He's the best in the business. He's forgotten more than I've ever known!' my dad said to me and Iain, with his arm around Brian's shoulder.

Just as everyone was laughing and joking around, I noticed Whopper Napper walking towards us with a light switch in one hand, with wires popping out the bottom. 'Alright, lads. Have any of you got a red marker pen by any chance?' he said, looking over at me, Iain and Decka standing chatting.

'Aye, I've got one you can borrow,' I said, rooting around in my pocket for my pen.

'So it's you who's been writing on the bog wall about me, you little bastard!' he shouted, lunging forward to grab me, but I was too quick, and I scarpered out the door, leaving everyone laughing their heads off behind me.

About half an hour later, I popped my head into the plumber's shop, and Whopper Napper had finally gone. I casually strolled back in and joined in with my dad talking to someone with his back to me.

'This is the boy, Andrew,' my dad said to the ginger, curly-haired bloke.

He turned to look at me, and I couldn't help but laugh. He was the spitting double of Krusty the clown from The Simpsons. He looked at me wondering what I was laughing at. I apologised and shook his hand.

My dad gave me a strange look and said. 'This is K– Dave Thirlwell.'

Hearing my dad almost calling him Krusty set me off laughing again.

'Sorry, I just can't stop laughing at a joke I heard earlier.'

He just looked at me, a little confused, and smiled. Then I heard one of the lads do an amazing Krusty the clown laugh, and it sent me off into a hysterical laughing fit, so I ran out of the shop again, and when I got outside, bent over and laughed my head off.

Iain came out a few minutes later to see what was going on. I explained the Krusty crack, which set him off laughing too.

Iain handed me a fag, and we sat outside enjoying our fags in the sunshine.

'Bit of a result, this, Reg!' Iain said.

'Aye, I think I'm taking to this place, like,' I agreed.

As we stood there smoking, Fat Kev came over with a big, stocky bloke with dark hair in his early twenties. He wandered up with his safety helmet clutched under his arm. 'Alright, lads. I'm Mick,' he said, reaching out and shaking our hands as we introduced ourselves.

Fat Kev asked Iain if he could pinch a fag. Iain got his pack out and handed him one and a lighter.

We stood chatting about the place and how it was much better than Wear Dock, and then Mick announced he was going to speak to someone and headed inside.

'Full of shit, him, by the way. Don't believe a word that comes out his mouth,' Kev said, nodding towards Mick.

'He seems areet,' Iain replied.

'He is. He's sound as a pound, but he constantly lies. It's like he can't help himself! If I've been to Tenerife, he's been to 'Elevenerife', you know what I mean?' Kev said, chuckling away to himself.

'He's called Mick Fleetwood, but the lads call him Fleetwood Mac,' he said, stubbing his fag out. He told us all once he was going to Miami for his holidays and one of the lads saw him in Magaluf.' He laughed and headed into the shop, singing, 'Tell me lies, tell me sweet little lies.'

I was just about to head in myself, but I was suddenly grabbed from behind and put in a headlock.

'You gonna stop calling me Whopper Napper, you little prick,' he yelled, as he squeezed my neck tighter. Iain looked on, laughing.

'Aye, sorry!' I squealed, as his grip got tighter.

He swung me around, which sent me flying into the bins that were sat next to the door. I climbed up the door to get to my feet, and he punched me in the ribs.

'Alright, that's enough, you prick!' Iain shouted and pulled Whopper Napper back.

'This isn't over!' he yelled in my face and stormed off into the plumber's shop.

'Bloody hell, that was a bit harsh,' Iain said, helping me to my feet.

'I was only having a laugh with the prick,' I replied. 'I thought he was only messing about at first, but the dickhead was serious!'

An hour or so after the carry-on with Whopper Napper, I decided to leave it and hope things would blow over, and I thought I'd just keep out of his way. I stood chatting to my dad about the car.

'Tommy, one of the lads, is fixing my car for me in the fitter's shed, so you don't have to worry. Apparently, it's only a bracket come loose, which is why the fan belt is...'

My dad waffled on, but I wasn't really listening. I was too busy wondering what to do about Whopper Napper. I didn't want to go running to Decka again, but I wasn't going to put up with his bullying, I thought.

'Anybody in there?' my dad shouted, waving a hand in front of my face.

'Sorry, dad. I was miles away,' I said.

'You okay, son?' he asked, suddenly all serious.

'Aye, champion,' I replied and wandered off to the toilets.

I sat there on the toilet, pondering what to do, when I heard someone go into the next cubicle. I sat reading the graffiti. 'Fleetwood Mac choked Linda Lovelace.' It made me laugh after hearing Kev saying he was always talking shit.

Suddenly, out of nowhere, I heard a noise above me. I looked up and a massive bucket of Swarfega soap was emptied over me. I quickly pulled up my pants and jeans, threw on my overalls, opened the toilet door and saw Whopper Napper creased with laughter when he saw me covered in the bright green, sticky soap. I looked in the mirror. I looked like I'd just been gunked on Noel's House Party. Even I found it funny when I saw myself in the mirror.

I looked at him, pondering my next move. I put my green, Swarfega-covered hand out in front of me and said, 'Look, we have got off to a bad start. I'm sorry for the drawing – it was just a joke, and I didn't know you didn't like being called that! So, it's up to you. We sort this outside or shake on it here and now and forget the whole thing.'

I was thinking to myself: shit, if he chooses to take me outside, he will kill me! I'm good at hurting myself, not other people!

He stared into my eyes and said, 'Look...'

Suddenly, Dicky walked in and started laughing at me. 'Bloody hell, Andy, what's happened?'

I smirked and said, 'Some twat got me with Swarfega when I was on the bog!'

Whopper Napper walked out, and I explained to Dicky I was sat there having a dump and someone chucked the bucket over me. I got myself cleaned up as best I could with the paper towels, but my arse was itching like mad. The Swarfega had even gotten in my boxer shorts.

I headed back in the workshop eventually after cleaning myself up. My dad was stood there, dressed ready to leave. 'Haway, man, ya tit. Hurry up, it's time to go!'

I quickly got my overalls off again, chucked them in the corner of the workshop and followed him up the bank. Back in the car, my dad was just about to jump in the driver's seat when he saw a cassette sat in it.

'I must have been sat on the bastard,' he shouted, and popped it in the cassette player. 'Ring of Fire' came blasting out of the speakers.

We eventually arrived back home in our square, and outside of Mrs Patterson's house was a big yellow skip with an old green toilet, sink and a big pile of broken tiles and concrete.

'Shit, I forgot about helping Harry!' I moaned.

My dad headed into the house, and I headed towards Mrs Patterson's house next door. I knocked on the little brass knocker on the old wooden door, but got no answer, so I popped my head in the window and saw Mrs Patterson jump to her feet; she was waving to me and made her way to the front door.

Eventually, after hearing her rattling about with keys, the door opened, and she let me in. Mrs Patterson must have been about 90. Nobody knew how old, as she always said, 'None of your business' when anyone asked. She also never told anyone her first name. She was in good shape, though, for her age, however old that was. She walked to the shops, no problem, but her face was so old full of wrinkles. She was a lovely old soul who took a shine to me, but she seemed to hate everyone else.

She told me Harry was upstairs, so I headed up, and she gave my bum a squeeze as I moved past her.

'Hey, I'm not that old, you know,' and she gave me a wink and a smile.

I quickly scarpered upstairs to the bathroom and saw the crack of Harry's arse as he was bent over the toilet, fastening it to the wall.

'Hey, you've done a canny job, Harry!' I said, as I admired the pretty impressive bathroom – all gold taps and the brilliant white, ceramic bathroom suite.

'I'm just about done now. It's taken me all day,' he said.

'What can I do to help?' I asked, wondering what use I could be to him.

'I'll just need a lift with her old bath! It weighs a bloody tonne! Actually, you can see if you can get that flusher working. She insisted on an old-style pulley chain. It was a pain in the arse to fit, but I can't get it to flush,' he said, taking off his glasses and cleaning them on his T shirt.

'Is it okay to stand on this?' I said, pointing to the toilet.

'Aye, just be careful – it's taken me all day to get this far.'

I carefully climbed onto the toilet bowl and reached up to the old-style flushing cistern fastened about six feet off the ground. I very carefully removed the ceramic lid, handing it down to Harry. I looked Inside and pulled the chain.

I noticed the ballcock was catching against the side of the cistern, so I gently tried to bend the rod attached to the ballcock to try and free it from getting caught. I explained to Harry what the problem was, and he passed me up a pair of big, heavy Stillson grips. I gently gripped the bar and twisted it, freeing the ballcock from the side of the cistern. 'Try that, Harry!'

He pulled the chain, and to my amazement, it worked.

'Wow, you're a natural, son!' He smiled and handed me the ceramic lid.

Still having the Stillsons in my hand, it was a bit tricky to put back on, but I was very careful, and I just about managed it. I carefully lay the Stillsons on top of the cistern and tried the chain again.

'Result!' Harry shouted, as he helped me down from the toilet bowl. 'Right, now the bathtub,' he said, pointing to the bedroom to my left. 'It's cast iron, so be careful.'

Grabbing the tap end, I struggled with the weight of the other end, but managed to lift it and manoeuvred it to the stairs. I headed down first as Harry clung onto the top, easing it down the stairs. We somehow managed to lift it down, and after a few minutes of struggle, we got it out of the front door and into the skip.

'Right, Mrs Patterson, we're all done. Wanna see?' said Harry. 'I've just got to have a quick clean up and get my tools, and we'll leave you in peace!' Harry said, wiping sweat from his brow.

'It's always nice to have young men around the place,' she smiled and winked at me.

Then she tried to give a big wad of ten-pound notes to Harry, who point-blank refused. 'No, no, no! Please put your money away or I'll never help you again,' he said, looking very insulted. 'Quick, hurry up before she asks again.'

He pushed me up the stairs. We went back into the bathroom and Harry began putting his tools away, while I bent over with the dustpan and brush, picking up the bits of dust. Mrs Patterson walked in, saw me bent over and said, 'Ooh, very nice!'

Harry laughed and we stood up, ready to go.

'Wow, very posh. I love it – thanks, Harry,' she said, admiring his very professional job.

Just as we were about to leave, I noticed the Stillsons still sat on top of the cistern. I told Harry, and he said, 'Grab them for me, will you?'

I stepped onto the side of the toilet bowl and reached up for the Stillsons. Just as I touched the handle, my foot slipped off the side of the toilet and went into the toilet itself, and then I fell backwards to the floor with a crash, my foot still stuck in the toilet. Then I looked up and saw the Stillsons wobble on the top of the cistern. Suddenly, they tipped off the edge and came crashing down, smashing against the side of the sink and breaking a big chunk off; then they crashed onto the toilet bowl, which cracked, and then the whole thing broke completely in half, releasing my foot and covering the bathroom floor with water.

I lay on the floor in shock and looked over to Harry and Mrs Pattison where they stood, open-mouthed.

'Oh dear!' said Mrs Patterson, as I stumbled to my feet

Harry looked at me like he was going to kill me when I handed him the Stillsons.

'Sorry!' I shouted and legged it down the stairs and out of the door as quickly as I could. Remembering the cricket bat incident, I thought I'd better go to Pikey's to hide out rather than go home.

CHAPTER 8

The thief

'We've slept in again!' my dad yelled.

That quickly snapped me out of my wonderful sleep. All my worries came flooding back – Harry, Whopper Napper. I was wondering which one was going to kill me first.

My dad popped his head into my room again. 'Haway, man – get up, ya tit!'

I quickly got out of bed and got my work clothes on, sprayed some Lynx under my pits and ran down the stairs, where my mam gave me my rucksack and popped a piece of toast in my mouth. I ran outside and jumped in the passenger seat of my dad's car. Luckily, there was no sign of Harry, but the skip was still there with the broken sink and toilet sitting on the top of the pile of rubble.

My dad sped out of the square, and I breathed a sigh of relief as we drove up St Luke's road.

'You owe me a hundred quid,' my dad yelled.

'What?' I gasped.

'You heard me! Harry was raging last night when you scarpered! I had to drive down to B&Q with him to calm him down and buy a new bog and sink! And bloody fit it!' my dad moaned.

'Shit, I'm sorry dad,' I looked on, shocked.

'You would have been sorry if Harry had got hold of you last night! Where did you go anyway? I never heard you come in.'

'I stayed around Pikey's after footy for a bit. His mam made me some tea,' I replied, gutted, wondering how I was going to pay the hundred quid back.

'Right, straight after work, get your arse to the shops, get Harry some cans and Mrs Patterson some chocolates and go and apologise!' my dad ordered.

I agreed. 'Can I borrow £20?' I asked.

We arrived at the bus stop and Dicky jumped in. 'Morning lads!' he shouted.

'Morning Dicky,' dad and I shouted back at the same time.

'Remember you said you'd pick Fat Kev up, Fawlty?' Dicky reminded my dad.

'Shit, I forgot all about that!' my dad snapped, looking at his watch.

We headed down South Hylton Bank and Dicky spotted fat Kev stood at the bus stop. 'There he is, Basil.' Dicky pointed.

'Morning lads!' Kev said, as he got in the back stinking of drink.

'Thought I might have missed you. I slept in – went out for a few last night,' Kev shouted forward to my dad.

'Bloody hell, you smell like Duncan Disorderly!' my dad replied.

'Hey, Fawlty, would you mind stopping off for Fleetwood Mac on the way past Hastings Hill? He was in the club last night, and I said I'd ask you,' Kev asked my dad, who didn't look very happy but agreed anyway.

'What's up, like? Is his Ferrari getting fixed, like?' Dicky laughed.

'He's full of shit, man. He told the lads he cycles all the way to work in thirty minutes. Billy Animal's seen him getting off the train with his bike yesterday morning! Anyway, his bike's knackered. He left it at work, so that's why he's asked for a lift!' Kev said, shaking his head.

'Where is he?' my dad said, pulling into The Hastings Hill pub car park. There was no sign of him.

We sat there for a few minutes and still no sign of him, so my dad suggested we go to his house.

'Do you know where he lives, Kev?' my dad asked, looking in his rear-view mirror at him.

'Aye, Krusty gave us a lift last night – we dropped him off at the big posh house at the top of Sevenoaks Drive.' Kev pointed up the road, so we headed around there.

'Hey, it's a lovely area, this, like. Worth a few bob, these pads!' Dicky commented, as we pulled up to the big, posh house where Kev pointed out Fleetwood Mac lived.

We drove up to the immaculate four-bedroomed, detached house, with double gates with two concrete, sculptured lions on the top of the pillars. My dad pulled up in his clapped-out Volvo and began sounding the horn. 'Haway, Mick!' he yelled out the car window.

We sat and waited a few minutes as a few curtains twitched, but still no sign of Mick.

'Andrew, go and give him a knock,' my dad said.

I got out, walked up to the house, pushed open the big wooden gates and walked up the drive of the house. There was a black, brand-new, sporty-looking Mercedes parked on the drive, which I admired as a walked past. I rang the bell on the expensive-looking double glass doors and heard a musical chime. A couple of minutes later, I saw movement behind the glass doors and the doors eventually opened. A little grey-haired bloke in his sixties dressed in striped pyjamas and slippers looked at me suspiciously. 'Yes?' he said in a posh voice.

'Is Michael here? We're here to pick him up for work,' I asked.

'Michael?' he said with a confused look. 'There's nobody lives here called Michael.'

'Very sorry, must be the wrong house! Do you know a Michael Fleetwood?' I asked.

'I've lived here for thirty years, son, and I've never heard that name.'

'Sorry to have bothered you,' I said and ran back to the car.

'He doesn't live there!' I said as I climbed in.

'He's full of shit,' Kev shouted. 'He probably lives at Pennywell, the lying bastard!'

My dad sped off back down the road and there was Mick Fleetwood stood outside The Hastings Hill pub. He pulled up and Mick jumped in.

'Cheers, Fawlty!' he shouted as he jumped in, wondering why we were all staring at him open-mouthed.

'Ya full of shit!' Kev shouted.

'What you on about?' Mick shouted back.

'We've just been to your house you said you lived in. Some old bloke answered the door and said he'd never heard of you!' Kev shouted, annoyed.

'That's my dad – he's got dementia, man,' Mick snapped back.

'I bet that's your Mercedes parked in the drive and all, is it?' Kev shouted.

'No, that's my mam's. They're staying with us for a while,' Mick replied.

'Aye, about thirty years,' I whispered to my dad.

He looked at me, confused, and put the radio on. Natalie Imbruglia's 'Torn' came on. My dad turned it up to cover Kev and Mick arguing in the back.

We eventually got to the Dockyard and pulled up in the car park next to the security gate, and we all got out and walked down the bank. When we got to the workshop, all the lads were stood there looking at the notice board. There was a sign that said, 'Safety officers wanted. No experience needed. All training will be given', and underlined, it said, 'Permanent position. If interested, please sign below.'

'I'll have some of that!' my dad said, signing his name underneath John Jenkins' name.

'Put my name down!' Krusty shouted over.

My Dad couldn't resist. He wrote, in big letters, 'KRUSTY'. Everyone started laughing, apart from Krusty, who snatched the pen, scribbled Krusty out and wrote, 'David Thirlwell.'

I ran to put my overalls and helmet on before anyone noticed I was late. I found them where I'd left them, climbed into the legs, and then put my hand in the arms, only to find they'd been cut off.

'Bastards,' I muttered, as I kicked off my trainers and went to put my boots on. I slipped my foot in the left boot and went to move, but the boot was stuck solid to the floor.

Iain saw me struggling and came over, laughing.

'What's happening?' he asked, as I eventually managed to get my foot back out and noticed my boots had been screwed to the floor. Jimmy saw us and came over.

'Someone been playing funny buggers, young'un?' he asked.

'Aye,' I replied, showing him the boots screwed to the floor.

'Haway, lads, there's a meeting in the bait room. Afterwards you can go to the store and get some new boots and overalls and a locker, so the buggers can't get at them,' Jimmy said, patting me on the back and walking away.

'Seems sound, him,' I said to Iain.

'Aye, big change from the baldy prick,' Iain replied.

Five minutes later, we were all gathered in the bait hut for our meeting. It was big enough to hold all 15-20 pipefitters. The room was quiet, and we heard a whistling getting louder, and in walked Jimmy, whistling, followed by two other blokes wearing white overalls.

'Right, lads, this won't take long! Just want to warn you all, there's a thief about. There are tools going missing, and even food. I just wanted to ask you to keep your valuables in your lockers or don't bring them to work at all.'

I started going red for some unknown reason. I always do in these situations; my brain tells me they're all thinking, 'It's you!' even though it isn't. As I sat there burning up, Iain looked on suspiciously.

'What's up with you?' he whispered.

'This always bloody happens! It used to happen at school,' I explained, getting redder and redder. A few people noticed, which made it even worse.

'Anyone caught will be sacked immediately! Personally, I can't think of anything worse than stealing off your own work mates, but these things happen! Just be vigilant lads!' Jimmy said, shaking his head.

The taller bloke behind him piped up. 'Can you return all tools to the store, please, lads. We just want to count everything up and see what's missing. For you lads who don't know me, I'm Ronnie, by the way, and this ugly bastard is Tommy!'

He pointed over to the big, heavy-set bloke with dark hair stood next to him.

'Alright, lads, the bloke wants his boat,' Jimmy smiled and walked out, whistling.

There was a bit of chatter as the bait room emptied, and a few people put sandwiches in the fridge and pies in the oven as they walked out. Big Brian whispered in my dad's ear and put a big sausage roll in the glass oven and a big bottle of Pepsi in the fridge.

Iain and I headed out to the office and Jimmy called us in. The two other bosses were rolling about on the floor, fun fighting. Ronnie had Tommy in a headlock, and he was rolling around trying to escape as Iain and I looked on, laughing.

'Ignore them two nutters. Here are your keys for your lockers. Get yourselves over to the store and get new overalls and boots – here's a chitty,' he said, handing us a piece of paper each and our locker keys as the two bosses screamed at each other in the corner.

Just as Iain and I were walking past the dock towards the store, I heard Whopper Napper behind me, laughing and joking, walking about ten metres behind us and heading the same way.

'Don't look now, but I think Whopper Napper is walking behind us,' I said to Iain, who instantly turned around and looked.

'Aye, he is, Reg!' he replied.

'Why did you turn around, man?' I said, discreetly.

'He wasn't looking anyway – he's with SuperTed!' he laughed.

'SuperTed?' I said, looking puzzled. I couldn't help but look myself, wondering who SuperTed was. I looked around at Whopper Napper, who was walking with and talking to a small, stocky lad wearing glasses and another lad in his late teens, even taller and thinner than me and a face full of acne.

'Which one's SuperTed?' I asked, still baffled.

'The little one with glasses,' Iain said, smirking.

'Why do they call him SuperTed, then?' I said, thinking he looked nothing like SuperTed.

'Have you seen his mate?' Iain said, laughing.

I still didn't get it and was still thinking about it when we walked in the store. The store at this dockyard, like everything else, was a lot more modern and seemed to have everything; it was huge with a little counter at the front. Larry came to the counter smiling, as always.

'Alright, bonny lads. This place is more like it, eh? Anyway, what can I do you for?'

Iain and I handed him our notes of paper.

'Stick your boot sizes and overall sizes on there,' Larry said, giving us back the bits of paper and a little blue bookie's pen.

We were busy filling the forms in when the door opened behind us and Whopper Napper walked in with SuperTed and the spotty lad. It then dawned on me when I saw the spotty lad close up why they called his mate SuperTed, and I burst out laughing. Whopper Napper stared at me for a little while and then walked out of view as I carried on filling the form in.

A few awkward minutes later, Larry passed the overalls and boots over and said, 'Try them on – make sure they fit.'

We did so, and then Iain and I stood there nodding at each other.

'Aye, they're areet!' Iain said, and Larry gave us a yellow helmet each.

'The apprentices here have to wear yellow hats. Here you go.'

We popped our hats on and signed a form, ticking the items we had received. Suddenly, Larry looked at me and started laughing.

'What?' I asked.

'Yellow definitely isn't your colour! Next,' he shouted, and Whopper Napper went to the counter, ignoring me and Iain.

Iain looked at me and laughed.

'What?' I said, and Iain said the same.

'Larry's right – yellow isn't your colour.'

I walked out of the store and SuperTed and Spotty both looked at me and laughed too.

'Is it that bad?' I laughed myself. I couldn't help but feel paranoid with everyone laughing, but I soon forgot about it as we headed on our way over to the plumber's workshop.

We walked over to the dock gate and I could hear someone shouting in the distance. I looked about but couldn't see anyone. Then I heard it.

'Knobhead!'

I looked up, and Billy Animal was on his way up the crane ladder, laughing and shouting, 'Knobhead!'

I looked at Iain, puzzled. 'What's he on about?'

Iain just laughed and said, 'God knows. He's off his head!'

My dad was walking towards me laughing with Dicky and Krusty, who were both smirking. None of them had any boots or overalls on, and they all had their bags on their shoulders.

'Where are you going, like?' I asked.

'We are going on night shift – we're off home,' my dad replied.

'How am I gonna get home?' I asked.

'Don't worry, knobhead! I've left my car keys in your bag – you can drive home! You've got your provisional, haven't you? And Kev will be going with you – he can drive if you're scared!' my dad said, while I looked at him a little shocked after hearing him calling me a knobhead.

'How are you getting home then?' I asked.

'K– Dave is taking me home,' my dad, laughing, having nearly called him Krusty again. 'You'll have to get in yourself somehow tomorrow, though, son.'

As we headed for the plumber's shop, Kev came up to us, smirking.

'Alright, lads, I'm leaving! I've just been fixed up with a nice job in Norway,' he said, rubbing his hands together. 'Any chance you can bring the car down later, so I can chuck my toolbox in the boot. I've put my notice in – I'm finishing at the end of the shift.'

He looked very pleased with himself.

'Aye, no bother mate. I'll have a word with Jimmy Whistler, make sure it's okay,' I replied.

As Iain and I walked into the plumber's shop, there was a big cheer, and Dot shouted over, 'Knobhead!'

I realised there must have been a reason people kept calling me that. I put my hand on top of my helmet and felt something on the top. I took it off and there was a six-inch cock made of insulating foam stuck to my hat with double-sided duct tape.

'The bastard! Was that Whopper Napper?' I laughed.

Jimmy came whistling over to us. 'Alright, lads, put your stuff in your lockers. You're gonna give Brian a hand on the fresh water,' he said, pointing us to the bait room.

We headed in and soon found our lockers. Brian followed us in, slid the oven door open and said, 'It's still there!'

Iain and I put our stuff in our new lockers and looked at Brian examining his sausage roll.

'Some bugger nicked my pie yesterday. I know who it was, I'm positive – just got to prove it,' he said and winked, placing his sausage roll back in the oven.

We headed back out into the workshop and Brian asked how my brother was.

'Aye, he's champion. I didn't know you knew him,' I replied.

'Aye, he's mates with my eldest,' he explained.

Brian explained what job he was doing and talked us through it, drawing a little sketch on the bench with chalk. Iain and I looked on, baffled. Brian explained how we have a lot to learn, but over time, we will pick it up, and any problems, we could always come to him. He seems like a decent bloke, I thought, while he started showing us how to use the hand benders.

Suddenly, there was a loud shout from the canteen. Brian stopped what he was doing and ran over; Iain and I followed.

Fleetwood Mick was in there with a pie on the floor. Brian stared at him and said, 'What you up to, Mick?' and eyed him up suspiciously.

'I was just checking my pie to see if it's cooked, and I've burned the bloody thing. I pulled it out, but burned my hand,' he said, holding his hand up and blowing on his fingers.

'What did you think I was doing, like? I'm not the bloody thief!' Mick shouted, looking a little pissed off.

'Hey, I never said you were,' Brian said, heading back out into the workshop.

'My dad's gone on night shift. I've got his car keys, though, if you need a lift,' I said, watching Mick scoop his burned pie off the floor.

'Aye, cheers. My bike still isn't fixed.'

I explained I hadn't passed my test, but as long as he or Kev had a driving licence, I'd be fine.

We headed out to see Brian for the next hour or so. He taught us how to make offsets in pipes, all the while keeping an eye on who was coming and going in the canteen.

'Right, lads, breaktime!'

We went off to wash our hands and then followed Brian into the canteen.

'There ya go – got the bastard!' Brian shouted, pointing to a sausage roll on the floor.

A few blokes came over to see what he was on about.

'Look, I pushed a big wooden peg inside the sausage roll and put it in the oven, and someone's tried to bite into it,' he said, pointing to it on the floor.

'Hey, that's half a tooth there, look!' One of the lads pointed next to the sausage roll.

'Who's not here?' Brian said, looking around the room.

Iain and I eventually sat down at a table at the back of the room and watched carefully as each person walked in to see if they were missing a tooth.

'Dot's not here. Kevin's not here. Fleetwood Mac's not here. Decka isn't here,' Brian shouted, just as Decka walked in.

'What's up? Decka asked, noticing the room had gone quiet since he'd come in.

Brian explained about the peg and the tooth. Decka laughed as he examined the tooth.

'Hey, that's a front tooth, that! Well done, Brian, lad,' he laughed, patting him on the back.

A few minutes later, JJ walked in, sat down and started reading his paper without a saying a word.

'Alright, John?' Decka shouted over, at which he looked confused. He looked over his Daily Mirror and just nodded.

Iain and I looked at each other thinking the same thing, wondering if it was him.

'You heard anything about the safety officer's job yet, like?' Brian asked, looking at John.

'Na, not yet. I only signed the form this morning,' he said, as the room made a sort of disappointed groan as his teeth seemed intact.

He looked around, wondering what was going on, when the door opened and Micky Fleetwood walked in singing, 'No... matter what they tell you. No matter what they do...'

He suddenly stopped, realising everyone was looking at him.

'What? It's won awards, this voice, man!' he shouted and sat down opposite John.

The door opened again, and Kev walked in, picked his bag up off the table and quickly walked back out.

'It's got to be him!' Brian shouted.

'He's a tight bastard, aye, but he's not a thief, surely?' Decka said.

'Well, where's he gone? Actions of a guilty man, that's all I'm saying!' Brian said, sitting down and picking up his paper.

The door opened and Dan walked in. All eyes quickly turned to him as he looked on, wondering what was going on. He sat down opposite me and Iain as everyone watched him carefully.

'What's going on?' he whispered, running his hand over his hat, making sure he didn't have a big cock on top like I did earlier.

We explained what had happened, and he showed his full set of teeth off to everyone who looked on and then carried on reading their papers.

'You seen Fat Kev?' I asked.

'Aye, he's sitting outside in the sun with his top off. What a sight!' he said, laughing.

'Prime suspect!' Iain muttered.

After dinner, we headed out into the workshop, and Jimmy asked us to go back into the bait room for a toolbox talk. I went out to tell Fat Kev, but there was no sign of him, yet his rucksack was still there. I followed the rest of the lads back into the bait hut and we sat back down in our seats.

'Right, lads, this won't take long. We're starting an overtime rota,' Jimmy said, pinning a sheet up next to the microwave.

'If any of you want to work Saturday or Sunday, put your names on the sheet. Also, we're missing two pairs of Stillsons out of the store. If anyone has them, bring them back, please,' he said, and walked out, whistling.

We headed back into the workshop and Brian eventually came out and carried on from where he left off, showing us how to bend offsets in pipes. We were stood there, trying to take in everything he was saying, when Iain nodded to me. I looked round and Fat Kev was heading into the canteen with his bag. Brian didn't notice and carried on chatting away. Dot came over, watching Brian, and when Brian looked at him, he gave him a teething smile.

'I heard I was a suspect, like,' Dot shouted. 'All the years you've known me!' He shook his head.

'I never said you were a suspect!' Brian shouted back.

'Hey, you know who ya mates are,' he said, wandering off, winking at me and Iain.

The afternoon dragged on, and eventually, Jimmy came around giving all the new lads a clock card and pointed to the clocking machine where we had to swipe our cards when we left.

'No clocking each other out – there's a camera up there,' Jimmy said, pointing to a camera up in the ceiling above the clock.

'Jimmy, is it okay to bring my dad's car down here? Kev wants to put his tools in the boot, as I'm dropping him off tonight,' I asked Jimmy.

'Aye, no bother, son. You'd better go now, though, as there's not long left.'

I quickly ran into the canteen to my locker to get the car keys out of my bag and up the bank as quick as I could. When I got to the security hut, I explained to the young security guard that I needed to drive the car in the yard. He passed me a green pass and told me to stick it on the dashboard.

I ran over to the car park, jumped in my dad's car and drove up to the security barrier. I stopped with a jump and stalled the car as the guard lifted the barrier to let me through.

I eventually pulled up outside the plumber's shop and saw Kev standing outside with his rucksack and tools. I threw the keys to him and ran inside to get ready to go. I ran to my locker, took my helmet and overalls off and chucked them in the locker, quickly put my trainers on and ran to join the line for the clocking machine. I noticed Jimmy at the front of the line looking in everyone's bags as they clocked out. Kev, at the front, shook his head, zipped his rucksack up and headed to the car. Fleetwood Mick did the same. I eventually got to the end of the line, swiped my clock card and opened my rucksack for Jimmy to have a look inside.

He took the rucksack and peered inside.

'Sorry to have to do this, son. See you in the morning,' he said, handing me back my bag back.

I ran to the car outside the plumber's shop. Fleetwood Mac was sitting in the back seat and Kev was in the front.

'Sorry to keep you waiting lads,' I said, as Kev handed me the keys.

I turned the key in the ignition and began reversing but stalled. Mick laughed.

'Take your time,' he said, and I tried again, this time successfully reversing out, and shuddered up the bank.

The security guard waved us through, and I handed him the green pass, tried to drive through the barrier and stalled again. I started the car up again and off we went.

'I used to be a driving instructor you know. I'll give you some lessons if you want,' Mick shouted from the back.

'Bollocks!' Kev shouted, as I stalled, yet again, at a roundabout.

'It's true. I used to work for B.S.M,' Mick said, leaning over from the back seat.

I managed to get the car going again and headed down towards the A19.

'Hey, I can't believe they searched us for them Stillsons on the way out!' Mick shouted.

'Bit out of order, like,' I replied.

'It's a good thing he didn't look in your boot,' Kev said, smiling, with half his front tooth missing.

'Ya fucking joking, ain't ya?' shouted Fleetwood Mac.

'Hey there loaded, man. They'll not miss a couple of pairs of Stillsons,' Kev shouted back.

Ten minutes or so later, I pulled off the A19 to Sunderland and carried on to Pennywell.

'Shit, sorry, Mick – I've driven past yours. I'll drop Kev off first then turn around,' I said, looking in the mirror at Mick.

I pulled in at a bus stop and Kev jumped out. I opened the boot, and he got his tools and the two pairs of Stillsons he nicked as I watched him, shaking my head.

'Cheers, Andy. Probably see you around,' Kev said, and headed down the road, loaded up with bags and boxes.

I quickly ran into the shop next to the bus stop and picked up some cans for Harry and a big box of Milk Tray for Mrs Patterson, jumped back in the car and chucked them on the back seat next to Mick. A bus was sounding its horn for me to move from the bus stop, so I started stressing, trying to get my seatbelt on as quick as I could. I tried to pull away as quick as I could, but I stalled again. My nerves got the better of me and the bus driver was still sounding his horn, and I stalled for a second time as I moved into the road, and a car had to slam on its brakes on to avoid hitting me.

'Jump out, mate – I'll drive,' Mick said, quickly jumping out of the back seat and opening the driver's door.

I got out and jumped in the passenger seat, and Mick drove us away from the angry drivers.

'You've just got to take your time, man. Don't stress!' Mick said, as we headed back up South Hylton Bank. 'Haway, go and drop your stuff off and ask your dad if I can take you for a lesson. I need to go to Boldon anyway to pick a crank up for my bike,' Mick said, as he turned onto my road.

'Down here, isn't it?' he asked.

'Aye, first square after the bus terminus,' I replied.

We pulled into the square and I jumped out and ran to Mrs Patterson's house and knocked on her door. I waited a couple of minutes, but there was no sign of her, so I popped my head in the window. She saw me and jumped out of her chair, waving, and came to the door. After a couple of minutes of hearing the sound of rustling of keys and bolts being unlocked, the door flew open, and Mrs Patterson reached out to give me a hug. I kissed her on the cheek, handed her the chocolates and apologised for the toilet and the sink.

'You didn't have to do that, you silly sod!' she said, and smiled.

I explained I was in a rush and waved goodbye, and she stood waving at the door as I ran to Harry's house. I opened Harry's gate and rang the bell, and a few seconds later, the door opened, and his little brown boxer dog shot out of the door and the gate.

'Bloody hell, man!' Harry shouted, chasing after him.

Seeing what had happened, Mick jumped out of the car and quickly managed to chase the dog and grab him by his black, spiked collar before he escaped out of the square. Harry ran out, relieved at getting Rambo back, and thanked Mick.

'He's a topper. I used to breed these,' Mick said, handing the collar to Harry.

Harry quickly dragged the dog in the house and shut the front door.

He turned to me. 'You're like a bloody curse to me, you, son!' he yelled.

'Sorry, Harry, I've brought you these to say I'm sorry!'

I handed him the Co-op carrier bag full of cans. He smiled and said, 'Cheers son.'

'Look, if there's anything I can do, just name it,' I said, and Harry started thinking something over.

'There is something! You can take that dog for a walk – he's driving me up the bloody wall.'

I explained I was just about to go and take Mick to Boldon, but I would as soon as I come back.

'Take him with you – he loves a ride in the car. He'll just sit there with his head out the window, and it'll give me a chance to paint the doors without him jumping all over the bloody place.'

'Aye, okay. No bother,' I replied.

My dad came to the front door and said, 'What's Fleetwood Mac doing here?'

'He's going to take me for a driving lesson. Is it okay to borrow the car?' I asked, as Harry came out and handed me Rambo on the lead.

'Aye, Krusty is taking his car anyway, but be careful!' he said, as Rambo began humping my leg.

'Off!' Harry shouted at him, and he handed him a dog chew when he did as he was told. 'Don't let him off the lead. And here are some chews – he goes mad for them!' he said, handing me a bag of spiral sticks. 'Please be careful.' He kissed the dog on the head.

I opened the car's rear door, and Rambo jumped in and sat on the back seat with his chew in his mouth, happily munching away.

'Do you want me to drive?' asked Mick.

'Aye, please. I'll drive back,' I said, jumping in the back with the dog.

We eventually pulled up to a pub in Boldon Colliery next to the train tracks called The Beggar's Bridge. I jumped out with Rambo on the lead and we walked into the pub. As soon as we stepped inside, the barmaid shouted, 'Sorry, no dogs!'

I left with the dog and took him to a patch of grass by a red and white fence, where he started sniffing around. Mick popped his head out of the pub door and said, 'You want a pint?'

'I'd better not, mate,' I replied, thinking I can't really leave the dog outside.

After a few minutes, I realised I really did need a piss. I stood there for a few more minutes while Rambo had a dump. I started dragging the dog towards the pub, as I really needed the toilet, but he was still sniffing away. I decided I was going to tie his lead to the fence while I ran in to the bog. I tied his lead in a double knot, dropped a couple of dog chews down on the grass and ran as quick as I could into the pub.

I saw Mick sat at the bar with some bloke sat next to him with a cap on. They were chatting away, so I just ran past them and into the toilet.

A few minutes later, I ran back out as Mick was shaking hands with the bloke, and he quickly downed his pint and followed me outside with his new crank for his bike.

We walked out the door, and I looked over to where I'd left the dog, and it was gone. Not only the dog, but the fence too.

'What the hell?' I shouted and ran to the spot Rambo was last seen. 'Rambo!'

'Please don't tell me you tied it to the level crossing barrier!' said Mick, pointing to the raised barrier I'd left the dog tied too.

I couldn't breathe. I couldn't look up. I started panicking and fell to the ground shaking. I looked over and saw two dog chews on the grass and his turd, and I almost started crying.

'Oh my god, what have I done!' I screamed.

Mick tried to calm me down, putting his hand on my shoulder.

'His lead's still on the barrier! Maybe he escaped!' said Mick.

I couldn't think about it. I was devastated and burst into tears.

A man in a high-vis jacket came over, seeing the state I was in, and helped me to my feet.

'Did you tie that dog to the barrier?' he said, staring into my tear-filled eyes.

'Yes,' I struggled to say.

'Can you come this way, please?' the bloke asked.

Mick and I followed him. He took us into a little wooden gatehouse next to the tracks. He opened the door and Rambo came running out to greet me. I fell to my knees, grabbed his collar and hugged him, and he immediately wiggled loose and began humping my arm. I reached into my pocket and gave him the full bag of chews, and he immediately let go and started munching away.

'What the hell possessed you to tie him to the barrier!' shouted the bloke.

'I had no idea! And I needed a piss,' I stuttered, smiling, relieved to see Rambo was okay.

'Well, it's lucky for you I spotted him there before the gate lifted, you bloody idiot,' the bloke shouted.

'I'm sorry,' I replied, climbing back to my feet and shaking his hand. 'Thank you!'

'Come on, let's get his lead,' the bloke said and led us outside, as I gripped Rambo's collar as tight as I could.

I decided to let Mick drive back, as I was in no fit state. I sat with Rambo in the back seat, thinking thank god he's okay.

BOOK 2

CHAPTER 9

October 1997

My alarm was blasting, but I didn't want to get up. I reached over, pressed snooze and rolled over.

'Five more minutes,' I muttered.

'For fuck's sake! Will you turn that fucking alarm off – I'm trying to get some sleep!' my dad screamed, standing at my bedroom door as my alarm beeped full blast.

'Billy!' I heard my mam shout from the bedroom, obviously not happy with my dad's choice of words.

I looked at the alarm clock. It was 7:15. I had five more minutes before Decka picked me up. I quickly got up, jumped into my work clothes and sprayed my Lynx, but it was empty. I ran into the bathroom. I ended up using my mam's Impulse deodorant, quickly brushed my teeth and legged it down the stairs.

I could hear music blasting from outside and a horn beeping, so I grabbed my bag and ran into the square, where Decka was parked up in his bright yellow Saxo with The Prodigy's 'Smack My Bitch Up' up on full blast. Colin was in the passenger seat; he jumped out and pulled the seat forward for me to climb into the back seat.

'How was your weekend in Paris?' I asked Colin.

'It was class,' he replied.

'Was it hot?'

'It was red hot – it was like being abroad,' he replied, and Decka and I laughed.

'Cheers for this, Decka,' I shouted over the music.

'Are you wearing perfume?' he replied, looking at me strangely.

The drug dealer next door opened the front door and ran over to the car.

'Turn that shit off or I'll...'

'Or you'll what? You tosser,' Decka interrupted.

'That's fighting talk where I come from!' the druggie yelled over the music.

Suddenly, Decka took off his seat belt, jumped out and stood with his arms outstretched, towering above him.

'But it was a rough area, so I moved away from there,' the druggie shouted, seeing the size of Decka, and quickly ran in the house.

Colin and I burst out laughing as Decka jumped back in the car. It was lucky Harry never came out with his cricket bat or it would have been World War Three, I thought, as Decka wheel-span out the square.

As we approached the A19, Decka was chatting away, but I couldn't hear a word over The Prodigy's 'Breathe' blasting.

'Sorry,' Decka said, turning the music down seeing me straining to listen. 'I was just saying to Col we were working on Cunifer pipe yesterday and I got a bollocking for not wearing a mask. They reckon it's banned in America because it's carcinogenic!'

'Aye, it is,' Colin agreed. 'They reckon it causes cancer too!'

Decka and I burst out laughing again.

'What?' Col asked, wondering what was so funny.

'That's what carcinogenic means, ya daft bastard,' Decka said, laughing.

We were flying down the A19 doing 120 miles an hour, and I was gripping the seats in terror.

'Dear me, are you going for the land speed record here, like?' I said, looking at his speedometer.

We got to the Dockyard in record time, and with my ears ringing, I was seriously contemplating if I should get the new Metro for the rest of the week.

We eventually clocked in and went to our lockers. I took my fleece jacket off and hung it up in the locker and then got ready into my overalls and boots as Iain came in and started getting changed next to me.

'Areet,' Iain said, watching me put my locker key on top of the locker.

'Aye, champion,' I replied.

We sat down and had a cup of tea while the other lads came in in dribs and drabs.

'Reet, who's in?' Iain shouted, shuffling a pack of cards '£1 a man, switch – winner takes all.'

'Aye, I'm in,' I said, rooting around for a pound in my pocket.

Colin, Dan and Decka pulled up a chair and all put their pounds on the table as Iain dealt seven cards each and turned a card from the pack over, which was three of spades.

'Your go, Colin,' Iain said, as he examined his own cards.

Colin put down a three of diamonds, and it came to my turn. 'Seven back to me, seven back to me, hearts,' I said, putting down two sevens and a Jack of clubs.

'What the hell ya doing? It's seven, miss a go, not back to me, and what ya deeing with the Jack?' Iain asked.

'Any Jack changes suits, and eights miss a go,' I said, as Colin and Decka nodded in agreement.

'Bollocks!' Iain and Dan shouted at the same time. 'Ace changes suit, man!' Iain said.

'Does it, bollocks! Ace of hearts pick up five, and Ace of spades blocks,' Decka shouted, and Colin and I agreed.

'Pick up five? What you on about!' Dan laughed, as everyone started shouting over each other with different rules.

Dot came over. 'I'll settle this. Next card decides,' he stated and turned the top card over from the pack, which was a ten of diamonds.

'There you go. Whose turn is it next?' Dot asked.

'Mine!' Dan shouted.

'Fifty-two card pick up,' he said, scooping up all the cards and chucking them on the floor as we all looked on, shocked. 'Now, shut the fuck up – we're trying to have a quiet cup of tea, man!' he shouted, and walked off as we continued arguing.

'Mackem rules, man. They just make it up as they go along,' Iain muttered to Dan as he picked the cards off the floor.

Jimmy came in, whistling away as always. 'Reet, lads, listen up!' he shouted. 'The Edinburgh Castle is moving to the quay, and we have a Norwegian ship coming in tonight. We need some volunteers to go on nights tonight for a while. Anyone interested?'

Iain and I popped our hands up, and we seemed to be the only ones, we noticed, as we looked around

'I dunno if they'll let apprentices go on nights, but I'll ask the question. Anyone else?'

Nobody else volunteered, so Jimmy walked out, whistling away.

'What do you wanna go on nights for?' Decka asked.

'My dad reckons there are no gaffers about, and you can do what ya want. Plus, it's extra money, and I'm skint,' I replied.

Five minutes later, I headed into the workshop while Iain went to his locker for his fags, and I joined Brian by the bench next to Fleetwood Mac. The two of them were laughing when I walked up.

'Here he is – Frank Spencer!' Brian laughed.

'I thought I was bad, but tying a dog to a level crossing…' Brian said, wiping a tear of laughter from his eye.

Jimmy walked over just as Iain quickly caught up with us by the bench.

'Right, Andy and Iain, you can go on nights for this week, but be back on days for Monday, as you start college next week. Report to Paula on Monday and she'll explain all the information, but I think your college day is Thursday.' Jimmy said, as Iain and I looked at each other excitedly.

'Are you okay for getting home?' Jimmy asked.

'Aye, we'll just jump on the Metro,' I replied, not wanting anything to stop us going on nights.

'Good. Get yourselves home and try get some kip. You work 7.30pm 'til 7:30am and have Friday off,' Jimmy said, as Iain and I looked at each other, grinning again.

We returned to the lockers to get changed, and I quickly threw my overalls and boots back in the locker and put my fleece on, not knowing Iain had stuck a big sign on the back of it saying, 'I love bum fun'. We walked out through the workshop and there were roars of laughter as we passed Brian and a few other blokes, figuring they were laughing about the dog incident. I just smiled as we walked past and headed up the bank.

A few minutes later, we got to Hepburn Metro station, where I walked over to the ticket machine to buy my ticket.

'What ya deeing man!' Iain shouted. 'I never pay. There's never any guards on this time of day, man,' he shouted, leading me to the platform.

We eventually jumped on the Metro bound for South Hylton, Iain jumped on with me, but said he'd have to change to the Shields line in a couple of stops. We stood in the carriageway, as the train was full, and I could hear giggles behind me. I looked around, confused, as Iain stood smirking.

Iain got off the train eventually and I found myself a seat next to an old lady as the Metro whizzed out of Pelaw station. I sat looking out of the window at the cranes in the distance thinking, 'Life is good'. The train eventually pulled into Sunderland city centre and, to my horror, a ticket inspector got on in a bright yellow high-vis jacket. I jumped out of my seat and walked as quickly as I could to the other doors away from the inspector, but just before I got there, there was an announcement: 'Stand clear of the doors, please', and the doors slid shut and the Metro began moving.

I began walking down the Metro, weaving in and out of passengers as discreetly as I could, but I could feel everyone's eyes burning into me and heard a few more giggles. I walked to the end of the Metro and the inspector came running over towards me. I put my hands up in the air in panic, and he laughed.

'Don't worry, I'm not going to shoot you,' he said, looking at the horror on my face. 'Turn around,' he said, laughing, which I did.

He pulled the 'I love bum fun' sign off my back and handed it to me as the rest of the passengers giggled. Then, to my amazement, he wandered off, laughing, and carried on where he was, collecting tickets as I stood there red-faced.

The ticket inspector was getting closer to me stamping other passengers' tickets. Luckily for me, the train came to a halt, and again, the announcement came: 'Stand clear of the doors, please'. The doors opened and I ran out onto the platform. As I left the train, I spotted two ticket inspectors checking tickets as people left the platform. I panicked and ran back onto the Metro. I quickly walked past the inspector, who didn't see me, as he was stamping someone's ticket as I walked past, and I sat down at the other end of the train.

After a nerve-wracking ten minutes, the Metro eventually pulled into South Hylton, where I got off. The ticket inspector from the train walked past me and said, 'Next time, get a ticket! It's lucky I know ya fatha.' He gave me a wink and walked off.

'What you done now?' my mam shouted as I walked through the front door.

'Nothing!' I replied, holding my hands up. 'I'm going on nights with dad.'

She made me a cup of tea while I took my shoes and jacket off and lay on the settee, and after a few minutes, I began to nod off.

'Will you not speak to me like that, Billy?' I heard my mam shout, as I woke with a jump on the settee.

'Well, where's my bloody shoes? Why do you have to move everything, woman!' my dad yelled back, stomping upstairs and slamming the bathroom door.

'Chuck him in the Tyne when you get to work, will you!' my mam shouted, as I sat up and looked up at the clock above the fireplace.

'Shit, it's 6:30!' I shouted.

'Language,' my mam snapped back. 'You'll get there on time if your dad finds his shoes!' she said, picking up my cold tea from the floor.

'I'm not bothered about that – I've missed Neighbours,' I replied.

CHAPTER 10

Night shift shenanigans

Eventually, my Dad found his shoes, and I put the video recorder in the boot, while my dad looked on, shaking his head. We pulled out of the square and headed up towards the A19. We pulled into the bus stop on Hylton Road and Dicky and Krusty jumped in the back seat.

'Morning lads,' my dad said, as they climbed in.

'Ya mean evening,' I corrected him.

'Shut up, man, ya tit. Worse than his mother, him,' my dad snapped, while looking in the rear-view mirror to Krusty and Dicky.

'Where's Pikey working these days, Andrew?' Dicky shouted over.

'He's in Holland at the minute, Dicky,' I replied.

'Aye, he's got nowhere to run to now, Dicky, when his mam hoys him out,' my dad piped up.

Dicky laughed and said, 'You been a naughty boy again, young'un?'

'Aye, he bloody has!' my dad interrupted 'Can't control his bladder when he goes out with his mates on a weekend! Keeps coming back home and pissing around the house!'

I sat there, my cheeks burning red, as my dad ranted away.

'Tell them what's in the boot,' my dad said, nudging my arm. 'Go on, tell them!'

'My video,' I replied, looking out of the window, annoyed.

'Tell them why.'

My Dad began nudging me again.

'Because I came in Saturday night and pissed all over it. And it won't work!' I shouted over to Dicky and Krusty, who burst out laughing in the back.

'It's bloody brand new – not even paid for yet!' my dad shouted.

'I'm gonna ask Andy the Sparky to see if he can fix it. Useless tit!' he muttered, looking at me and shaking his head.

We finally arrived at the dockyard and the security guards let us through the gate. It seemed as though all the office staff had gone home and there was plenty of parking available onsite. As we drove down the bank, a group of about ten lads were walking past the dock; my dad slowed right down behind them, turned his engine and lights off and rolled slowly behind them. As we got a bit closer, my dad honked his horn and the lads nearly shit themselves in fright as we looked on, laughing.

'Ya daft bastard! You could have given me a heart attack!' one of the older lads shouted at my dad.

'Hey Andy,' my dad shouted to a dark-haired lad wheeling his bike.

'Will ya see if you can fix the boy's video if you get a chance? The silly bugger pissed all over it at the weekend.'

All the lads, including Dicky and Krusty, burst out laughing again.

'Aye, bring it round, Fawlty. I'll have a look if I get a minute,' Andy replied, shaking his head.

'Cheers, bony lad,' my dad shouted out the window as he started the engine and headed off down towards our workshop.

He parked up and we headed through the workshop and into the bait room. It felt very strange, as there wasn't a soul in sight. I walked over to my locker and got my overalls and boots on, and eventually, I sat down and started to read my paper. A few minutes later, Iain came walking in.

'Cheers for that sign on my back, ya dick!' I shouted, laughing.

Iain laughed and replied, ‘Funny that, mate! Didn’t you wonder why everyone was laughing at you?’

‘I did wonder,’ I said, thinking I’ll get the twat back.

Eventually, Jimmy Whistler came in, whistling the same tune he always did.

‘Right, lads, listen up! I’m off home now. There’s not really a lot to do tonight. The ship’s in the dock and there’s a list in my office of the jobs I want doing. Just share the work between yourselves, and if you get it finished, treat yourself to a beer each. There’s a room next to the galley – the captain said it’s okay to have a couple each, but don’t take the piss! Okay, lads – have a good night. Any problems, leave a note for day shift. And any safety incidents, the BFG will be in his office,’ Jimmy said, leaving us all with puzzled looks.

‘Who’s the BFG?’ Dicky asked.

‘The Big Fat Geordie. Night shift safety officer,’ Jimmy replied.

We all looked at each other and laughed as he walked out.

‘That man is a gentleman and a scholar. Free drink!’ my dad said, rubbing his hands together.

‘We’d better not take the piss, though, lads, eh,’ Dicky replied.

‘I’m not gonna take the piss!’ my dad snapped, looking insulted.

Eventually, we went to the office and looked over the job sheet, and the lads decided Dicky and my dad would work together, and Iain and I would go to work with Krusty. Dave Thirwell. He was as a nice enough bloke. He took us on the Norwegian ship, The Lod Brog, and showed us around, explaining how the ship needed a full refit and was eventually going to be cut in half and a section put in the middle to extend it.

‘It hasn’t gotta be done by tonight, has it?’ Iain joked.

‘A year’s graft, I reckon,’ Krusty stated, looking around at the old, crumbling pipework.

We walked towards the galley and noticed my dad and Dicky by the door of the next compartment with cans of Norwegian beer in their hands.

‘Hey, canny drop, that!’ Dicky shouted over to Krusty, raising the can.

We headed over to have a look and, to our amazement, there was a room full of cans.

'I reckon if we climb over to the back, they'll not notice how many we've drunk,' my dad said, grinning. He grabbed a beam on the deck head and began climbing up over the top of the cans. We heard a thud as he dropped to the other side of the cans and out of sight.

'Hey, there must be a couple of thousand cans here, lads,' my dad shouted over.

'Well, we'd better get stuck in then, Marra, eh!' Dicky shouted over and popped open another can.

'Haway, lads, let's rattle this job off,' Krusty said to me and Iain, and he walked out of the room, with us reluctantly tagging along.

He led us to the engine room and showed us three pipes that had to be removed, and eventually, all three of us began undoing bolts on the flanges of the pipes. It was a nice, easy job, and things went smoothly for once, only taking us an hour at most. Once the pipes were dismantled, we headed up the stairs towards the gangway, each with a pipe on our shoulders. Krusty stopped us just as we were about to step onto the gangway.

'Shh, listen!' he said and raised an eyebrow as he strained to hear the faint sound of singing.

'Beer, beer, beer, tiddly beer, beer, beer!'

You could hear my dad and Dicky singing at the top of their voices from the deck below.

'Bloody hell, man!' Krusty shouted, heading back on board and sending us over to the workshop with the pipes. We dropped the pipes on the workshop floor.

'They must be getting hammered, those two,' I laughed.

'Aye, I know. Haway, what the fuck are we waiting here for? We've done our graft – let's go back and get some grog!' Iain said and started walking back towards the door of the workshop.

We got back to the ship, walked over the gangway and went down the stairwell to the galley. Before we even got to the next level, you could hear my dad and Dicky singing The Irish Rover at the top of their voices. As we got there, Krusty stood watching from outside the room, laughing at my dad and Dicky, who were now making trumpet noises.

'Hey, I used to play the trumpet in the Salvation Army years ago,' my dad said, proudly, sipping another drink from his can.

'You in the Salvation Army?' Dicky laughed.

'Aye, hey, listen to my story,' he said and ushered us in closer. 'We had a big concert one night, and there was this one rich kid – right smug little twat, stood there in his immaculate suit and shiny shoes. Anyway, he pulled out his brand-spanking-new trumpet out of his case and stepped onto the stage and began playing. To be fair, he was okay, but not great. We were all left a little disappointed, expecting great things. Next up was Little Timmy. Now, Little Timmy was a quiet young lad. He came from a very poor family. He wore a tatty old suit, and he was wearing old, battered shoes with holes in the toes. He stepped up nervously onto the stage with his battered old trumpet and the room suddenly fell silent. He stood there nervously with the audience watching; he took a deep breath, and when he blew on that trumpet...'

We looked on in anticipation.

'He was shite! Even worse than the rich kid!' he said, sending us all into stitches with his story. He threw his car keys to me.

'What?' I asked.

'The video. Go and take it to Andy the Sparky!'

I walked out while Iain popped open a can and joined in with my dad and Dicky, while Krusty looked on. I walked over to my dad's car, lifted my piss-smelling video out of the boot and headed over to the electrician's place. I walked up to the door, gave it a shove with my back and pushed the handle down with my knee as I struggled with the video, but the door was locked. I walked around to the side door, which was also locked, so I gave it a gentle tap with my steel-toe-capped boots. After a couple of minutes, a light came on, and I heard locks being undone and the door opened.

'Ah, young Fawlty,' a bloke dressed in a dressing gown said, yawning. 'Stevie said you'd be coming. Haway in,' the lad said in his thick, Geordie accent.

I followed the bloke into a big, dark warehouse, where he turned the light on. I noticed he had a bed in the corner of the room made up with insulation and a sleeping bag on top.

'Sorry! I hope I didn't wake you,' I said, looking at the bed.

'Nee bother son, I'll have to go and do a bit of graft soon anyway!' he said, stretching.

'Just put the video on the bench there – I'll have a look at it, or I'll get Steve to when he gets back from the pub,' he said.

'Pub?' I laughed.

'Aye, they've gone through the secret passage,' he said tapping his nose.

'Secret passage?' I asked, laughing.

'Haway, I'll show you, but this is top secret, okay?' he warned, suddenly taking on a serious tone.

He took off his dressing gown and slippers and got ready into his overalls and boots; then
he walked me up the bank. He walked me by a hedge and a big wire mesh fence. He pointed over to a little gap in the hedge and we walked through it. He lifted a little hook in the fence, and to my amazement, I noticed someone had made a door in it. It swung out like a giant cat flap. I would never have noticed it if he hadn't shown me; it was disguised so well.

'The pub's just a five-minute walk through those bushes. You just have to jump over the wall at the end – the security guards have no idea,' he said, smiling proudly.

I was tempted to go for a pint, but I thought twice. Knowing my luck, I'd get caught and sacked, so I thought I'd just head back.

'Sorry, I didn't catch your name,' I said, stretching out a hand to him.

'I'm Paul – or Junior Hacksaw, as the lads call me,' he said, shaking my hand.

'Junior Hacksaw?' I asked with an inquisitive look.

'My dad worked in the yards a few years ago and was known as 'Hacksaw', so they call me Junior,' he said.

'I see. Is he retired?' I asked.

'He retired a few years ago from the yards. He became a roofer, but he passed away shortly after.' He looked up to the roof. 'Dad, if you're up there...'

He laughed and walked back to the electrical hut.

I had a slow walk back. Just as I was about to head to the dock, I noticed Krusty walking towards me.

'Alright, son, will you give me a hand to do your dad and Dicky's job? Those two are in no fit state,' he said, sighing and shaking his head

'Yeah, no bother. Are you not having a drink, like?' I asked.

'No, someone's gotta drive us home in the morning, and Jimmy trusted us to finish the job,' he said, looking a little bit annoyed.

I ended up grafting my nuts off with Krusty for the rest of the night. The two pipes my dad and Dicky were supposed to take out turned out to be a nightmare. After about three or four hours of draining oil from the pipes and then struggling undoing seized-up bolts, we eventually finished all we had to do. Dave and I took the pipes up the stairs and off the boat, then over to the workshop.

'Cheers, son. It's nearly 2am now, so we will have a quick cuppa, then head back over and get the buckets and have a quick clean up. Then we can relax for the rest of the shift, eh,' Krusty said, wiping a bead of sweat off his forehead.

'Sounds good to me,' I replied. 'But I must go to the bog first.'

I headed to the toilet block. I sat there, bloody knackered. I would normally be tucked up nicely in bed by now, I thought, as I rested my head back against the toilet cistern.

Suddenly, I awoke with a jump. My legs had seized up – I'd been in a seated position for so long. I stood up and fell forward into the door. Luckily, I managed to grab a peg on the back of the door to stop me falling to the floor. I stretched my legs to try and get the blood flowing again. For a moment, I wasn't sure where I was. I came around eventually and realised I must have fallen asleep on the toilet. I had no idea of the time, but I noticed daylight coming through the frosted glass windows above the cubicle. I got myself sorted out, got my overalls back on, flushed toilet and walked out of the cubicle like John Wayne over to the sink to wash my hands.

I crept out of the toilet block and into the sunlight and wandered down to the ship. I walked over the gangway and down the stairs towards the galley. As I approached the room next to the galley, I heard snoring. My dad and Dicky were flat out, snoring their heads off, a pile of about thirty empty cans lying next to them.

'Dad, wake up!' I yelled.

He woke and jumped in a fright, a confused look on his face.

'Shit. Dicky!' he yelled.

Dicky jumped into to the land of the living, his grey hair sticking up on end. 'Shit, what time is it?' he said, rubbing his eyes. He looked at his watch. 'Shit, it's nearly 8 o'clock. Day shift will be coming on board soon.'

He quickly jumped to his feet, gathering the empty cans and chucking them over the back of the pile of unopened cans.

'Haway, quick!' my dad shouted, as we got ourselves together and headed off the ship.

We walked over to the workshop. 'Bloody strong stuff, that Noggie beer,' my dad said, as
we walked in the workshop.

There was a cheer of laughter as the day shift lads were busy having their early-morning toolbox talks. We walked into the bait room with our heads down. Krusty was sat fast asleep in a chair, snoring, and Iain was sprawled out on the floor by the lockers fast asleep.

I ran over and wrote 'Twat' on Iain's forehead in black marker and then woke him up. Iain jumped to his feet just as Jimmy Whistler came walking in and stood there silently as we stripped out of our overalls. He looked over at John fast asleep.

'Lads, I've gotta say, I'm proud of the effort. I didn't expect you to work an extra half an hour! And I can see you got all the pipes out.'

Dave woke up and looked around, confused.

'Hope you haven't been asleep there all night, Dave,' Jimmy shouted.

'Na, he's done his bit with the rest of us,' my dad laughed, while Krusty gave him a look of daggers.

'Get yourselves off home, lads. It looks like you could do with some sleep,' Jimmy said with a smile.

Iain asked my dad if he could get a lift to the Metro station.

'Cheeky twat you are, son!' my dad winked. 'Of course, I'll drop you off – no bother.'

CHAPTER 11

End of an era

The three years of our apprenticeship flew by, and all the apprentices were asked to stay on and work as tradesmen. We were told the order books were full and we could end up having a job for life. Quite a few of the apprentices decided to work elsewhere, but Iain, Colin and I, and a few others, decided to stay on and get some experience under our belts, as we all felt we weren't quite ready for the world of contracting just yet.

Thursday, 10th August 2002

My dad came to the flat to pick me up, and for once, I was stood outside waiting for him. I climbed into the passenger seat, as Dicky was sat in the back.

'Bloody hell. Has your lass kicked you out?' my dad muttered, not used to seeing me up and ready for work.

'Can we stop at the shop, so I can get some food for my dinner, dad?' I asked.

'Aye, son – I fancy a pie anyway,' he replied.

'Have you still got your trumpet, Fawlty?' Dicky piped up from the back seat, which set us off laughing.

'What you on about, Dicky?' My dad laughed.

'You told me before you used to play the trumpet in the Salvation Army. I wondered if you still have it?' Dicky explained.

'You thinking of taking it up, like? I said, laughing.

'No, I just wondered,' Dicky said, wondering why we were laughing.

'I think I've still got it in the garage somewhere. I've got a violin, like!' my dad said.

'Can you play it?' Dicky asked

'No, but I always wanted to try, and I tried it, and I couldn't play it! It's bloody harder than it looks, so it's stuck in the garage now. Hey, but you'll like this. When I bought it, the bloke in the shop asked if I would like a bow, so I told him, 'Na, don't bother gift-wrapping it, mate!" my dad said, laughing.

We eventually stopped off at a little paper shop in Hepburn that sold freshly baked pies.

'I'm just going to go and get some money, dad. I'll be two minutes,' I said, running to the cash point about a hundred metres down the street.

After I got my money out of the machine, I ran to the shop, where my dad was already back in the car, moaning.

'Hurry up, ya tit,' he shouted out the window as I ran into the shop.

As quick as I could, I bought my pie and my paper and jumped into the car outside the shop. 'You fat bastard!' I said, as I jumped in the passenger seat, as there were about twelve pies sat on the passenger seat. I looked up and some big, fat bloke with a bald head stared at me from the driver's seat.

'You fucking what!' he yelled.

'Shit, sorry, wrong car,' I said, quickly jumping out and looking to the car behind, where my dad and Dicky stared out the window, laughing their heads off.

Eventually, we arrived at work after about ten minutes of laughter and telling them what I said to that poor bloke in the other silver car. We walked down the bank as usual, but the atmosphere was far from normal. Normally, people were laughing and joking, but not this morning; everyone had concerns after the recent news that Cammell Laird were on the verge of going bust. We walked quietly down the bank, headed into the workshop and clocked in as usual, then went to the bait room and began getting our overalls on with the others.

Jimmy came in a while later with Ronnie and Tommy. 'Take a seat, lads,' he said, with a solemn look on his face. 'We have all read the papers, lads, and as you probably have heard by now, Cammell Laird has gone into receivership. Sorry to be the bearer of bad news if you didn't know, but this is our last day today, lads. You will be paid for the rest of the week, so today just pack up your tools and belongings and say your goodbyes.'

Jimmy smiled sympathetically. The room fell silent, and Iain and I looked at each other, shocked.

'So, this is it, eh,' I said, looking at Iain.

It was worrying for me, as I'd just moved in with my girlfriend, Tina, and we had only just gotten our first mortgage.

'There's loads of graft out there, man! We will find something,' Iain said, seeing the look of concern on my face.

The bosses went around shaking everyone's hands and thanking them for their hard work while the lads packed away their tools and other belongings. There were loads of blokes just standing around in groups chatting. Whopper Napper and a few other electricians walked in the workshop and came over, shaking hands and saying goodbyes. Finally, Whopper Napper got to me. 'See ya later, mate – it's been a laugh,' he said, reaching out a hand, to my amazement.

I shook it and laughed. 'See you again sometime.'

'I fucking hope not,' he said, winking, and walked away.

Ya better get used to this, son. I've had a lifetime of getting laid off,' my dad said, patting me on the back, noticing I looked a bit fed up with it all. 'But you never know, son, you might end up with a cushy job somewhere abroad, I'm too old in the tooth to travel now, but you have your whole life ahead of you.'

JJ came walking over and saw me and Iain standing together, while my dad walked off with Dicky. 'Alright, Dumb and Dumber?' he said with a wink. 'Good luck for the future, boys. Hope you both get fixed up with work soon.'

He then shook our hands. Decka came over as Iain and I looked at each other, surprised, at John's farewell. Decka group-hugged me and Iain.

'Canny emotional, this, ain't it!' he laughed, wiping a tear from his eye.

'Been a pleasure, mate!' I said, shaking his hand, and then Iain did the same.

'I might have a job lined up down South. I'll be in touch if they need any more pipeys,' he said, before walking off and saying his goodbyes to the other lads.

Colin came over and joined in the handshakes, and we all exchanged phone numbers. Iain and I both walked in the office. Jimmy got up out of his chair, as did Ronnie and Tommy, and each took turns wishing us luck.

'At least you got to finish your apprenticeships, lads. The first-years weren't so lucky,' Tommy said, patting me on my shoulder.

'If we end up back here again, we'll give you all a call. Thanks lads,' Jimmy said with a tear in his eye.

'Ah, you soft twat!' Ronnie shouted.

'I've got something in my eye, man!' Jimmy shouted back, as we all laughed.

As we were walking out of the workshop, Dot and Krusty both wished us well, as did a few others who were passing by. Iain, Colin and I walked out of the workshop and up the bank for the last time. I wasn't sure how Iain and Colin felt; they were both chatting away as if nothing had happened, but me – personally, I was devastated. This was the first job I really liked, and the laughs we had I'd never forget for as long as I live. As we neared the top of the bank, I noticed my dad and Dicky walking up ahead with their tool bags,

Shit, I've forgotten my tools, I realised. I said my goodbyes again and legged it back down the bank for my tools as Iain and Colin looked back, laughing.

Ten minutes later, I finally got to the top of the bank again with my tools. My dad was sat in the car, with Dicky in the back shaking his head.

'Bloody hopeless,' my dad said, as I climbed into the passenger seat.

Just as we were about to drive off, the security guard came over. 'Can I just have a quick look in the boot, lads? Sorry to have to do this, but there's loads of stuff gone missing.'

My dad switched the engine off, got out and opened the boot for the security guard. After he was happy that we hadn't smuggled anything out, my dad jumped back in the car and sped off. We headed right out of the yard, as our usual route to the left looked busier than normal. As we drove a little further up the road, Dicky burst out laughing and pointed over the road. There were about five of the lads passing tools and copper pipes over the wall and shoving them in the back of a white transit van.

'They must have come through the secret gate,' I laughed.

'The secret what?' my dad asked.

'The secret gate the lads use to go to the pub on a night shift.'

My dad looked at me, shocked. 'Why didn't you tell me about this secret gate, like?'

'Because it's a secret,' I replied.

CHAPTER 12

New adventures.

September 2002

After weeks of job hunting, I'd had no luck. Colin and Iain hadn't found work either. Decka had started a job down South at a place called Baldock near Stevenage. He said it was a good job working in a Tesco's main frame factory, and he was doing his best to get me, Iain, Pikey and Colin a start, as he knew they'd be needing a lot more lads soon. Pikey also was having no luck; he'd lost his job in Holland. Pikey and I searched for work together, sending CVs out to companies all over the UK. We would spend every day at the job centre ringing around, but we seemed to get the same result after every call: 'We have nothing available at the moment, but soon as something comes in, we will be in touch.'

We eventually gave up looking for work as pipefitters and started applying for all kinds of other jobs. Eventually, we found work in a factory in Washington with a company called BHD Windows; they made double-glazing windows and doors.

'I didn't train four years to do this shit,' Pikey said, as he put four stickers on yet another window on the production line.

It was his job to put a little sticky pad on the windows as they came to the end of the production line, and then my job was to stack them on a pallet. It got so repetitive; I was stacking windows in my dreams. Both Pikey and I hated it, but we persevered, as our only other choice was the dole.

I remembered having a hard time with John at Wear Dock, but he was a gentleman compared to our new boss, David Redmond, who did nothing but walk around all day policing everyone, talking down to us and just being a general dickhead. His smug, horrible, spotty face made everyone's life a misery, which resulted in a very dark atmosphere.

'I'm going for a shit,' Pikey said, and walked off.

Within seconds, the windows began piling up. I tried desperately to do Pikey's job with the stickers as well as my stacking job, but the conveyor belt was just too quick. The windows started piling up at the end of the rollers, and then suddenly, *smash!* About three windows fell from the rollers and smashed on the floor, followed by another, and then another. Dave Redmond slammed his hand on the emergency stop button and then came over, red-faced, full of rage.

'Where's Steve?' he screamed.

'He's had to run to the bog – he's not well,' I replied, trying my best to cover for him.

'Anyone who leaves their station must ask permission first!' he yelled.

Meanwhile, my phone vibrated in my pocket as he continued ranting about how much this was going to cost the company. All I could think was, 'Who's ringing me? It could be a job offer.' In the end, I held my hand up and said, 'Two minutes. I really have to take this.'

I pulled out my phone and answered the call, which infuriated him further. It was Decka.

'Areet, Frank,' he yelled down the phone. 'You and Pikey still want a job?'

He'd barely finished the sentence, and I replied, 'Mate, were desperate to get out of this place,' just as Dave was yelling, 'There are no mobile phones allowed on the factory floor!'

I barged out of the fire exit doors, setting off the alarm. 'Sorry about that, mate – my arsehole of a boss won't give me a minute,' I shouted down the phone.

'I've spoken to the boss and he wants you guys to start Monday,' he replied.

'Perfect. Cheers, Decka – you're a legend!'

I went back through the fire doors, where Pikey was stood while Dave was ranting. I totally ignored Dave and said to Pikey, 'We start Monday, mate – the Baldock job. Decka just rang.'

Dave was getting angrier and angrier by the second. Pikey put his head in Dave's face.

'Listen to me, you jumped-up prick. Andy and I are out of here to earn twice as much as you're earning in this shithole! So, shove your seven quid an hour up ya arse.'

Dave stood there, gobsmacked. 'You can't just leave a live production line!'

'We just have,' I replied, and Pikey and I walked out of that place happy as a pig in shite.

As we walked out, we bumped into the top manager, Trevor, who was a decent bloke, unlike Dave. Just as we were about to speak to him, Dave came charging over.

'These two are walking out with no notice! It's disgraceful the way they've just spoken to me,' he screamed at Trevor.

'I'm sorry, Trevor, but we're sick of this bloke's attitude towards us,' I said, pointing to Dave.

'Aye, he's been a jumped-up prick, and we've been offered a job for double the money we earn here,' Pikey said.

'If that's the case, I don't blame you, lads,' he said putting his hand out to shake.

'Cheers, Trevor. Sorry for the short notice,' I said, shaking his hand.

We walked out of that factory and never looked back.

CHAPTER 13

Mackem invasion

Colin, Pikey, Decka, Iain and I turned up at Baldock town just after 6pm on a sunny Sunday evening. All five of us had been crammed into his tiny little Saxo for over three hours and we were as stiff as a board.

'This is the place, lads,' Decka said, as we all stood, stretching.

The Goldcrest Pub. This was to be our home for the next few months. The building looked ancient. Baldock town itself was a little historic market town in north Herefordshire. It was a quiet little place – well, it was until we turned up.

We walked into the Goldcrest and told one of the girls at the bar we had rooms booked.

'We only have double rooms, so you'll have to share,' she said.

I didn't like the idea of sharing a room, but we weren't paying, so we couldn't really complain. Pikey and I decided to share, and Colin and Iain were going to have the other room.

She took us up the stairs while Decka got the beers in.

'Room number ten,' she said, handing me a set of keys, and walked us up the stairs to the room directly above the bar.

'It'll be a little noisy when the bar is open, but we close at 11pm every night,' she said, and unlocked the door to our room.

'It's a bit grim, ain't it?' I said, looking around the room.

'You're the lucky ones – you have Sky in this room,' the woman replied.

'What, there's a hole in the roof too, is there?' Pikey laughed.

The woman didn't see the funny side of his comment and walked off, with Iain and Colin following. I closed the door and looked at the room with a frown. There was barely enough room for one of us, never mind two, I thought. There was a big double bed and a single bed next to it. There was a sink in the corner and an old, portable TV on an old chest of drawers. Pikey plonked his bag on the double bed. 'I'll have this,' he said.

'That's not fair,' I moaned.

'Snooze, ya lose,' he said, unzipping his bag.

Pikey unpacked his bag, while I fiddled with the telly. 'Hey, we do have Sky!' I noticed, as I flicked through the channels. 'Bit of a dump this place, though, ain't it?' I said, noticing an inch of dust on top of the TV.

'It's not that bad, man. I've stayed in worse places,' Pikey said, while on his tiptoes pissing in the sink, as I sat on the end of my bed shaking my head.

After we settled in, we went downstairs to the bar, where Decka, Iain and Colin were already knocking back shots.

'It'll be alright, man. It'll just be inductions and that tomorrow,' Pikey said, grabbing himself a shot and necking it.

'Fancy a game of killer?' Decka said, laughing, putting a couple of pounds in the jukebox. 'Firestarter' by The Prodigy came on quietly in the background as we chatted at the bar.

'Hey, I can hardly hear that, man. Can ya knock it up a bit, pet?' Decka moaned to the barmaid, who walked away.

'Are you lads speaking a different language? I can't understand a word you're saying,' she muttered.

Iain noticed the sound system to the left of the bar, walked over and turned it up full blast.

'That's better,' he said, and we headed over to the pool table to play killer.

The barmaid came back as Decka wrote our names on the chalkboard next to the dartboard, and we each chucked a pound on the end of the pool table. I went back to the bar, where Colin was sat reading a Daily Sport newspaper.

'Are you lot deaf?' the barmaid yelled, as she quickly ran behind the bar and turned the music down a bit.

'Can I have four pints of lager, please, pet?' I said, and she stared at me, annoyed.

'Yes, but I'm not your pet,' she moaned, as she poured our beers.

'Bloody hell, Colin. I don't think she likes us much.'

'Speak for yourself,' Colin winked. 'I think I'm in here, mate,' he said, looking over his paper.

'Hey, I must say, Colin, you don't strike me as a Sport reader. It's an old pervert's paper, that, ain't it?' I laughed.

'I don't normally. It was just sitting on the bar. Hey, look, you've got Sky in your room, haven't you?' he asked, pointing to an advert in the paper showing a free adult TV channel launched on Sky.

'I know what he's like. All we will be watching is Top Gear and Dad's Army,' I said, nudging my head towards Pikey.

'Are you playing killer pool?' I said, handing Colin one of the beers the barmaid handed to me.

'Aye, I'll be over in a minute,' he said with a wink.

I took the beers over to the pool table, where the balls were set up ready to go.

'Same rules, but there are only five of us, so we will have two lives each. The first one out does a forfeit, and the winner takes the pot and decides the dare for the loser,' Decka said, chalking his cue while I rolled my eyes, as I knew it would be me who would be doing the dare. I was bloody hopeless at pool.

Decka took his shot and broke off, potting two. Colin was up next. He missed his shot on an easy red and left it hanging over the pocket. Hey, maybe I might have a chance, I thought, as I potted the red Colin missed. Pikey stepped up and potted a tricky green stripe and left Decka with a virtually impossible shot. Decka blasted the balls and got lucky as one ball dropped in as I chatted to Colin, and then Iain potted his shot.

'So, what's the score with the barmaid?' I asked Colin.

'She said she loves the accent, so I bought her a drink,' he said, smiling, as he leaned over the table to take his shot and missed an easy shot into the middle pocket.

'Bollocks,' he muttered, as Pikey rubbed his name off the chalkboard.

'Colin does the dare,' Decka shouted, as I stepped up and miscued, sending the white into the pocket.

Decka and Pikey battled it out after Iain was eventually knocked out. I missed another easy shot and finished third. I sat there chatting to Colin as two big, stocky blokes came to the pool table. Decka was busy setting the balls up, as they'd potted the first set.

One of the lads moaned, 'Hey, what are you doing? We're next – you've had your game.'

'We're playing killer. You can join in if you want,' Decka said, while carrying on putting the balls in the triangle.

One of the lads snatched the cue out of Pikey's hand

'What are you doing?' Pikey yelled, snatching the cue back and staring into the bloke's eyes.

Decka and Iain walked over, as did the barmaid, as she sensed it was about to kick off.

'As I said, you're welcome to join in, but don't go snatching cues, or you're likely to get it wrapped around your neck,' Decka yelled, and the lad stepped back, pulled a nervous face and walked away.

The other lad stepped up towards him, Pikey and Iain, almost eying them up, and then walked away with the other lad. Just as they were about to leave, one of the lads looked at Colin chatting away to the barmaid.

'I'd stay away from her if I were you. She's dropped more boxers than Mike Tyson,' he shouted.

'Leave now!' the barmaid yelled.

They laughed and walked out the door.

'Who were those pricks?' Pikey said.

'Just a couple of local dickheads,' she said and walked back behind the bar, shaking her head.

After a while, we all decided to call it a night, as the bar was getting crowded, and we were stood waiting for ages to be served, except for Iain, who decided to stay for a few more.

'Colin slipped away to his room before doing his dare,' Decka moaned, as we headed up the stairs.

'Probably didn't want to be shown up in front of the barmaid,' I commented.

'It'll keep,' he said, smiling, and headed off to his room.

I got to the room and Pikey was pissing in the sink again. 'I wish you wouldn't do that, man!' I moaned. 'It's gonna stink.'

'That's what it's there for, man. Why else would there be a sink in the room? They call it the Geordie en suite,' he laughed, zipping himself up and jumping onto the bed.

I sat on the bed, turned the TV on and flicked through the channels, as Pikey threw a rolled-up pair of socks in my face.

'Ow, man,' I yelled, chucking them back in his direction. 'Hey, there's that channel Colin was on about.' I flicked onto Babestation.

There was a knock at the door. Pikey never moved, so I got up off the bed and left the adult TV channel playing as Pikey got ready for bed. I opened the door and Colin was stood there, naked, covering his bits with his hands.

'What are you doing?' I said, laughing my head off as he came running in.

'Can I borrow a pair of shorts and a T shirt? Decka dared me to run to the toilet naked as part of my forfeit, and he shut my door, but I've left the key in the room and I'm locked out.'

Pikey burst out laughing and threw him a pair of shorts and a T shirt.

'Hey, are you watching that dirty channel?' Colin said, sitting on my bed.

'Hey, man,' I said, pulling him to his feet. 'I don't want your bare arse on my bed.'

There was another knock at the door, and I walked over and opened it, as I half expected it to be Decka. It was the barmaid from downstairs; she looked on in horror as Colin stood there, starkers.

'Look, I don't know what's going on up here, but can you turn the TV over, please? I don't mind you switching channels to whatever you want when the pub's shut, but we can't have Babestation playing in the bar,' she said, pointing to the TV.

I stood looking embarrassed as Pikey burst out laughing, and Colin quickly put his shorts and T shirt on.

'What, that controls the Sky in the bar?' I asked, cringing with embarrassment, pointing to the Sky remote.

'Er, yes,' she said, sarcastically, looking at me like I was dumb.

I changed the TV to Sky Sports, and I heard boos from the bar below. The barmaid walked out, and Colin ran after her, explaining that he'd been locked out. I sat on the bed and we burst out laughing, and then decided to try and get some sleep.

CHAPTER 14

The following morning, we all met at Decka's car feeling a bit worse for wear.

'My bloody head is killing,' Iain said, as we climbed into the car.

'I'm not surprised – you were smashed last night! You woke me up at one o'clock in the morning banging on the door to get in,' Colin moaned.

'Sorry. Mate. Hey, what's this about you having a gay orgy in your room last night?' Iain said, laughing.

After a short, ten-minute drive, we arrived at Tesco's mainframe building in an industrial estate in Letchworth. The security guard opened the gate for us, and we drove into the empty car park. We got out of the car and Decka took us into the main reception of the posh-looking modern building.

'What's a mainframe?' Colin asked, which is what I thought we were all thinking.

'It's like the God of Tesco. It's a massive computer that controls everything, from the staff being paid, to food deliveries, that sort of stuff,' Decka replied, signing a sheet at the reception desk. He passed it around and we all signed it as a quiet, nerdy-looking bloke looked on.

'I'm Tim. I'm in charge around here,' the guy said, directing us to the corner of the room, where there was a camera facing a white screen.

'Stand there while I take your photo for your passes,' he said, directing Pikey. Colin walked over too.

'One at a time, please,' he moaned, rolling his eyes.

'He's a pain in the arse, him. He's only a security guard, but he thinks he's in charge,' Decka whispered to me as Pikey stood getting his picture taken.

Just as Colin was about to get his photo taken, a big, tall, fat bloke in his late forties came through the doors. 'Aright, lads. I'm Glen,' he said, in a strong, south West Country accent.

'Any pipe turned up yet, Glen?' Decka asked.

'No, not yet. Probably in the next few days,' he replied.

'What are we supposed to do in the meantime?' Decka asked.

'Have you not got a ball? Don't worry, you're still getting paid,' Glen said, patting Decka on the shoulder.

After having our photographs taken, we were all given a pass on a lanyard to hang around our necks. Glen introduced himself to us and shook our hands, and then showed us around the place. He explained how we were eventually to make and fit sprinkler pipes in every computer room, once the pipes eventually arrived. He then showed us the workshop where eventually we would be making the pipes. The place was spotlessly clean. There was a pipe-threading machine and a saw in the corner.

'Aright, lads – listen up,' Glen shouted, as we all gathered around him. 'Lads – listen up. Decka knows the score here, but I just want to let you know. This place has to be kept spotless. That thing in there is the God of Tesco and is worth millions, so please be very careful.'

He explained how he would pop in from time to time, but most of the time, we would be trusted to be on our own. There would always be Tim, the head of security, here and occasionally a technician to monitor the computers, he said, and then pulled out a twenty-pound note.

'There's a cafe around the corner. Will one of you go and get me a breakfast?'

Colin said he would go, and Glen gave him the £20 note. 'Get yourself something with the change.'

The rest of us gave Colin a few quid and explained what we wanted, and he smiled and walked out as Glen continued showing Pikey, Iain and me around the place. About half an hour later, Colin came back; we were all sat outside the workshop on the step in the sunshine under the roller shutter doors. Colin handed the lads their breakfasts and he stood there with a red carrier bag in his hand. Glen put his hand out for his change.

'What?' Colin asked.

'Where's my change?' he said, looking at Colin.

'I thought you said I could get something with the change?' Colin said, lifting the bag.

Glen looked confused. 'I did. What did you get?'

'I got this T shirt,' he said, opening the carrier bag and showing him a navy-blue T shirt.

'You bought a fucking T shirt with my change?'

Glen looked on, shocked, as the rest of us rolled about laughing.

'Bloody hell! Glen said, looking pissed off. 'I meant a sandwich, not a bloody T shirt! Anyway, there are a couple of labourers coming this afternoon, Martin and Scott. If you lads can show them the ropes, I'm gonna head off. I've gotta be on another site.'

'Aye, no bother,' Decka said, still laughing away to himself.

Glen drove off and left us to it, as we all continued laughing at Colin.

'Seems okay, that Glen,' I said to Decka.

'Aye, he's no bother. I've hardly seen him since I've been here.'

'So, what can we do?' Iain asked.

'Nothing really 'til the pipe turns up. I've got a ball in the boot. Shall we play footy?' Decka said with a grin.

'Aye, why not,' we all agreed. We finished our breakfasts and headed out into the sunny car park for a kick-about.

Just as Decka nearly broke my leg with a tackle, he pointed over to two lads standing at the shutters.

'There's one of those pricks from the bar last night!'

The mouthy lad from the bar stood with his head down, and the other lad was tall and stocky with a shaved head. They both stood watching us play football. We eventually stopped and walked over.

'Alright, lads. I'm Martin. This is Scott. We're the new labourers.'

We all stood there staring at Scott, thinking he had some nerve after last night. We all shook Martin's hand and introduced ourselves, but nobody acknowledged Scott as he stood there with his head down. Martin looked confused.

'What's going on?' he asked in a strong, Southern accent.

'Ask him,' Decka said, nudging his head towards Scott.

Martin asked Scott what was going on.

'It was Mick acting himself again, pissed,' Scott said.

'It was you who was doing most of the shouting last night!' Pikey shouted over.

'You'd better not have fucked this job up for me or you'll get a kicking,' Martin said, staring at Scott with his fists clenched.

'It was nothing serious, don't worry, mate,' Decka said, smiling at Martin. 'But if he starts any trouble again, I'll help you give him a good kicking.'

He smiled and took the two new lads inside and showed them around.

'Of all the people to start, it had to be that dick,' Pikey said, shaking his head.

'The other lad seems alright. I'm sure he'll keep him in line,' Iain replied, as we headed inside ourselves.

About half an hour later, Decka came back from showing the lads the plant.

'Glen's been on the phone asking if we can start drilling and putting brackets up on the ceiling. There's a mobile scaffolding tower over there – we can use that.'

Decka pointed over to a dismantled pile of scaffolding pipes in the corner.

Martin, the new labourer, and I started taking the scaffolding tubes into the computer room as Decka showed the rest of the lads where the brackets were going. Martin seemed like a good lad, laughing and joking as we headed into the main computer room. It was a huge room with tiled white flooring, with a large computer in the middle making a continuous buzzing sound. All of a sudden, Pikey went whizzing past us on an office chair with wheels on. I looked back and Iain was running, wheeling a chair, and then he jumped up onto it on his knees and went whizzing past us too. Shortly after, Decka and Colin came flying past doing the same until they eventually rolled to a stop.

'Bloody hell, you take some beating you, Pikey,' Decka said, as they got off the chairs and walked up to me and Martin putting the scaffolding tower up.

Suddenly, a lady with dark hair appeared from behind the computer.

'Excuse me, would you mind not playing silly games around the computer,' she moaned, looking at the lads like naughty schoolchildren.

'Sorry, pet,' Decka said, as the woman walked away, shaking her head.

'Shit, I didn't even know she was here,' Decka said. 'Hey, it's darts and quiz night tonight in the bar, by the way. You all up for it?' he asked, as he joined in erecting the tower.

'What's that, like?' Colin asked.

'Well, it normally consists of darts and a quiz – the clue is in the name,' he said, sarcastically, laughing to himself.

'Yeah, it's a good night, a Monday, in the Goldcrest,' Martin agreed. 'I'll have a pop in and have a few beers with you.'

I suddenly thought I'd better not, as I'd had enough last night. 'I think I'll give it a miss tonight.' I said, as Iain handed me another scaffold tube that the other lads had brought in.

'What, you're not coming? What you gonna do? Stop in and watch Babestation all night?' Iain said, which set the others off laughing.

We finally finished putting the scaffolding tower up, and Decka explained where I was to drill the holes for the brackets. Martin went to the other room to get the drill, as did the others, leaving Iain and me.

'You okay doing this yourself? I feel like shit. I'm gonna head to the bog to sort my head out. I've got the Davies,' Iain said, rubbing his face.

'Got the what?' I asked.

'The Davies! Do you not get them?' he asked, looking at me surprised.

'Get them? I don't even know what they are,' I said, pulling the scaffolding along towards where Decka wanted the holes drilling.

Iain went on to explain the Davies are the symptoms you get after a night on the drink. They make you feel paranoid, and in extreme cases, you want to lock yourself away from the world. 'It's like the night of horrors the night after a good session. The only cure is another drink, but then the following day, you end up with the double Davies! Nowt worse,' he said.

'I know what you mean. I get like that every day after I drink, but why do you call it the Davies?' I asked.

'Remember that bloke at the dock, Davy, who was paranoid and didn't speak to anyone?' Iain said, wandering off to the toilet.

'Ahh I see! So, you feel like him?' I shouted and laughed to myself.

I tried again to move the scaffolding, but it wouldn't budge. I figured one of the brakes might have been on the wheels, so I walked around and checked them, but the brakes were off. I noticed one of the wheels had turned sideways, so I gave it a kick, and the tower began to move. I dragged the thing almost to where I needed it, but it came to a halt again.

'Bloody hell, man!' I yelled and pulled it again, but it was jammed solid, so I yanked it as hard as I could, and I suddenly heard a bang. The lights in the room began flickering and the buzzing of the computer suddenly stopped.

'Shit!' I muttered, thinking, what have I done now?

Suddenly, the dark-haired woman who moaned at the lads earlier appeared out of nowhere with a panic-stricken look on her face.

'Have you just pressed the emergency stop button?' she yelled.

'No, of course not,' I replied.

She quickly ran off, and I thought I'd better tell Decka. I ran into the workshop where all the lads were sat in the sun under the shutter doors.

'Lads, I think I've done something bad.' I explained what had happened.

'It's probably nothing to do with you, man. You can't knock an emergency stop button – it's got two plastic covers on. You need to open both to press it,' Decka said, putting my mind at rest.

It was probably nothing to do with me, I thought.

'Haway, let's go to the cafe around the corner before we get the blame,' Decka said, and we all left, except for Scott, who decided to stay, and Iain, who was still in the toilet.

We turned up at the greasy spoon cafe about a five-minute walk from the site. It was a nice little place, like an old country house, with the sun shining in through the windows. We sat at a table by the window drinking tea and coffee.

'Have you known Scott long, like, Martin?' Decka asked.

'I know of him. He and his mates are a bunch of lunatics – always causing trouble. I've had a few run-ins with a few of his mates over the years, but now they tend to steer clear of me, as they know they always end up worse off,' Martin said, smiling.

He looked a bit of a hard case, I thought to myself, but like Decka, he seemed like a reasonable bloke who didn't go looking for trouble.

'You into kickboxing, like, Martin?' Pikey asked, seeing the kickboxer tattoo on his arm.

'Yeah, I do a bit of competing. You'll have to come and watch one of my fights sometime,' Martin said.

We sat and chatted for half an hour or so, then started walking back to the site. We turned the corner to the normally quiet street. It wasn't quiet now. There were cars parked everywhere in sight and people running around with mobile phones, running towards the mainframe plant.

'What's going on here?' Colin muttered.

I suddenly panicked, thinking, I hope this isn't down to me. Just as we got to the gate, Tim, the security manager, came running over.

'You lot can clear off. You're not allowed in,' he yelled.

'Why? What's going on, like?' Decka asked, but Tim ran back to the building to sign in the queue of about twenty men who looked like they had the world on their shoulders as they shouted down their mobile phones. Scott and Iain appeared at the reception door being ordered off site by Tim.

'Go on, clear off, you bloody idiots.'

Iain dragged Scott back, who looked like he was going to go back and knock Tim out. They eventually got to the gate.

'What's going on?' Decka asked Iain.

'He reckons someone has pressed the emergency stop button. Not good when you've got the Davies, this carry on! There are about a hundred people in there going mental,' Iain said, pointing back to the building.

'Bloody hell, man. I'm sorry, lads, if it's me who's caused this,' I said, starting to seriously freak out.

'You will be sorry if it costs me my job,' Scott yelled in my direction.

Martin yelled in his face. 'Look, the lad's said he's sorry! It might not even be anything to do with him, so shut the fuck up.'

Decka was about to say something but his phone rang. 'It's Glen!' He turned away from us and listened to what Glen had to say.

'It's nowt to do with us, Glen. We haven't even started drilling yet,' he said, then listened again, nodding along and running his hands over his shaven head. 'You're joking! What about our tools and stuff?'

We looked on, fearing the worst. Eventually, he finished the call.

'Look, lads, we're being kicked off site – something to do with the computer going down. He reckons it's serious and the cost could run into hundreds of thousands,' he said, looking on shocked.

'Surely he couldn't have caused that by pulling a scaffolding tower?' Pikey said.

'I don't know what's happened, but Glen reckons they want us off site, and we're not allowed back in. Glen's gonna come back tomorrow morning and sit down with them to try and smooth things over. Until then, lads, were off site 'til at least midday tomorrow, so we might as well go and get pissed!' he said, smiling.

'Hey, what about my T shirt? I was going to wear that tonight,' Colin moaned.

Scott walked off down the road muttering something about me.

'I'll see you in the Goldcrest. I might as well go back and get the three Ss,' Martin said, smiling.

'What's that?' Colin asked.

'Shit, shower and shave! See you later, lads,' Martin said and wandered off down the road.

'Ow, Tim!' Decka yelled through the security gate.

'I've told you; you're not allowed on site!' Tim yelled, charging over.

'Look, I want my car, so either you open these gates, or I'll climb over them,' Decka yelled back at him.

Tim reluctantly let Decka into the car park to get his car, and he drove out as people were still running around like headless chickens.

A few hours later, we were back at the digs to get showered and changed. I was getting ready after already having showered when there was a knock at the door. I opened the door; it was Iain.

'Can I come in?'

'Aye, why aye,' I replied.

'Colin's doing my head in. He won't stop rabbiting on about the barmaid. He's polishing his shoes at the minute and getting all tarted up,' Iain said, laughing.

'Polishing his shoes? Do people still do that?' I said, laughing.

'Colin does! Where's Pikey?' he asked.

'He's having a shower. Shall we go down and have a pint?' I suggested.

'Aye, haway,' Iain said, and I put my trainers on and went down to the bar with him.

'Two beers, please, pet' I said to the barmaid.

She shot me a look of daggers.

'Sorry, I meant two pints of lager, please, madam.'

She stood looking at me with her hands on her hips. 'Madam?'

'Bloody hell, man! What do you want me to call you?' I said, not meaning to snap, but I'd had a very stressful day.

'My name is Dawn,' she said and began pouring our pints.

I fished my wallet out of my jeans and handed Dawn a ten-pound note. She gave me the change, and I said, 'Cheers, pet!' without thinking. 'Sorry, Dawn! Cheers Dawn,' I said, before she had the chance to moan again. She looked at me like she was about to jump over the bar and give me a slap.

Iain and I walked into the other room and decided to practise our darts, to prepare ourselves for the darts tournament on tonight.

'Bloody hell, Iain, I hope you're good at quizzes, as you're bloody hopeless at darts,' I laughed, as Iain hit the three, the one and the light above the board.

Decka came walking through the door with three beers. 'Alright, lads. Can I play the winner?'

'Aye, why aye,' Iain replied.

Iain threw another three darts. One hit the ten, one hit the outer board, and the other bounced out.

'You ever thought of going pro, Iain?' Decka said, laughing, as Iain picked his dart up off the floor.

I hit the double eighteen to finally put Iain out of his misery.

'You've got to follow through with your shot. You're letting go too early.'

Decka showed Iain hitting two twenties and a treble twenty. Iain stood at the oche and tried again.

'Right, now follow through,' Decka said, as Iain threw.

'I would, but these are the only clean jeans I've got,' Iain said, laughing.

We continued practicing our darts for a while until we got bored with it and sat down at a table next to the pool table. Pikey walked in carrying a tray of drinks over with beers and some Aftershocks.

'Good for the Davies, these, Iain,' Pikey said, putting the tray on the table.

'Aye, and they're lethal,' I laughed, reminding him of the carnage I caused in Harry's garden the last time I drank Aftershocks.

'Hey, check Colin out,' Pikey said, pointing to the bar, where Colin appeared looking extremely smart in pair of black trousers, a black shirt and shiny black shoes. Iain wolf whistled as he went to the bar.

'Can I have five pints of beer, please, pet, and one for yourself,' Colin said to the barmaid, as I put my head in my hands, thinking he'd blown it with the 'pet' comment.

'Certainly, Colin,' she said, to my amazement.

'Hey, how's he getting away with that? She was going to knock me out when I called her pet,' I said to the lads, quietly, so the barmaid couldn't hear.

'Good lad, he's steamed straight in there,' Decka said, laughing.

'Hey, he could be waking in the crack of Dawn in the morning,' Iain said, which set us off laughing as we sat and watched Colin laughing and chatting away to Dawn.

About an hour later, Martin came in and ordered yet another round of drinks and stood talking to an old bloke at the bar wearing a dicky bow tie. He eventually joined us with the tray of drinks.

'Hey, that's Dave – the quiz bloke. Are we paying in?'

'Aye,' we all agreed.

Martin explained you pay five pounds a man; that enters you into the quiz and the darts tournament, and the winning team overall takes the pot. Second place wins a bottle of spirits of their choice.

'What we gonna call ourselves?' Decka asked, as he signed our names and payed the fivers we all passed to him.

'How about the Nutcases from the North?' Dawn shouted over.

'How about the Northern Knobheads?' came a voice from the behind Decka.

We turned to look, and it was Scott and five of his mates who were all big, heavy-set blokes in their late twenties. Decka laughed it off.

'You lot in the quiz and darts like?'

'Yeah, could do with the money. It seems as though your numpty mate might have got me sacked,' Scott moaned, giving me a dirty look.

'Well, how about we make it Interesting?' Decka said, eying the lads up.

'How do you mean?' Scott replied, his mates staring at Decka.

'Tenner a man,' Decka said, looking at us. We all nodded in agreement.

We all sat back down near the pool table while Scott and his friends sat in the bar.

'It could end up kicking off, lads. Watch your backs – they're a bunch of lunatics, them lot,' Martin warned.

'It's alright – Colin there is as hard as nails,' Decka, laughed, unfazed by Martin's comment.

The quiz eventually began, and we were doing okay. I was doing well with the music questions and Pikey knew his sport.

'Who was the UK Christmas number one in 1993?' Dave, the bloke in the bow tie, shouted over the mic.

'Whitney Houston,' Decka whispered.

'It wasn't. It was Mr Blobby,' I said.

'You sure?' Pikey said.

'One hundred percent,' I said, remembering the year well, as it was the year that I left school, and I used to love Noel's House Party, which featured Mr Blobby.

'Final bonus question: Can you name a celebrity named after a body part? You get a point for each body part. You have one minute, then I'm going to collect the sheets in,' the bloke shouted, as we all put our heads together and whispered possible answers.

'Bellenda Carlisle!' Iain suddenly came out, with which set us off laughing.

'Michael Foot. Former Labour leader,' Pikey came out with.

'Nice one, Pikey,' Decka said, writing the answer down.

'Dr Legg from EastEnders,' Colin blurted out, which Decka wrote down.

'Hey, you never know, he might accept it.'

The clock was ticking, and my mind was totally blank.

'Tony Handcock,' Pikey whispered.

'Good one!' Decka laughed and wrote it down, as Dave the quiz bloke picked up our sheet and walked off.

'Hey, we done alright there, I reckon,' Colin shouted.

'Aye, I think your Dr Legg might have clinched it for us! Well done, lad,' Decka joked, as Colin stood up smiling and went to the bar to talk to Dawn.

Dave shouted over the mic shortly after. 'The results of the quiz, ladies and gentlemen,' and we all turned to face him.

'In fifth place with 52 points is the Golden Girls.' The table of old ladies behind us frowned with disappointment.

'In fourth place with 55 is Shaz and Dave.' Shaz and Dave sat booing from their table next to the window.

'In third place is Hitchin Quiz Masters with 57. Not this time, lads, sorry,' he announced, as the table of blokes by the door gave a groan of disappointment.

'In second place with 58 points, who will play the winners at darts, is...' There was a drumroll as the announcer tapped his fingers on the mic. 'Baldock Bellends,' he said, which set the room off laughing.

'I changed their name on the sheet,' Decka laughed, as we cheered, thinking surely, we must have won.

'And the winners with 60 points is the Northern Nutters. Well done, lads. Your answer to the bonus question, Tony Handcock, earned you 4 points, which clinched it,' which set everyone off moaning, especially Scott from the runners-up table.

'Why did they get 4 points? I thought you said it was one point an answer?' Scott yelled.

'I didn't. I said one point per body part. Toe Knee Hand Cock,' he said, which set the room off laughing.

'I couldn't accept your answers 'Bellenda Carlisle' or 'Dr Legg', though,' Dave said, laughing.

We had a brief break before the darts started, so I went to get the drinks in. 'Six pints please, pet,' I said, instantly regretting what I'd said. 'Sorry, Dawn,' I quickly corrected myself as she snatched my twenty-pound note.

'Are you deliberately trying to wind me up?' she shouted.

'No, honestly,' I replied, but she gave me my change with a look of hatred.

I carried the drinks over to the lads as they were discussing the rules. We were going to play the Baldock Bellends at darts. We were told each team member had to all throw three darts, and the highest scorer of each team played each other in a game of 501 for the prize money. We sat there quietly confident, as Decka was a cracking darts player, and I wasn't bad myself, and Martin said he wasn't a bad player either. The time arrived, and we all stood at the board as the Baldock Bellends took their throws. Scott hit the highest score amongst his team, scoring 85.

I threw first and hit three twenties. Not bad, I thought.

Pikey came forward and hit 41.

Colin stepped up next and scored a respectable 58.

Then Decka threw 65, which put him in the lead.

Martin scored 60, so Iain had to hit 66 to play Scott in the final, which was highly unlikely, given his previous attempts. Iain stepped up and threw his first dart. He hit treble 12. He looked over at us, quite shocked, and threw his second dart, which landed in double 13.

'Shit, he only needs a ten, and he's playing in the final,' Colin said.

'Where did you go to school?' Decka laughed, but his expression soon changed when Iain hit a 20 with his third dart, taking his total to 82, which meant he was playing Scott in the final.

'Bloody hell, man. How did that happen?' Iain said, as he came back to the table to get his drink.

Decka pulled a sneaky grin, then walked over to Scott and his mates.

'Look, lads, I'll be honest with you. I can see you're a canny player, but we have a bit of an unfair advantage here with Iain. We were only talking earlier about him going pro. How about we split the pot, forget the bet and play this match as a friendly?'

Scott thought for a few seconds, weighing up weather or not Decka was being honest. He chatted to his mates, and after a little conferring, they agreed.

'Right, lads, nearest to bull throws first,' the bloke announced.

Scott threw first, hitting the outer bull. Iain stepped up, threw his dart and missed the board.

'I think the lad misunderstood me. I said nearest bull, not nearest the radiator,' Dave said over the mic, laughing.

Scott started the game and scored one hundred. Iain stepped up. His darts seemed to improve a little as all three darts hit the board, but he only scored 7, with Scott looking on, raging, realising he'd been conned. Iain's darts seemed to be improving again, as Decka had advised him to aim for the left-hand side of the board, as there was less chance of hitting low numbers, and it seemed to be working, as he kept hitting trebles.

'Scott, you require double 20,' Dave shouted, as Scott got himself ready to throw.

Scott threw his darts and hit single 20, then hit double 10 to win the game.

'Give me that fucking money,' Scott yelled at Dave, who looked gobsmacked and a little frightened, so he quickly gave Scott the envelope full of cash.

Decka stood up and stared into Scott's face and said, 'We had a deal. You'd better hand over half.'

Scott's four mates edged over next to Scott, staring at Decka.

'You'd better get out of our way or you and your mates are going to get a good kicking,' Scott yelled in Decka's face.

'How about just you and I settle this outside?' Decka suggested, staring down at Scott.

Out of the blue, one of Scott's mates suddenly swung a punch at Decka, catching him in the side of the face. Quick as a flash, Decka swung a punch straight back at him, connecting under his chin, sending him flying over the pool table. Martin appeared. He quickly spun around and kicked one of Scott's mates across the face, which sent him flying into a table, smashing the table itself to pieces, drinks flying everywhere. Iain joined in and punched the other lad in the chin, who was just about to swing a pool cue over Decka's head.

Pikey, Colin and I were about to run in to try and help, but there was no need, as Martin punched Scott in the jaw, sending him backwards into his mate. The two of them fell to the floor, but they quickly got up and scarpered out of the pub.

'Right, that's it – you're all barred!' Dawn yelled over to Decka.

'What are you talking about? We live upstairs,' Decka shouted back, holding his cheek where the lad had just punched him.

'I want the lot of you out first thing in the morning,' she shouted, pointing to the door.

'Haway, man, pet! It was them who caused the bother, not us,' I said, pointing to one of the lads lying on the floor out cold.

'Stop calling me pet!' she screamed and ran towards me. I quickly shot out the door away from her. She continued yelling at the rest of the lads to leave.

They followed me out shortly after and we all headed upstairs.

'Hey, that bastard took off with the money,' Decka shouted, as we walked up the stairs.

'It's okay, I've got the runners-up prize. Fancy a little nightcap?' Iain said, waving a bottle of vodka in the air.

Pikey, Decka and Iain all went off to Iain and Colin's room, while Martin left to go home. I decided to go to the room to bed, as I'd had enough to drink, and I could barely even walk up the stairs. Colin stayed downstairs trying to apologise to Dawn.

CHAPTER 15

The following day, I woke up with the hangover from hell. I climbed out of bed and looked over towards Pikey, who was up and ready and putting his trainers on.

'What time is it, mate?' I said, but he totally ignored me.

'Pikey?' I shouted, but he walked out of the room and slammed the door. 'What's up?' I yelled, but I heard no reply.

Shortly after, there was a knock at the door. I climbed out of bed, noticing black stains all over my pillow.

'What the hell is that?' I muttered and headed over to the door. I opened the door and Decka and Colin were stood there. They immediately started laughing their heads off.

'Look at the state of you,' Decka said, laughing.

'You okay? You look a bit off colour,' Colin said, as Decka started laughing in kinks.

'Haway, we have to get out – we've been kicked out,' Decka said.

I suddenly got flashbacks of the fighting in the bar last night.

'Shit! I'll just have a quick shower,' I said.

'There's no time. Dawn said she'll call the police if we're not out by ten,' Colin said, frowning.

I jumped into last night's clothes and chucked the rest of my clothes in my bag and eventually followed them downstairs. Pikey was stood at the bottom of the stairs and turned away when I passed him.

'What's going on, like, mate? Why are you ignoring me?' I asked, but to my surprise, he walked out of the building and totally ignored me again.

Dawn stood there with her usual miserable look as I walked past her. 'I'm sorry.' I said. as I walked out. but she totally ignored me too as I handed her the key to the room.

Everyone was crammed in the back of Decka's Saxo when I walked out of the door. Decka got out of the car, still laughing, and opened the boot for me.

'What's going on? Why is Pikey ignoring me?' I whispered, as I tried desperately to squeeze my bag on top of the other bags already in there.

'I'm keeping out of it,' Decka said, climbing back in the driver's seat of the car.

I jumped in the passenger seat and looked at Pikey, Colin and Iain crammed in the back seat. Iain looked rough, but he still managed to burst out laughing when he looked at me, as did Colin, but Pikey sat there, stony faced, staring out the window.

'Haway, mate, please tell me what's up.'

'Fuck off,' he replied, to my shock. I turned away and stared out of the window wondering what I'd done. We had been mates since school and I'd never seen him like this before.

'Where are we going?' I asked Decka, who burst out laughing.

'We're going to the laundrette to pick Pikey's stuff up and then how about the greasy spoon?' Decka said, looking in his mirror.

'Aye, sounds good,' the lads agreed in the back.

'Why the laundrette?' I asked Decka, who smirked.

'Ask Pikey,' he said.

I looked back at Pikey.

'Because you pissed all over my bag full of clothes last night, you prick!' he screamed.

Everyone burst out laughing.

'Shit. Mate, I'm sorry – I'll pay for the laundrette,' I said.

'I know you will, and you can pay for my taxi I had to get this morning! And I'm never sharing a room with you again. You're a fucking nightmare,' he yelled.

We stopped at the laundrette. Pikey ran in to get his stuff and eventually managed to squeeze his bag back in the boot. I jumped in the back seat and apologised again to Pikey. 'I'm sorry, mate. I'll get you a breakfast.'

Pikey pulled a little smirk like he was starting to come around. 'I want a full English with double everything, you prick.'

After a while, Pikey calmed down and we headed into the greasy spoon.

'Why is everyone staring at me?' I said, feeling everyone's eyes burning into me.

'That's the Davies, that. Mind you, you do look a bit off colour,' Iain laughed.

I decided to go to the bathroom to freshen up a little, as I had rushed out of the Goldcrest without even washing. I went to the toilet and afterwards went to the sink to wash my hands. I looked in the mirror and saw my face. It was jet black.

'The bastards,' I muttered, laughing, as I tried scrubbing what looked like boot polish off my face. I walked back into the cafe where the lads were laughing and cheering.

'Twats. No wonder everybody has been giving me dodgy looks. 'You look a bit off colour!'' I said, laughing, looking at Iain and Colin.

We sat eating our breakfasts, chatting about where we were going to stay if we still had a job.

'I'll have a word with Glen when I see him. Don't worry, somewhere will come up,' Decka assured us, just as his phone began ringing in his pocket.

'Hello Glen,' he said and listened to what he had to say. 'Okay Glen. Yes Glen. Okay Glen, we'll head down now,' Decka said and hung up.

'Who was that?' Colin said, laughing.

'We have to go down there now,' he said, drinking the rest of his coffee and giving Colin a look like he was about to give him a slap.

Ten minutes or so later, we arrived at the mainframe site and parked on the road out front, where Martin was stood outside the gate.

'Alright boys,' he said, smiling.

'How's the face, Decka? Looks a bit swollen,' Martin asked.

'I'll live! Which is more than I can say for Scott if he turns up,' Decka replied and pressed the call button on the gate.

Tim came out of the reception and walked over to the gate without acknowledging anyone, pressed the button that opened the gate and walked back into the building. We walked into the reception, where Glen was stood in a suit along with three other blokes all suited and booted.

'Alright, lads – this way, please,' Glen said, guiding us into a big conference room.

There was a huge, brown table that almost filled the room, with seats around it and a big TV at the front.

'Take a seat, lads,' Glen said.

We sat down and the room filled up with about ten very smartly dressed men, as well as the female technician from the computer room. A tall, thin bloke in his mid-forties stood up and stood at the front of the room in front of the TV screen, where there was a frozen image of the computer room.

'Hello. My name is Murray Black. I'm the owner of EA Group,' he said in a very posh accent, and then introduced us to each of the people around the table. They were all the top representatives from Tesco's and the company directors from EA Group.

'First of all, I'd like to take you through the events of yesterday. At 11:21am, Mr Andrew Carter was pulling a scaffolding tower through the mainframe computer room. As you can see, the wheel locks,' he said, pointing to the TV screen showing a video of me caught on CCTV kicking the wheels.

'Andrew again pulls the scaffolding, but the tower stops' Murray said, then pointed to a little grey area under the tower. 'Andrew is unaware the scaffolding is stuck on the emergency stop button, and I'm guessing he presumably thinks the wheel is locked. Is this correct, Andrew?' he said, looking at me.

'Erm... yes, this is correct,' I replied, burning bright red.

'Andrew then proceeded to pull the scaffolding with extra force, which ultimately resulted in the emergency stop button being torn from the wall,' he said, pointing to the video moving in slow motion. 'May I ask, Andrew – had you any idea what had happened at this point?'

'No, not at all,' I replied, nervously.

'As everyone here knows, Tesco's mainframe computer went down for one hour because of this incident at a cost of almost £85,000. Tesco stores as far as Scotland were affected. Deliveries throughout the rest of the UK came to a standstill, and Tesco is still recovering. Staff may not be paid on time and food deliveries have been affected. I'm not trying to scare you, Andrew – I'm just informing you of the severity of your actions,' he said, staring, as well as the rest of the room, directly at me.

'I'm very sorry,' I replied.

'Luckily for EA Group, we have insurances in place for such incidents, and we accept that this was a freak accident and the emergency stop button should have been better protected, but I speak for everyone at EA Group. We are very sorry, and we assure you an incident like this will not happen again.'

Murray sat down opposite me, and a man with grey hair in his late fifties stood up.

'I accept this was an accident and I'm happy for the lads to continue with the work. However, if any similar incidents occur, I suggest we get another company in to complete the work. We also require anyone who works here to receive a full safety induction and given information on the importance of the Tesco mainframe computer. This cannot happen again. Do I make myself clear?' he said in a stern voice, to which everyone nodded.

The Tesco people left the room and left us sitting with the EA Group owners and staff.

'Lads, we have had a very lucky escape here, but any more horseplay and you're out! Do I make myself clear?' Glen said, with a look of seriousness on his face.

'Horseplay? It was an accident – you saw for yourself,' Decka said in our defence.

Glen pressed rewind on the video recorder and pressed play. You could clearly see Pikey go flying past the camera on an office chair, followed by Decka, Iain and then Colin.

'Lucky for you lot they didn't see this!' Glen said, pointing to the screen while we sat looking like naughty school kids.

The owners and directors finally left, and we were told we could resume work. Just as Martin and I were about to head into the computer room, Glen shouted us back. He gathered us all in the workshop.

'I need to have a word with you all. Firstly, where's Scott? And secondly, what the hell happened at the Goldcrest last night? The owners have told me that our staff are not welcome back there. Why?' Glen asked.

'There was a bit of an altercation with some of the locals. They didn't take it too kindly because we won the quiz,' Decka explained.

'A bit of an altercation? We have been billed for a damaged pool table, a damaged table and chairs, a cleaning bill for a room that stinks of piss – shall I go on?' Glen yelled as we lowered our heads.

'This is your final warning, lads. I've got you a couple of rooms in an old couple's house in Letchworth. Now, please be on your best behaviour. You're not kids,' Glen said, handing Decka a piece of paper with an address written on it.

'Where's Scott?' Glen asked again.

We all shrugged our shoulders and pulled faces like we had no idea.

'One more thing. The damage to the Goldcrest is coming out of your wages. Think yourself lucky we didn't sack the lot of you,' Glen said and eventually left the site.

The lads eventually drilled the holes for the brackets. They wouldn't allow me anywhere near the computer room, so I just stayed in the workshop chopping brackets for them.

'That's all we can do here for now 'til the pipes arrive, so we might as well get ourselves moved into the new digs,' Decka said, dusting himself down.

Martin agreed to stay on 'til 5pm in case the pipes turned up, and we eventually headed off in Decka's car to our new digs.

We arrived at the address Glen had given us, and we pulled up into the drive of a very posh, Victorian, large detached house with a beautiful landscaped garden.

'Bloody hell, this is a bit flash, ain't it?' I commented, as the lads stood admiring the house.

'Must be worth a mint, this place,' Pikey said, as he looked up at the house.

We walked to the porch and rang the bell. After a few minutes, a very posh-looking couple came to the door.

'Mrs Taylor, hi. We're the lads from EA Group. We believe our boss booked a room for each of us,' Decka said, sounding like a perfect gentleman.

'Hello, I'm Mary, and this is my husband, John. Come in, boys, but please take your work boots off,' Mary said, sounding very prim and proper.

'This area is out of bounds,' she said, pointing to the living room and the kitchen. 'Your rooms are upstairs,' she said, as she walked us through the posh passageway with cream carpets and fancy oil paintings on the walls. I noticed there was also a framed photo of a body builder on the wall holding a trophy. Mary saw me looking.

'That's my son, Thomas. He lives with us, but you'll hardly see him – he works as a DJ most evenings. Either that or he's weight training,' she said, proudly.

She showed us three very nice, large double bedrooms. They were a big improvement on the Goldcrest. Very fancy with large TVs and spotlessly clean. Colin and I agreed to share the room at the back of the house, while Pikey and Iain decided to take the larger room at the front. Decka was to have his own room at the other side of the building. Mary then showed us the bathroom we were to share next to her son's room.

'Have a nice stay, lads,' Mary said, handing us the keys and heading back downstairs.

'Hey, good luck sharing with Frank Spencer,' Pikey said to Colin as we headed down to the car to get the bags.

'Good luck sharing with Iain! His farts smell worse than the fitters' fridge at Wear Dock,' Colin replied.

We eventually got settled in and unpacked.

'You okay, mate?' Colin asked me, as he noticed me sitting on my bed staring into space.

'No, mate. Not really. I'm thinking of packing all this in. I'm gonna end up seriously hurting myself or somebody else with my calamities.'

Colin sat down on his bed next to mine. 'You'll be fine, man. Accidents happen. Besides, what else could you do?'

'My brother, Dave, runs a company selling windows. He said I could work for him when I pass my driving test. My fifth driving test is in two weeks and I'm feeling quite confident this time,' I replied, seriously thinking about it.

'I'm thinking the same, to be honest. I've applied for my Australian visa – my brother lives out there. It's got to be better than this,' Colin said, looking outside, seeing the rain lashing against the window.

I lay on the bed watching Countdown while Colin went in the shower. There was a knock at the door. I got up off the bed to answer it. I opened the door; it was Iain.

'Are you coming for a pint and a bite to eat? Decka and I are gonna get a taxi into Baldock,' he said.

'I'm sick of the sight of drink, mate. I think I'll just have a quiet one,' I said and sat back down on the bed.

'Haway, man! You'll be bored out of your skull stuck in here all night. Plus, you don't have to drink.'

I thought for a little while and decided I would. In the end, Pikey and Colin ended up coming too. Decka phoned a taxi and it eventually dropped us off in Baldock town. We decided to steer clear of the Goldcrest after last night's antics and went to a bar on the corner called the George and the Dragon. Martin had recommended the food yesterday, so we thought we would give it a try. Just as we were about to walk in the door, Colin said, 'After my bait, I'm going to go to the Goldcrest try and talk to Dawn.'

'Be careful, Colin. If Scott and his mates turn up, there'll be hell on,' Decka said.

'Have you got your phone on you?' I asked.

'Yeah.'

'Well, ring me if they come in. We will be here, and we will come straight up,' I replied, starting to feel a little worried about Colin.

'Hey, this is alright, though, ain't it?' Decka said, looking around the modern-looking pub with three-seater sofas everywhere and big screens with Champions League football on.

'Have you got any menus, pet?' Pikey said, asking the young barmaid.

She handed us five menus. 'It's steak night tonight, lads. Beer and a steak for £5,'
she said, smiling.

'That'll do me. Champion,' Iain said, rubbing his hands together.

Eventually, our steaks arrived.

'Jesus, how can you eat your steak like that, Decka?' Pikey asked, as he watched him tucking into a rare steak with blood everywhere.

'It's the best way to eat it, like this. Look at his well done, man – it's ruined,' he replied, pointing to my well-done steak.

'I like mine a little red, but bloody hell, a good vet would get that back to life,' Pikey said, which set us off laughing.

I decided to text Martin and ask him if he fancied a pint.

He replied saying, 'I'm training tonight, mush, but if things kick off, give me a ring.'

Colin headed off to the Goldcrest, and rather than head back to the digs, we all decided it was better to stay in close proximity to Colin in case Scott and his mates came back for revenge.

Iain came over to the table and put a tray of Aftershocks down.

'No way!' I said, laughing. 'It always leads to disaster.'

'Haway, man, there are no pipes at work! Nice easy day tomorrow – might as well,' Decka said, downing an Aftershock.

Pikey downed his. 'Be rude not to.'

I gave in and drank mine.

'Cheers, Iain,' I said, shaking my head.

'Hey, I feel pissed already, me – that's my last one,' I said, downing my third Aftershock.

'Aye, after you get your round, ya tight bastard,' Pikey yelled.

'I was still going to get you all one, just not me,' I replied, thinking, tight? Me? I felt a bit insulted, as I always thought of myself as the opposite.

I headed over to the bar. I'll show them tight, I thought, and ordered four TVRs.

'TVRs?' the barmaid said, looking at me strangely.

'Four tequila, vodka and red bulls, please,' I explained.

I took them over to the table. The lads were all laughing at me.

'Told ya a bit of reverse psychology works a treat on him,' Pikey said, laughing, as he took a sip of the drink and pulled a face like it was harsh. 'Jesus wept! What's in that?'

Decka necked his in one. 'Nice, that.'

Iain did the same. 'Did I tell you about my neighbour?' he suddenly came out with.

'Eh?' Decka replied.

'I got caught stealing my neighbour's knickers off the washing line!' Iain said, as we looked on, laughing. 'Aye, true story. I nearly shit her pants when she turned up at my door'

We carried on drinking and telling jokes. I was starting to slur my words and kept messing up my jokes, but Iain was on form, as always.

'Anyway, this young couple get pulled over on the motorway by the police,' Iain slurred. 'Listen, man – it's a good one, this,' he said, as we all quietened down.

'The policeman knocks on the window, so the bloke in the car winds the window down,' Iain said.

'Probably for the best with the cars flying past. He wouldn't be able to hear otherwise,' Decka interrupted, laughing.

'Shush, man – it's a good one, this,' Iain yelled, then carried on as we sat there laughing.

'Anyway, the policeman says, 'Excuse me, sir, do you realise you were doing 90 miles an hour in a 70 zone?' The bloke replies, 'Sorry, officer, I wasn't aware of that.' The wife chips in, 'You lying bastard. I've been telling you for miles to slow down.''

'Typical woman,' Pikey shouted.

'Shh, man!' Iain yelled back.

'Anyway, where was I? 'Also, sir, do you realise you have a taillight out?' the policeman said. 'No. Sorry officer, I wasn't aware of that. I'll get that fixed immediately.' Anyway, the wife shouts, 'You lying bastard. I've been on to you for weeks to get that fixed.' So, the bloke loses his temper and screams at his wife, 'Will you shut up, you silly cow!' The policeman said, 'Does he always speak to you like this, madam?' The woman replied, 'Only when he's had a drink.''

We all went into kinks of laughter.

'It's the way he tells them,' Decka said, laughing, wiping a tear from his eye.

We carried on drinking the night away, and I decided to text Colin, as he'd been gone a few hours.

'Are any of you coming home this weekend?' Decka suddenly came out with. 'My ex has just text. She said I can have the bairn this weekend,' he said, looking at his phone.

'I didn't know you had a kid, Decka! I thought you said you hated kids,' I said, surprised, as I'd had no idea.

'I do hate kids. They're like farts. You love your own, but you hate everyone else's,' Decka replied, laughing. 'Aye, I've got a little lad. I don't see him as often as I'd like,' he said, with a look of sadness in his eyes.

The conversation stopped as Colin came bursting through the doors and ran over to our table with a serious look on his face.

'What's the matter, Colin?' Decka said, immediately jumping to his feet. 'Has Scott turned up?' he shouted, as Colin struggled to get his breath.

Colin held his hand up. 'No, no. I just had to tell you… I'm bloody knackered – I've run all the way here,' he said, struggling to catch his breath again.

He suddenly threw a wad of cash onto the table.

'Scott was in the pub earlier. He gave that to Dawn. It's half the quiz and darts money. He said he doesn't want any more bother,' Colin said, finally catching his breath. 'And guess what? I'm going on a date with Dawn,' he said, smiling from ear to ear.

'Hey this calls for a celebration. Five TVRs and a drink for yourself, pet,' Decka shouted over to the barmaid and patted Colin on the shoulder.

'Dawn also said we can move back in as long as we behave ourselves and he stops calling her, pet,' Colin said, pointing at me. 'I'm going to head back. I just had to tell you,' Colin said excitedly and bolted back out the door.

'What do you reckon? Shall we move back in?' Iain asked.

'I'm quite happy where I am, to be honest,' Pikey replied, as Decka and I nodded in agreement.

'Bit out the way though, ain't it? Let's sleep on it, eh?' Decka suggested, as the barmaid shouted over that our drinks were on the bar.

The following morning, I woke up on the bed, fully clothed, with my head spinning.

'Shit, what time is it?' I said, noticing Colin was up and already eating a bowl of Frosties.

'It's alright –we have half an hour yet,' Colin said, putting his bowl on the bedside cabinet and spraying Brut under his jumper.

'You got any pop?' I said, struggling to speak, as my mouth was so dry.

'No, I haven't, mate. There's some milk on the windowsill,' Colin replied.

'Dear me, what time did we get in last night? I can't remember a thing,' I said, sitting up.

'We got back just after twelve. Do you not remember us carrying you into the taxi?' Colin said, laughing. 'You were steaming. You were telling a load of lads in the bar you were from Birkenhead. Do you not remember doing the Scouse accent?'

'I can't remember a thing,' I replied.

About half an hour later, we locked the room. I'd hunted high and low for my phone, but it was gone.

'I must have left it in the bar,' I said to Colin, as we walked down the stairs, with Pikey, Iain and Decka close behind us.

'Excuse me, lads, can I have a word?' Mary the landlady said, standing at the bottom of the stairs in her dressing gown.

'Yeah, sure. Everything okay?' I asked, as she stood staring at me, looking angry.

'Has anyone lost a mobile phone?' she asked.

'Yeah, me,' I said, relieved, thinking she must have found it.

'Can you describe it, please?' she asked.

'Yeah, it's a Nokia 3310 with Homer Simpson on the cover,' I replied, wondering why she was quizzing me.

'Can you tell me what it was doing in my son's room?' she asked, standing with her arms folded, studying my reaction.

'I've no idea. I had quite a bit to drink last night, you see, and…'

Mary quickly interrupted. 'It's a little more serious, I'm afraid. Forgive my language, but somebody has pissed all over his room.'

I stood there, shocked, rooted to the spot, as I heard one of the lads behind me snigger. 'Oh my God. I'm so sorry. I don't normally drink. you see. I... I…' I struggled to get my words out; I was so embarrassed.

She handed me the phone.

'You're lucky we stopped James from breaking all your doors down. He was going to kill you last night,' Mary shouted and explained how he came in from his deejaying set at three o'clock in the morning and jumped into a bed that was soaking wet.

'I want you out of this house! Come back after work and get your things,' Mary said, opening the door for us to leave.

The lads all rushed past me and ran out the door.

'I'm so sorry. This is all my fault. I'll move out, but please don't punish the lads. They'll get sacked. I don't normally drink, you see, and I was given shots at the bar. I think I may have been spiked,' I lied, trying to weasel my way out of it.

'Just leave. We will speak about it later,' Mary yelled, pointing to the door.

'I'm so sorry,' I said, and I quickly ran to catch the lads up as she slammed the door behind me.

I climbed into the passenger seat of the car in a state of shock. I looked over at Decka, who was slumped over the wheel in hysterical laughter, as were Colin, Iain and Pikey in the back seat.

"Somebody's pissed all over his room',' Pikey said, mimicking Mary's posh voice.

CHAPTER 16

We eventually arrived at work, where Martin was waiting outside the gates ready to go in. We all struggled to climb out the car, as all the lads were hung over as well as me, but more so extremely embarrassed after this morning's events.

'Alright boys,' Martin said, laughing, looking at the state of us.

The lads were all still laughing their heads off as we walked towards the gate.

'What's up?' Martin asked, wondering why everyone was laughing except me.

Pikey explained to Martin what had happened, bursting out laughing throughout the story.

'Bloody hell, you really are Frank Spencer,' Martin said, joining in with the laughing.

'Hey, it's taken my mind off the Davies anyway,' Iain said, as he rang the buzzer on the gate.

'Hey, where are you going to take Dawn on your big date, Colin?' Pikey asked.

'I'm not sure. Can you recommend anywhere nice?' Colin replied, looking at Martin.

Tim came to the gate and, again, didn't acknowledge us; he just pressed the button that opened the gate and walked away.

'There's a new Greek restaurant my mate Mick the Greek works. I've never tried it, but I've been told it's nice,' Martin told Colin, as we walked through the gate.

'I want to take her somewhere special. I want to impress her – I get the impression she thinks I'm a little bit thick,' Colin muttered.

'Whatever gave her that impression?' Iain said, laughing.

'Hey, why don't you do what Andy did in Greece? That'll impress her!' Pikey said.

'What did you do in Greece?' Colin asked me as we walked through reception.

I explained to Colin how I went to Zante in Greece with my girlfriend, Tina. One day, I walked past a Greek restaurant while she was back at the hotel. A tout asked me if I'd like to eat in the restaurant that evening, so I stopped and chatted with him for a while, and I came up with an idea to impress her. The tout had agreed to my idea and came to our table when we arrived later that night. Tina and I looked at the menu and decided what we wanted to eat, and I began speaking to the tout in Greek.

'What, you speak Greek?' Colin said, looking amazed.

'No,' I laughed. 'I pretended I could speak Greek. I started doing my best Greek accent, obviously speaking gibberish, but to her, it looked like I was speaking the lingo, and the tout was replying to me in Greek and writing in his little notebook while she stared at me with her mouth open in disbelief,' I said, laughing. 'Hey, you should have seen her face – it was so funny.'

'So, did you tell her in the end?' Colin asked

'Why, aye. I only did it for a laugh. The other Greek waiters didn't look too impressed, like,'
I said, laughing.

'I can't do a Greek accent, though,' he said, as we walked into the workshop.

'It's easy, man – I'll show you. They just speak with loads of Ks and make that sound at the back of the throat that Scousers make,' I replied, demonstrating the accent.

'Hey, it's really good, that! You really do sound Greek,' he said, laughing, and wandered off practising.

'We'll try it out on Tim later,' I shouted, as Colin wandered off to the toilet.

'Hey, Martin,' Decka shouted, handing Martin his share of the quiz and darts money.

'What's this?' Martin asked, looking puzzled.

'Scott handed half the money over to Dawn. He said he doesn't want any bother,' Decka replied.

'Cheers, mate,' Martin replied and put his money in his wallet.

'Look, lads, what are we going to do about this digs situation? Shall we just move back to the Goldcrest?' Decka asked.

'I don't think we're gonna have much choice, thanks to the serial pisser here,' Pikey replied, laughing.

A few hours later, a wagon turned up with our pipes on the back.

'Ah, bollocks! Today of all days. I've got the hangover from hell here,' Iain moaned, slumped in the corner of the workshop.

We all made ourselves busy and began unloading the six-metre lengths of pipe off the van and laying them in the workshop. We finally all sat down, knackered, as the van drove off. Tim the security guard suddenly came running in.

'You can't leave all that pipe stuff there – it'll have to go outside,' he yelled.

'You're bloody joking, ain't ya? It's taken us all morning to put it there,' Pikey replied.

'Well, you'd better get it moved; otherwise, I'll be on the phone to Glen.'

We sat there and looked at each other, red-faced and out of breath.

'Haway, then, let's get it shifted,' Decka said, sighing, and we all began putting the pipes outside.

Tim pulled a smug look and walked away. Decka lay two lumps of wood on the ground outside of the workshop behind Tim's Mercedes parked to the left of the workshop.

'He wants them outside, he can have them outside,' Decka said, laughing, knowing full well Tim would struggle to get his car out with the pipes piled up behind it. We took turns taking a length of pipe out with one on each end. Colin was practicing his Greek as we did it.

'Hey, you're getting there, Col,' I said, laughing, as he did actually manage to nail the accent.

'Are you really going to go ahead with this?' Iain asked, laughing, throwing a pipe on his shoulder.

'It's just a bit of fun. It'll break the ice a bit. I'll tell her afterwards,' Colin replied. 'Did you tell your mate Mick the Greek what I have planned?' he asked Martin.

'Yeah, your table is booked for 8pm and you're going to speak to him in Greek. I've explained everything to him. He was laughing and said he's happy to play along,' Martin replied.

'I wish I could be a fly on the wall for this,' Decka said, laughing, wandering out the workshop with a pipe on his shoulder.

We finally finished moving the pipes outside and sat down in the shelter from the rain, absolutely shattered and soaking wet.

'Shall we call it a day, lads? We'd better head back and see if we still have a roof over our heads tonight,' Decka said, wiping a bead of sweat from his brow.

We locked the workshop and headed to Decka's car.

'See you later, lads,' Martin said, as he walked out of the gate.

'Hey, you're leaving a bit early, aren't you?' Tim yelled from the window of his office.

'It's only an hour! We worked through our break – not that it's got anything to do with you, ya prick,' Decka shouted back, muttering the last bit quietly so only we could hear.

Tim eventually came outside and opened the gate as we climbed into Decka's Saxo.

'See ya later, Tim,' Decka waved and smiled sarcastically, as did we all, as we drove past him.

'He's gonna be raging when he realises that he has to walk home tonight,' Iain said, laughing from the back seat.

'Serves him right – he's a right jumped-up dickhead,' Decka said, laughing.

I sat there quietly contemplating what I was going to say to Mary. 'I'm dreading speaking to Mary,' I said, rubbing my face, as the others started laughing all over again, which set me off.

'Please don't make me laugh when I go in,' I said, cringing at the thought of explaining myself to Mary and her husband.

The lads were in kinks of laughter; it was infectious, and I started laughing as we got closer to the house.

'Haway, please stop laughing,' I said, seriously.

The lads decided to give me a break and quietened down, so Decka turned the radio on and Afroman's 'Because I Got High' came on. We sat in silence for a little while listening to the music, until Decka started singing, 'He pissed all over his room, because he got high,' which set everyone off laughing again.

'I got kicked out of my digs, because he got high,' Pikey started singing.

Everyone joined in singing as we pulled into the street, 'Because I got high! Da, da, da, da, da."

Decka stopped the car just before we got to the house. He wiped a tear from his eye and said, 'Haway, lads, we really need to stop laughing. If we turn up laughing, it's going to piss her right off. She'll tell Glen, and we will be out,' he said, trying to control his laughter.

Everyone calmed down and sat quietly. Decka drove up to the house and in through the gates. Suddenly, Iain started laughing hysterically and pointed to the side of the house, where there was a mattress leaned against the wall. Everyone else started laughing again.

'I give up,' I said, as I climbed out of the car and left them to it.

I walked up to the house nervously in the heavy rain and pressed the bell. Mary came to the door and told me to come into the living room. I took my work boots off and followed Mary into the room. I noticed her husband sat in an armchair reading the Daily Mail.

'Sit down, please,' Mary said, and she took a seat on the sofa.

'Andrew, as you know, you caused a lot of trouble last night. We have had to throw the mattress away, so I'm going to need to buy a new mattress, and with cleaning costs and for the inconvenience, you will have to pay a hundred pounds,' Mary said, getting straight to the point. Her husband didn't once take his eyes away from the newspaper.

'Okay, I understand. I'd just like to say that this isn't typical behaviour, and I'm so sorry. I'd understand if you'd like me to leave,' I replied, putting my head down in shame.

'We all make mistakes. He's done worse,' she said, pointing to her husband, who looked over his newspaper at her.

'You what?'

'Let's just see how things go, but you might want to avoid James. He was understandably very upset last night,' Mary said, as her husband shook his head and frowned.

'Your rent is paid until the weekend, so I think it's probably best all round if you all leave on Friday. I'll not say anything to your boss, providing you're all on your best behaviour for the rest of the week,' Mary said.

'Okay, no problem. I'll have to go to the cash machine to get your money. I'll give you it later, if that's okay,' I said, thinking I'm going to be at a loss this week with all the damage costs.

I headed out to the car, where the lads were still sat waiting. I climbed into the passenger seat and explained to the lads we had to move out at the weekend, and I explained about the money I had to give her.

'It's no bother, man – we can just move back into the Goldcrest,' Decka said, seeing my worried face.

He then pulled out a wad of cash. 'Here, use my quiz money to go towards the mattress,' he said, shoving the money into my hand.

'No, it was my doing,' I said, handing him it back.

Pikey handed over his money, and Iain and Colin.

'Go on, give her that lot. That with your share will cover it,' Decka said, looking like he wasn't going to take no for an answer.

'Are you sure, lads?' I said, smiling.

'Why, aye,' the lads agreed in the back seat.

'Cheers. I appreciate this,' I said and got back out of the car and went to pay Mary. The lads climbed out of the car and followed me into the house.

Mary came to greet us in the passage. 'My goodness, it's really coming down out there, isn't it,' Mary said, peeking outside at the rain.

'Aye, it's piss… chucking it down,' Pikey said, quickly correcting himself.

I handed over the money and apologised yet again.

'It's done now, so let's say no more about it,' Mary smiled, looking like she was beginning to accept the fact that I was genuinely sorry. 'I've had to do a lot of washing today, and I have had to put a few things on your radiators in your rooms. Sorry for the inconvenience. With this rain, I have no other way of drying the clothes 'til we get the drier fixed.'

'No problem,' Iain replied, as we headed to our rooms.

'Look at them,' Colin said, laughing, as we walked into the room, pointing to a big pink pair of Mary's knickers on the radiator.

'Hey, she's old enough to be your grandmother. Don't go eyeing her knickers up,' I said, laughing.

'Hey, there's only one pair of knickers I'm interested in,' Colin said, winking.

I lay on the bed while Colin went to have a shower, and soon after, I nodded off to sleep. I woke up a couple of hours later to a knock at the door. I got off the bed and opened the door.

'Sorry, did I wake you up?' Iain said, and walked in.

I sat back on the bed and rubbed my eyes, trying to wake myself up, as Iain jumped on Colin's bed.

'Pikey's fallen asleep, and I'm bored out my brains. Decka has gone to drop Colin off for his big date, so I thought I'd come and see my mate, Frank,' Iain said, laughing.

I looked around to see why he was laughing, and he had Mary's knickers over his head.

'Put them back, man. I'm in enough trouble,' I said, laughing, as Iain put them back on the radiator under the window.

'Hey, do you mind if I smoke?' Iain asked.

'No bother, mate, but make sure you lean out the window,' I said, thinking that we can't be too careful, already being in their bad books.

'Can I have that after you, mate?' I asked, pointing to his fag.

'I thought you'd packed it in?' Iain said.

'I have, but you've set me on now, plus I've had a very stressful day,' I said, taking the remainder of Iain's cigarette.

I took a couple of puffs and didn't enjoy the taste, as I hadn't smoked for so long, so I decided to flick it out the window. I flicked it only for a gust of wind to bring it back in, and it fell onto the radiator.

'Shit, it's gone in her knickers!' I shrieked, and quickly tried to grab the fag, but it burned straight through the knickers and fell to the floor. I quickly picked it up before it had a chance to burn the beige carpet and threw it out of the window, this time successfully.

'I don't believe this,' I said, picking up the knickers with a fag burn in the gusset.

'What?' Iain said, trying to see what I was looking at.

'Shit!' Iain shouted and fell back on Colin's bed, laughing.

I decided to put Mary's knickers under my pillow in case she came up for her washing.

'Shit, she's going to think I'm some sort of weird pervert,' I said, thinking this day couldn't get any worse.

Iain decided to go back to his room, and I noticed I had four missed calls on my phone. Three of the calls were from Martin and one was from Colin. I decided to ring Martin first. 'Hello, mate, you been trying to ring?' I said.

'Yeah, do you have Colin's number?'

'Aye, why like?' I asked.

'It's probably a bit late now, but my mate Mick the Greek's granny has died, so he's not at work tonight. I wanted to warn Colin not to speak Greek,' Martin said, sounding concerned. 'I've been trying to ring you all night.'

'Aye, sorry mate, I fell asleep. I'll try and ring Colin now. Cheers,' I said, and hung up.

I was just about to ring Colin when there was a knock at my door. I opened the door and Mary was stood there. 'Hi, Andrew. I hope I didn't wake you. I've come for the washing.'

I stood there nervously as she collected the washing from the radiator and looked around with a confused look on her face.

'I must be going mad,' she muttered, and walked towards the door with her basket of clothes. Just as she was about to leave, Pikey walked in the room.

'What's this about Mary's knickers?' he said, laughing, as he walked in and saw Mary stood there.

'I can explain!' I said, as Mary ran out of the room looking extremely embarrassed.

'Shit!' I muttered. I went over to my pillow and showed Pikey the knickers with the fag burn.

Mary's husband suddenly barged into the room and grabbed the knickers out of my hand. 'Out! Now!' he yelled.

An hour or so later, we were all packed up in the car ready to go. Mary and her husband didn't come out of the living room.

'Did you pack Colin's stuff?' Decka said.

'Shit, Colin,' I said, suddenly remembering Martin's phone call.

Just as we were about to drive out of the garden a taxi pulled up and an extremely pissed off, soaking wet Colin climbed out of the back.

'You alright, mate?' Decka shouted out of his window.

'No, I've just been chased around the streets by a load of Greeks,' Colin replied.

'Aye, well, you'd better jump in. We've been kicked out because of this pervert,' Decka said laughing.

Colin explained how he sat down in the restaurant with Dawn, and all was going well until he winked at a waiter called Michael and started speaking Greek. The waiter walked away and came back with two blokes, and Colin tried again, only this time, one of the blokes went for him, so he ran out the door, leaving Dawn behind, and they chased him around the rainy streets of Baldock until he finally decided to hide in a bush until they gave up and left. He then ordered the taxi and tried to ring Dawn, but she wouldn't answer.

'I think I've blown it,' Colin said, frowning with disappointment, as the rest of us couldn't help but laugh.

We eventually arrived at the Goldcrest, where there was a young lad standing at reception.

'You got any rooms, mate?' Decka asked.

Luckily, they had plenty of rooms, so Colin and I took a room together on the top floor, and Pikey, Iain and Decka had to share a family room at the back.

'Is there no shower up here?' I asked the lad, as he showed us to our rooms.

'I'm afraid not. Everyone has to share the one downstairs,' he replied, handing us the key.

It was similar to the room Pikey and I shared downstairs, but it was slightly bigger.

'I'm going for a shower, mate,' I said and walked out, leaving a fed-up looking Colin sat on the bed.

Just before I left, I turned to Colin and said, 'Look mate, I'll try and explain to Dawn what happened. You never know, she might come around.'

'I doubt it very much. She hates you,' he replied, as I went for my shower.

After showering, I went to head back to the room with my towel wrapped around me and my work clothes under my arm. I was in a world of my own, thinking how embarrassing the last few days had been. Without thinking, I walked into the room Pikey and I shared last week. There was a big, stocky bloke laying on the double bed in his boxer shorts and a woman sat doing her make up without a stitch of clothing on.

'Shit! I'm sorry, wrong room,' I yelled, as the lady covered herself with her hands and screamed, and the bloke jumped off the bed and ran towards me.

I quickly ran out of the room and up the stairs to the room I should have gone to. Just as I was about to open the door, the bloke grabbed my shoulder, span me around and punched me in the eye.

'Ow! It was an accident – I stayed in that room this week and got confused after my shower,' I shouted, covering my eye.

'Yeah, well, make sure you don't get confused again – otherwise, you'll get more than that,' the bloke yelled and walked off down the stairs, cursing under his breath.

'What a bloody day!' I shouted, as I stormed into the bedroom and slammed the door.

CHAPTER 17

The final straw

Friday, 22nd September 2002

The last few days had been an absolute nightmare. Life in the Goldcrest was bad. We weren't welcome in the bar, and Dawn still wasn't speaking to Colin, as she thought he was some kind of racist idiot. At work, things weren't much better. Glen had found out about us getting kicked out of the digs, and also, Tim had been on the phone to say we had been leaving work early and blocked his car in with the pipes.

We climbed into Decka's car to go to work. Iain and Pikey had their bags in the boot, as Decka was planning to try and sneak them off to the train station for a long weekend at home; we were going to try and cover for them. When we arrived at work, all the EA Group company directors' cars were there.

'Shit, you didn't kill Tesco's again, did you, Frank?' Decka said laughing.

'I bloody hope not,' I replied.

We parked the car up outside the gates and pressed the button. Tim came reluctantly walking over and opened the gate.

'Morning,' he muttered, and walked back into the reception as we followed a few metres behind.

'Bloody hell, he must have got his end away last night. Did he just say good morning and smile?' Iain shouted.

'It was probably just a bit of wind,' Pikey said, laughing.

'Can you come into the conference room, lads,' Glen shouted over, as we were about to head towards the workshop.

We followed him inside, wondering what was going on.

'I wonder what all this is about?' Martin asked, as we sat around the big table waiting for everyone to come in.

One of Tesco's top bosses sat down, stony faced, then the others came in and sat down.

'Alright, lads, I'll keep this short,' Murray, the EA Group owner, said as he stood at the foot of the table.

'The hours of work here are as follows. 7am 'til 5pm. No leaving early, as Tim informs us you have been.'

'Aye, only because we worked our break,' Decka interrupted.

'That's beside the point. You don't get paid for your break – it's unofficial. Also, Tim informs us you deliberately blocked his car in by stacking pipes behind his car. We will not accept behaviour like this. You are representing EA Group. If you can't do that in a professional manner, I'll have to ask you to leave. Is that understood?' Murray yelled, looking around at all of us as we all sat nodding.

'Also, the accommodation situation. Your bad behaviour there has got to stop. You're not bloody children, now grow up,' he yelled and stormed out, slamming the door.

Glen stood up next. 'From Monday, I will be onsite every day, so this childish behaviour stops now. Is this understood?' he yelled.

Again, we sat nodding.

'Now go and start doing what we pay you to do and do some work,' Glen yelled.

Decka looked like he was going to shout back, but he controlled himself and got up to leave the room with the rest of us.

'Grass,' Martin muttered to Tim as we walked past the reception, where Tim was stood with a smug look on his face.

We headed into the workshop, and Pikey and I went into the computer room and measured and sketched up a few pipes for the lads to make up. As the day went on, we worked flat out making pipes and fitting them in the computer room with no problems, but the atmosphere wasn't as jovial as normal; everyone was snapping at each other.

'Has Glen pissed off yet? We've got a train to catch,' Pikey moaned.

'I'll check if his van is still there. If it's not, we'll slip away. I'll run you to the train station – we're due a bit of breakfast anyway,' Decka said and walked outside the workshop to check the car park.

He came back a few minutes later. 'All the cars have gone. Haway, I'll drop you off,' Decka said.

Martin, Colin and I continued fitting the pipes when they went. After a while, I looked at my watch and realised an hour had gone by, and there was still no sign of Decka. Just as I was passing a pipe up the scaffolding to Martin and Colin, Glen came charging over.

'Where the fuck is the rest of your lot?' he yelled in my face.

'They've gone for a breakfast – they'll be back in a minute,' I said in a bit of a fluster, as I wasn't sure what to say for the best.

'Tim said they left over an hour ago! You lot are taking the piss out of me,' Glen shouted and charged out of the computer room, red-faced, and slammed the door.

'Shit, I'd better ring Decka and warn them Glen is back,' I muttered. I quickly rang his phone, and he answered after a couple of rings.

'Alright, mate. Glen's back and he's not happy. Tim's told him you have been gone over an hour,' I said down the phone.

'I'm going to end up knocking him out. I'll be back as soon as I can. They're on the train now, and I'm stuck in traffic. I'd better go – there's a copper,' he said.

'What shall I say to Glen?' I asked, but it was too late – he'd gone – and Glen was charging towards me.

'You know the fucking rules on mobile phones,' Glen screamed in my face. 'Now where the fuck are they? No more bullshit.'

I really didn't know what to say, so I hesitated and said, 'I'm sorry. I don't know. They went for a breakfast, I think.'

'What do you mean you 'think'? Are you thick or something?' he yelled, with his nose stuck in my face.

'Hey, there's no need for that,' Martin shouted down from the staging.

Glen walked out of the computer room again raging.

'I've had enough of this prick,' I said, seriously contemplating walking out.

I climbed up the staging and helped Martin and Colin screw the pipe into the tee piece when I noticed Decka walking towards us.

'Bloody hell, man, the traffic is murder out there,' he moaned and looked up at the progress we had made while he'd been away.

'Hey, you haven't done too bad. How's Glen been?'

'Don't ask!' I replied.

'He's been shouting and bawling at Andy – he had his nose in his face,' Martin yelled.

'Has he now!' Decka shouted and went to look for him.

'Don't, mate. Just leave it,' I shouted, thinking I really didn't want Decka to be fighting my battles for me.

Glen walked into the computer room and saw Decka charging towards him.

'What's this about you yelling at Andy?' Decka shouted in Glen's face as I covered mine.

'You lot are taking the piss. Where the hell have you been?' Glen shouted back.

'Don't you go speaking to me like that or I'll knock your teeth out. I've taken them to the digs – they've both got food poisoning,' he lied.

Glen immediately stopped shouting when he saw the look in Decka's eyes.

'You lot are going to get me sacked. I've got the company owner in there going mental. They want this place finished by next month,' Glen said, shaking his head. 'First of all, Tesco is nearly killed, then the damage at the digs. I think we need to replace you all' Glen said, nervously.

'This is all my fault, not theirs,' I said, pointing to the lads. 'I pissed all over the digs. I nearly killed Tesco's. I dropped the fag in Mary's knickers! Not them!' I shouted, while Glen looked at me strangely. 'Sack me, not them. In fact, you know what – I quit,' I said and began to walk out.

'Don't be daft, man, Andy – we're a team!' Decka said.

'I know, mate, but you'd be a better team without me. I'm sorry for everything, but I've made my mind up. I'm out of here,' I said and walked out as the others looked on, shocked. I walked in the workshop and started packing my tools away. Decka came over.

'You okay, mate?' he said, patting me on the shoulder.

'I'm fine, bud – I'm just sick of my calamities causing problems for everyone. I even managed to screw things up with Colin and Dawn!' I moaned.

'You'll be fine, man, haway – it's not too late,' Decka said.

'My mind is made up, Decka, but thanks for everything,' I said, meaning every word.

'Come on, I'll take you back to the digs,' Decka said, picking my toolbox up.

'No, it's okay. I'll get a taxi. He's already in a right mood – I've gotten you in enough trouble already,' I replied.

'Well, if your adamant about this, hang about at the digs. I'll take you back to Sunderland tonight. I'm going home to see the bairn anyway,' he said smiling.

'Okay, cheers,' I said, patting him on the arm.

'You sure I can't change your mind? It's only been a few accidents, man, nothing major,' Decka said, standing at the door.

'I'm sure, mate.'

I sat on my own for a little while and I realised I'd made the right decision. I'd had enough. I needed a fresh start.

I eventually said my goodbyes to the lads and phoned for a taxi to pick me up at the gate in ten minutes.

'Keep in touch,' Martin said, as I shook his hand on my way out.

Colin stood there looking shocked. 'I'll see you back at the digs before you go,' he said with a frown.

I didn't acknowledge Glen; I just walked straight past him and out.

Tim walked out and opened the gate for me. He didn't say anything, just walked away after pressing the button to open the gate.

'Thanks for everything,' I said sarcastically, and I walked out and sat on my toolbox outside.

I rang my driving instructor, Ken, back in Sunderland. He mentioned there might be a cancellation for a test earlier in the week, and luckily for me, he managed to get a late driving test booked for the following Monday morning. If I passed, I was planning on going to work for my brother selling windows. I'd reached the conclusion that I'd be better suited in an environment where I couldn't cause millions of pounds' worth of damage with my calamities. If I were to fail my driving test, I wasn't sure what I was going to do, but I did know I'd had enough here at Baldock.

The taxi eventually arrived, and I jumped in, and after telling him where I was going, I just stared out of the window for the short journey back. I climbed out after paying the driver and walked into the Goldcrest. Dawn saw me walking inside with my toolbox. I decided I'd had enough of trying to apologise and walked past her with my head down.

'Are you leaving?' she asked.

'Yeah, I've had enough. I'm going home tonight,' I replied. 'Look, can I have a word about Colin?' I asked, as she was about to walk away.

'What about him?'

'Look, he's a nice lad with a heart of gold. It was my daft idea to speak Greek. He had it all planned with Martin's mate, Mick the Greek. He was going to pretend he was speaking Greek to impress you, just for a laugh, to break the ice, but Mick's Grandma died, and he didn't turn up, and… well, you know the rest,' I said, looking at Dawn, who looked at me like she seemed to be coming around a little.

'He's not a racist or an idiot. He just thinks a lot of you, and I bollocksed it all up, like I do with everything. I'm sorry,' I said, and walked away with my head down.

I'd seen her smile for the first time and thought to myself that maybe I've done something right for once.

'Tell him to pop into the bar tonight. I'll have a chat with him,' Dawn said, and walked away.

I headed up the stairs towards the room and saw the guy who punched me the other night walking towards me with his wife, dragging a case down the stairs. I stood aside to let them pass and gave them a nervous smile. The man looked at my black eye. 'I'm sorry about that. I just lost my temper,' he said.

'I'm sorry for barging in. It was an honest mistake. My mate and I stayed in that room – I just got confused, that's all.'

The wife looked at my eye. 'Bloody hell, Derick – he's just a kid.'

'I said I'm sorry, woman!' he moaned, and they started arguing as they walked out of the door.

I got back to the room, packed my things and lay on the bed and texted Colin: 'Dawn wants to meet you in the bar tonight, mate. I've explained everything, I'm sorry.'

He replied shortly after: 'Okay, thinks' which made me smile. He'd done really well learning to read over the last few years, but he still made the odd mistake when texting.

I lay on the bed feeling a little better about things, but I knew I couldn't go on living like this. This past week had been a wake-up call. I decided there and then that I was going to stop drinking to extremes, try to change my ways and stop and think a little more.

Decka eventually returned from work with Martin and Colin. I said my goodbyes again, shook their hands and promised to keep in touch. Decka and I eventually hit the road, and I left my life of pipefitting behind me.

Or so I thought at the time.

EPILOGUE

I finally passed my driving test on the Monday, my fifth attempt, and my brother, Dave, true to his word, got me a start for Budget Windows, a company in Stockton Teesside. I bought myself a new suit and a cheap little runner from my cousin, Paul – a Vauxhall Astra. My new life had begun – what could possibly go wrong?

Colin and Dawn made up and even had a brief romance, but the job finally came to an end when the work was completed, and sadly Colin left. He finally got his visa through for Australia and went to live with his brother, where he lives today. He still keeps in touch with his friends and family. The last I heard he was working in a mine out there doing really well for himself. Decka continued working for EA Group; he went on to do a number of jobs for them in and around London. We still keep in touch and go for the occasional sensible few beers and remain great friends.

Martin went on to work in security, and he also made money fighting gypsies in street fights. Martin and I still keep in touch occasionally to this day.

After Baldock, Pikey and Iain decided to work in the oil industry, and they completed their offshore survival training and found work on the oil rigs shortly after. We're still all good mates, and Iain and I see each other as often as we can.

Pikey and I still remain best mates to this day (after he forgave me for pissing in his bag). I myself went to work for my brother selling windows for a while, but it didn't really work out. It turns out you can cause chaos selling windows after all, so I went back to the world of pipefitting, normally causing chaos wherever I went, but that's a story for another day.

A LITTLE NOTE FROM 'FRANK' ABOUT THE CHARACTERS

This story is a fictional story based on my own experiences working in the world of shipyards and contracting. A lot of the characters in this book are based on real people or, in some cases, are real people. For instance, 'Pikey' (Steven Pike) – my best mate.

We met in school and worked together a few times, including being apprentices together. I got permission from Pikey to include him in this book, and he is just as this book describes him. What you see is what you get. He is a downright hilarious character and a top lad. We were even best men at each other's weddings and will always be friends for life.

Iain Hunt is based on a real character a great lad I met on my first day at the shipyard. I've worked with Iain a number of times since, and I can honestly say he is the nicest lad you'll ever meet, and at the same time, the funniest person too (I wish your name was spelled 'Ian', though – it's a pain in the arse to keep spell checking it, haha!).

Martin. His character is also a real person. A great lad to work with and party with. We had some great times in Baldock. Everything that was written about Martin is true in real life. Top lad – Martin 'Hitman' Lowey.

My dad (Billy Coates, aka Basil Fawlty). My dad really did work in the dockyard when we were apprentices, and also worked with me in Norway a few times. I can honestly say that without my dad, this book would not have been possible. He is, in real life, exactly as he is in the book; he has funny bones. He just makes everyone laugh and is an absolute gentleman with a heart of gold. Loads of the stories in this book my dad told me about from his years in the shipyards – for instance, the drinking on a night shift. That actually happened, although I wasn't there at the time.

Dicky. Dicky was also based on a real character. He is just as he is in this book – a lovely bloke. My dad used to take him to work and we would all laugh and carry on all the way to work, as we do in the book. Happy times. I worked with him as an apprentice for a while and the man never had a bad word to say about anyone.

Blue. There was a bloke in the yard nicknamed Blue, who was a lovely bloke. The character in this book is nothing like him. Blue was certainly never described as a pervert. I used the name, only I hardly knew Blue from the actual shipyard, but every encounter I did have with him he was just simply a very nice, down-to-earth family man.

Billy Animal. There was a 'Billy Animal', and in real life, he was as he is in the book – an extremely funny man. I hardly knew him personally; however, I did get the train with him a few times, and he'd have the whole carriage in kinks of laughter with his singing and jokes. A great bloke.

Dot. There was an actual Dot (although this story doesn't reflect in any way him as he truly was). He was another real character in the yard who always had everyone laughing and was a real wind-up merchant. All the stories about Dot are fictional. A great bloke, though.

JJ. There was a JJ, but the stories about him are fictional. Don't get me wrong; in the early days, he made our lives a misery, but in our later years as apprentices, he'd laugh with us about how useless Iain and I were. He turned out to be a decent bloke once we got to know him. His character doesn't reflect how he is in real life.

Jimmy Whistler. Just as he is in the book – a great bloke and a pleasure to work for.

Decka. Decka is a fictional character, but I did sort of base him on a mountain of an apprentice called Dave Robson, who was built like a brick shithouse, but a top lad. He is also based on one of my best mates, Stevie (Jackie).

Colin. Colin is a fictional character. He isn't really based on anyone, but I wanted a Trigger-type character. There were plenty of people like him in the real yard, me included.

Billy Chocolate (the NVQ bloke). Exactly as he is in the book, although in real life, he was called Billy Temple. Top bloke.

Larry (the happy store man). He's based on a couple of characters. One was a store man in Norway we nicknamed Larry for the same reason, and the other was a friendly store man at Wear Dock whom we nicknamed Ned Flanders (he really did look like him). Another top bloke.

Fleetwood Mick. Another fictional character, but there were a lot like him.

Fat Kev. Fictional character.

Big Brian. He was based on a real character. A top bloke just, like his character in the book.

Drunken Duncan. He is also fictional.

Photo Finish. A fictional character, but there was a bloke nicknamed 'Photo Finish' in Barrow-in-Furness for the same reason.

Gavin (the safety guy with a lisp). He's fictional, although there was a safety induction that I went to at Amec years ago and the exact same thing happened where he said 'shaftey'.

Paula. Based on a real character. The poor woman was demented with the apprentices.

Whopper Napper. Another fictional character; however, I've heard there is a 'Whopper Napper' out there somewhere, but he's a nice lad, apparently. This character was based on all those people over the years I've met and no matter how hard I try, they just simply don't like me. There's one here in Plymouth, and he's got a massive head whom I actually nickname Whopper Napper (not to his face, though).

Krusty. There was a bloke who was the absolute spit and double of Krusty, and a lot of the stories are true about him. He was also a top bloke.

There were a lot of characters I never used. I found it so much easier to write about fictional characters rather than real people in case I portrayed them in a way they didn't like. If you worked with me at the time and you never got a mention, I'm sorry! You are in there, just through other characters. This story could never have been written without you.

Incidents that actually happened:

The Portsmouth fat bloke's boxer shorts incident

This did actually happen exactly how I explained in the book.

Hammer horror

This story actually happened as it was written in the book.

The crane game

Yes, we actually did do this. When I look back and think now about how dangerous it is, it's scary. Luckily, nobody was ever hurt or dropped in a tank.

Falling through the roof

That did happen, but it happened in Hepburn in real life into a canteen, not an office. There's still a patch on the ceiling to this day where I fell through.

The flood

That did happen, but not to me; it happened to a bloke called Alfie Redpath, a top bloke who is sadly no longer with us.

The gun incident (Colin sent to the shop with the note)

That story actually happened, but it was a bloke at my dad's club whom it happened to. They sent him to the bookies down in South Hylton.

Tesco's mainframe

That happened exactly as it does in the book. I'll never live that down. The only thing I'm not sure about is the cost.

Pissing in Mary's son's room

I am ashamed to say that in my younger days, I used to get hammered, and on many occasions, I'd get up during the night and piss everywhere, including on videos, PlayStations – you name it. The incident at Mary's house happened exactly as it does in the book, except it was in a place called Cranfield near Bedford Sewage Treatment Plant, where we were working at the time. I was sharing a room with a mate at the time, Ryan Jones, who recently reminded me of the Mary's knickers incident, which also happened. They never threw us out, though, surprisingly. I did have to pay her £100 for a new mattress, and her son kicked the grill in on my car in a rage. I can't say I blame the lad. Ryan was in kinks all day, especially the drive back to the house, which happened exactly as it does in the book, with the mattress and the song 'Because I Got High'. The only difference was it was only me and Ryan. I still cringe thinking about it now. Ryan was also an apprentice at the dockyard at the same time as me. Top lad.

The poo incident in the van

It did happen, so I'm told, but not with Iain; it was Iain's mate. The story stuck in my head from when Iain told me years ago.

The dog incident (the railway crossing)

That also was based on a true story, but it wasn't me. Pikey told me about this story; it happened to one of his mates offshore. Sadly, it didn't have a happy ending for the dog, unlike in the book.

People I'd like to thank:

Mam. Thank you for being the best mother I could ever wish for, and apologies for my calamites over the years. I love you.

Dad. Thanks, dad, for getting me into pipefitting in the first place and all of your funny stories that you've told me over the years. You are the biggest contributor in this book; it could never have been made without you. Thank you, and I love you.

Dave, my big brother. Thanks, Dave, for all your shares on Facebook and your support and being a canny boss when I sold windows for you. Well tried (I was bloody hopeless!). I love you, bro.

Natalie, my sister. Special thanks to my little sister, who has been so supportive, has told everyone about my books and has even contacted radio stations. I'll never forget your help. Also, thank you for just being you – my fantastic sister. I love you.
Stevie Mckinee (Jackie) Thank you mate for always being there for me, you're a true friend and you are a real life Decka top lad always in my corner.

Deborah Richardson, my cousin. Thank you so much for your comments on Amazon very much appreciated and so glad you enjoyed it. X

Carol Anderson, my cousin. Thank you so much for your kind words on Amazon and good reads, and I'm so glad you enjoyed the books. x.

To everyone who rated my book:

I'm new to this writing lark and I doubt myself constantly, and when I hear positive comments, it really helps me and gives me the confidence boost I need to carry on and write more. It really is a huge help. Thank you.

Ryan Jones. Cheers, mate, for sharing and the nice comments. You're a true gentleman and another great character from Wear Dock and Hepburn.

Donna Warwick. Thank you so much for rating and commenting on allow me to be Frank. I really appreciate it.

Louise Welsh. Knowing you're an avid reader like myself, I was really worried about how you'd rate it, and I was absolutely buzzing when I saw your comments. Many thanks – it means so much to me. Your comments were so kind and blew me away. I really can't thank you enough.
Still the nicest comment I have ever had about my books. Thank you.

Victoria Fowell. Thank you for your comment on Amazon. I must admit, I was worried, as I heard you're a teacher. I thought I may have got a 'D' for my bad grammar. I was over the moon to see you enjoyed it. Many thanks. I really appreciate it.

B19 Dwc. Thank you so much for your comment on Kindle. Your support means a lot.

Graham H. Thank you for your kind words on Amazon – you're a top bloke. Much appreciated.

Joanne Finn. Many thanks for your kind comments on Amazon. I am so glad you liked it.

Deborah Potts. Thank you so much for your kind words and also your assistance in spotting a few spelling errors that went un noticed.

Nicola Wood. Thank you so much for your comments on Amazon means a lot.

Brian Jukes. Thank you too for your kind comments on Amazon it means so much to me.

To all the other people who commented who didn't leave a name, thank you so much, and I'm overjoyed you liked it enough to comment. Thank you so much.

'FORGET YESTERDAY, LIVE FOR TODAY AND LOOK FORWARD TO TOMMORROW.' Thank you whoever left that review. I especially liked that one.

Thank you everyone for your support.

Steven Pike. Gave me a massive confidence boost when I had the Davies recently and was doubting myself. Thank you, mate. Your support is always really appreciated – you're a ledge.

Minty, your advice was priceless – always appreciated fuwtwotftndot.lu. (that's not a grammar error, ha!).

Phillip Lawrence. Thanks for your support and great advice. Check Phil's music out on all major platforms. His stage name is 'Philthlike.

Paul Gollop. Many thanks for fixing my cover issues and your great photoshop work.

Sarah Wildblood. Special thanks for your great work on editing and proofing, and just being generally great. Many thanks.

Dad, aka Basil Fawlty.

Trevor Gillespie, 'Tremendously nice' Tom, John Young, and my best mate, Steven Pike. All great lads and amazing characters.

The apprentices at Tyne Tees Dockyard – 1998.

Some of the world's best pipefitters and all-round great blokes. Tyne Tees Dockyard, Hepburn:
Pikey and Paul Lamb (with the scarf); Big Iain, top left; Fast Eddie and Jimmy Emerson, middle right; Alfie Redpath, RIP; Dot, bottom left; and Dad, bottom right.

The original plumbing shop where it all began. I'll never forget that place.

Picture courtesy of Wylie Bell many thanks.

Printed in Great Britain
by Amazon